The Mouth of Babes

Tosin Coker

NINEFORMATION

INTERACT WITH THIS
AUTHOR ON
NUBIANSCRIBES.NiNG.COM

First published in Great Britain 2007 by N9neformation

British Library Cataloguing in Publication Data. A catalogue record for this book is available from the British Library.

ISBN 978-0-9557483-0-1

www.N9neformation.com

Acknowledgements

Well as usual, I'm the last to find out the juicy low-down about myself. That I had a book in me was a wild fantasy not worth giving any real focus to. All the while others around me would point it out and I'd think, 'If only you know how wrong you are, I just don't have what it takes'. But damn, I done wrote my first novel. How'd that happen?

To my family; Mummy, from as far back than I can remember, you always said I should write a book, but I could never see the potential you so keenly perceived. Thank you for believing in me before I was strong enough to believe in myself.

Tara, Dele, Nike, Seun, forever my inspiration; your love, support and tireless hugs have kept me strong and focused, I couldn't have done this without you. Love no limit. Funmi, love to the max. Thank you for everything.

I'm simply incapable of adequately conveying the words with which to perfectly express gratitude to all those who supported me in this endeavour, so I'm gonna just say it as it is. Kay Bridgeman, it was you who made this book happen by setting the mission parameters of this story. Back then it was simply meant to be a "2000 word feel good short story, that must mention a waterfall, black panther, mayo & a photograph...." Well damn, look what you done started! *Smile* Thank you for your unwavering support. Yvonne Allen aka Zayunu; I have picked your brain and taken you way back when to help me with my research for this book, I'm convinced we have matching imprints of our phone's handsets etched onto our ears for sure! $E=MC^2$ to da power of 9. Carill Allain aka Mubiyna; your enthusiasm and love have kept my head together. As I wrote this book, it was often for the sake of keeping up with the energy your vibe afforded me. Thank you.

Christopher Charles, I bow humbly before you in gratitude and respect. Thank you for being the model template of a god incarnate.

Sandra Tigano, (cover illustration) thank you for your energy, your skill, your support, your genius. Respect for you like whoa!

Last, but by no means least, my Sun and Moon; I cannot even begin to explain how you are, and continue to be my blessing. When I told you I had finally finished writing this book as we walked home that evening, the way you hugged me and cheered words of congratulations of how proud you were of me, rendered me weak. I could have collapsed right there and cried, for how overwhelmed your love made me feel. That evening, you made everything worthwhile. In that moment, I realised how nothing mattered more than making you proud of me. Thank you for your patience. Unconditionally, without limit - I love you.

To my peeps whose names I have not managed to include, know that your support cannot go without a mention, your support as been phenomenal. I thank you. I appreciate you.

Blessing Love & Light,

Tosin

For the divine soul essence within;

Don't forget to BE!

Prologue

He opened the door that exited onto the car park, and gesticulated for her to pass through.

"Ladies first," he grinned.

She returned his smile and obliged. As she stepped through, he admired the contours of her lower body through her above-the-knee skirt, and silently declared her to be a fine specimen of a woman. Together they walked around the building of the wine bar from which they had just departed and headed towards his car. The sultry night air was warm on the skin of her bare arms, shown off by the short-sleeved white blouse she wore. The sky held swollen clouds that threatened to rain again as it had done earlier. Aside from the distant traffic and the faint remnants of music that persisted from within the walls of the saloon, the only crisp sound were the couple's footsteps.

He offered to carry the coat she held draped over her forearm, the perfect excuse to make physical contact. As she accepted his gallantry, he lightly reached with his arm closest to her side to 'innocently' place his hand in the arch of her back. She looked up at him once again. smiling a polite thank you and their eyes locked. He slid his hand down over her ample buttocks and squeezed gently. Her eyes fluttered nervously. He noted her anxiety and quickly leant in to kiss her before she could utter rejection. He lightly stepped forward motioning her back against the wall bringing his hand from her rear, down to the rim of her skirt. He slipped his hand under and hastily reached up to her black lace thong, pushing it aside to stroke her womanhood. Her lower lips moistened to the cajole of his fingers. She barely had time to deny his procession before his fingers plunged into her. She kicked herself for the way her body responded, welcoming him to continue. She obediently complied with his unspoken request, and bent over as he prompted her to turn around. Until his member probed access in place of his fingers, she hadn't even realised he had unfastened his belt. She let out a gasp as he guided himself into her southern hospitality and let out a reluctant moan as he grabbed her hips and pumped harder and faster. He narrated murmured words of detestable appreciation as he aggressively thrust into her. Then as suddenly as his seduction had started, he let out a groan of satisfaction and withdrew. Leaving her empty and unfulfilled, his momentous sex trickling down her thighs. He tucked himself back in his trousers and planted a kiss on her cheek and thanked her, barely able to contain his pleasure at a job well done. She straightened up and tried to recompose herself, picking up her coat from where he had dropped it to the floor. He licked his fingers tasting the flavour her wetness that remained, looking devilishly into her eyes as he did.

As he drove her home, she remained silent and inexplicably frustrated at being left with a feeling of having been swindled.

She let herself in the house and leant back onto the door she closed behind her. The entrance to her three-bedroom home opened into a generous hallway. The walls were painted a cheery sunshine yellow dotted with framed mirrors and family pictures. The floor chequered in black and white tiles, bore the accent of a simple jute runner. Opposite the front door, across the hallway was the staircase, adjacent to which the hall continued to the kitchen and half bathroom. The bottom of the steps paralleled the entrance to the living room, and ascended to the upper corridor along which bedrooms and bathroom opened onto. A wave of panic swept over her as the familiarity of her surroundings threw images of the perfect husband she had just cheated on into her mind. Thoughts of what he would think and how he would respond tormented her as she dared to entertain the implications of him ever finding out. She slid down the door collapsing into a heap and wailed tears of sorrow and anguish for what she had done.

FAILURE IS

NOT

AN OPTION

"After much deliberation, the decision has been made to honour your request for reassignment to the mission. You have been cleared to initiate proceedings. All preparations are ready; the time will soon be nigh. Once the simulation has begun and you have been redeployed to aid recall, there will be no turning back. I cannot further impress upon you of the magnitude of this operation, failure is simply not an option. I know you are nervous, but you need not worry, I will be close by. You know the drill, stick to the plan as discussed."

"Thank you. I am grateful, for your lenience. I promise, will not fail this time, my genes will prevail."

"For Zauba-ah's sake, they had better. This N9ne Blood has never failed a mission, and never had an Initiate fall short. It would be most unfortunate if this situation could not be rectified.

"I will set the parameters of the simulation to that of your own T.H.O.R.T.S.; we shall commence without further delay."

Dialogue between a 'god and an angelic disciple'.

Location: Ouranos; Mental Realm density level five.

1

20TH JULY 2007

Maya climbed wearily onto the hospital bed upon which her daughter lay. She tenderly wrapped Teeny's favourite mink blanket in which she had carried her into Accident and Emergency, tighter around her comatose body.

Only seven hours ago, her usually boisterous two months short of an eleven year old had pushed aside her dinner plate, claiming to be more tired than hungry. On hearing this Maya had stopped in mid chew of the forkful of vegetable lasagne she had just piled into her mouth. She suspiciously narrowed her eyes in inquiry of her daughter's statement, before resuming a slower chewing motion. Mouth still half full she asked, "Are you okay honey? It's not like you to leave the table without having seconds".

"I'm fine. I'm just really tired, and I have a sore throat. It's making it hard for me to swallow," Destiny replied, forcing a weak smile that triggered Maya's 'mummy radar'.

She gulped the remaining bolus in her mouth, dropped her fork and jumped up from her chair in one motion and hastily skip-walked to her daughter's side to touch the back of her hand to her forehead.

"Hmm, you have a temperature. Might be coming down with something. Go lie down and I'll bring you some junior Disprol."

Teeny slinked off her chair in silent compliance and headed toward her room. Her protest free response was all the clarification Maya needed. It was still early; only 7.02pm and it was a Friday. Her daughter would usually be eagerly anticipating the evening's episode of Eastenders. She'd drown her mother's ears in a prelude of chatter in deliberation of what she expected to happen, versus what her best friend, Alysha's thoughts were on this all important subject after the last episode's dramatic drumbeat finish.

Maya walked over to the small, single-door upper cupboard at the end of the white Ikea kitchen unit, in which she kept her essential oils, vitamins and all-purpose medicines. Her slippers made a dull, rhythmic squelch, as they lightly suctioned onto the linoleum then lifted to slap the underside of her bare manicured feet. She tore two tablets from the paper coated foil wrap down the perforation that linked them to the other four in the tray and dropped them in a beaker, covering them in warm water. She gently shook the container to assist the dissipation of the soluble paracetamol for under children twelve, turned on her heel and made her way to the corridor that led to the stairs. Only when she climbed the second step, did she lift her head in time to see that the next step she took would have been onto her daughter's ankle. Teeny was curled in a semi-foetal position spanning five steps.

"Oh my god! Teeny?" Maya gasped.

She was met with a soft moan accompanied by the awkward shifting of her daughter's left shoulder as she sought more comfort from the navy blue carpet that covered the stairs. Maya rested the beaker out of the way on the step upon which she now stood and lifted her daughter from under her arms.

"Come Teeny, let's get you upstairs babe."

“So weak, Mummy, just so tired, I couldn’t climb any more,” breathed Teeny.

“I know. It’s okay, Mummy’s got you.”

Maya half carried, half dragged her daughter up the rest of the stairs. It wasn’t that Teeny was heavy, far from it. Her name nickname was a shortened, slightly altered version of her the name given to her at birth, Destiny. A playful reference to her petite frame that often had her mistaken for being no more than eight years old. Carrying Teeny up the stairs would have been a lot less strain had Maya taken a few more seconds to assess the best way to pick her from where she had lain.

With her foot, she kicked open the door that bore the school made plaque that read ‘Destiny’s Child’ on the front and entered. She tilted her body to shift her weight onto her right leg, jutting out her hip in a clumsy attempt to rest a fair amount of Teeny there. With her now free arm she pulled back the grey and cream mink blanket on which an image of a black panther looked poised to walk out of, along the length of the bed. She finally managed to tuck her daughter in, before running down the stairs to retrieve the now fully dissolved beaker of Disprol. By the time she returned, Teeny had already kicked the blanket to the left of her body and wrapped her arms around it like a giant teddy bear. It took a little coaxing, but Maya finally managed to get the little girl to drink the medicine. It was hard not to panic, whilst her ‘mummy radar’ was still active in the form of repetitious chanting her head, with which she tried to reassure herself that this was ‘*just a twenty-four hour bug that’s all*’.

She looked around the room, taking in all that was so typically her daughter – “a perfect example of precisely balanced contradiction”, her late mother would say. The pastel pink walls were dotted with pictures of luxury cars on black backgrounds, in white frames. Destiny easily favoured the classic silver Porsche 911 Turbo over the yellow Lamborghini Gallardo, the red Ferrari Enzo and blue Lotus Espirit Turbo saying it had a "cute bum" that made it look deceiving. "People think that something cute is less likely to be powerful," she'd reason. Her deep purple carpet was scattered with pieces of a Scalextric racing track and an 'eagle eye' Action Man, she had inherited from her reluctant uncle. Maya's brother had insisted that such a toy was for boys, not sissy girls, until she pointed out that being aged thirty-seven, he himself was no longer a boy and thus also failed to qualify retention of ownership.

On the wall opposite her bed, Destiny owned a selection of lip-glosses, fruity body sprays, neon rubber bracelets and hair clips that were neatly ordered on a little vanity table. Their presence insisted she couldn't be classed as tomboy despite how everything, save the colours of her room pointed to the fact. Propped up on the side of her vanity table was a custom-built skateboard that she proudly boasted to be her "best thing in the world". She could do tricks to make boys her age "Wow!" in coveted jealousy, and she had the scars of trial and error education to prove it. Her shelves held books on all her various subjects of interest, from Nancy Drew spy novels and skateboard periodicals to Greek myths and legends and a black history heroes series. These were kept in place with My Little Ponies that she still treasured, but had grown out of playing with. The wall to the left of her bed was coated in black board paint and acted as a forum for all her inspiration and contemplations. Her father, Derrick had hoped it would reduce incidences of her 'artwork' that seemed to pop up randomly around the walls of the house during Teeny's toddler years. Her friends thought it was awesome and would occupy themselves for hours until as recently as a couple of years ago. Nowadays they tagged it with "BFF", "da hotness" or "goofy riders rule", style comments. Or if they came unannounced and happened to miss her, they'd ask to leave a message on The Wall.

Maya went back downstairs and made an attempt to finish her now cold lasagne. She managed all but a couple of forkfuls before her 'mummy radar' softly gnawed at her again. She sighed and got up to scrape the remains of both hers and Teeny's plate into the bin. 'Just a twenty-four hour bug that's all,' she silently reaffirmed. She washed up the plates and straightened up the kitchen before walking out and into the living room to set the video to record Eastenders, before powering on her computer and succumbing to a mind numbing evening of solitaire.

'Just a twenty-four hour bug.'

She completed four or five games, losing all but one, before turning her attention to the phone, wondering whom best to call to take her mind of her daughters 'bug'. As if it heard her, the phone rang; it was Derrick, her ex-husband.

"'Sup M'y'? Just checking if Teeny's cool for our usual pick up tomorrow." He still greeted her with his pet abbreviation of her name that back in the good old days would have preceded a term of endearment such as "sweet", "queen" or even "goddess".

She smiled at the memory and answered, "Okay. You?"

"Well enough to know, that your voice is betraying you right now. Something's wrong, what is it?"

He always knew. She could never lie to him, no matter how insignificant or slight. All these years, he had remained intuitive to her every action and emotion. It was this intuition that alerted him to the affair she had had. He'd been away on business attending a series of work related seminars after receiving a well deserved, pay increased promotion. She wished she could blame being drunk on her thoughtless act, but she was teetotal. Not that being filled with reckless abandon, due to the effects of alcohol would have made her dirty deed any less damaging to hers and Derrick's nine-year marriage. She barely even remembered the name of the man that had swept her of her feet with his toned muscular 6’1” body that strained under his double-breasted suit. The sexiness of his dark chocolate skin was only matched by his perfect gapped-tooth smile, framed with a perfectly trimmed goatee. His hair was styled in neatly cornrow-ed braids, his hairline expertly trimmed to sharpen the finish. He had lent himself as a hero tending to her flat tyre, and had followed her home to make sure she arrived without further incident. The encounter could have ended there, but he offered to take her out for a drink, insisting that would be thanks enough for the loan of his assistance. Seeing as an opportunity had presented itself for her not to have to spend her evening alone, she naively obliged. When she had become convinced she was going to be late to welcome her daughter home, she had called to enlist her good friend, Nia; Alysha’s mother’s help. Nia had happily agreed to collect and keep Teeny for their planned sleep over date after netball practice earlier that evening.

The stranger’s glass of red wine and the pineapple juice she ordered had somehow ended with them having sex up against one of the more discrete the walls of the bar’s car park. That foolish little act had caused her to break Derrick’s heart, trust and eventually forfeit her marriage. All for a man with whom sex didn’t even remotely satisfy her as much as making passionate, attentive love to her husband.

“Teeny is ill, I don’t know what’s wrong with her,” she confessed.

“I’ll be there in an hour,” Derrick said without hesitation.

Without another word, he clicked down the phone. Maya hung up and cleared her throat, trying to choke back the tears that suddenly demanded passage from her eyes to her cheeks. A combination of the ‘mummy radar’ that continued to disturb her, relief that she wasn’t going to face whatever her alarm was sounding for alone, and finally, yet another reason to regret destroying the perfect relationship with the perfect man she had

had in Derrick. She often wondered if his gift of intuition perceived her nightly prayers for his heart to be healed and offer her a second chance.

She ran upstairs to freshen up. She couldn't help always trying to look her best for whenever Derrick came around. On this occasion she didn't have enough advance warning to psyche herself up into her brave, 'I'm doing okay without you face'. Every weekend she wore it like a foundation for make up. She still loved him with every fibre of her body, and he continued to be the source of her x-rated fantasies, but ego refused to let her beg his mercy again after she had done so unrelentingly for almost a year straight. If she was ever going to win him back, she no longer wanted it to be through pity of her pathetic performances of apology and promises of "never again".

She poked her head in on Teeny; she looked odd somehow. Maya ventured further into the room and touched her shoulder. She was hot, very hot and trembling all over. The baby hairs, too short to be pulled into her zigzag styled cornrows, that framed her mocha-skinned face, had shrunk into tight curls from the perspiration that beaded down her forehead. Her usually large coal coloured eyes, now squinted in retaliation to the sixty watt, bedroom light. The 'mummy radar' immediately intensified from the gnawing feeling, to heart palpitations. Maya ran to find the number for the doctor, wet some towels and dial the phone she still held in her hand all at once. The doctor's number offered her an automated answer machine message, listing out of hours numbers to call that included NHS Direct. Back at her daughters side she placed the damp towels on her head and neck whilst tightly wrapping Teeny in her panther blanket, against her weak protests of being too hot. She cradled her daughter in her left arm and began to dial the National Health Service with her right. 'Mummy radar' intensified further and manifested as a knot in her stomach.

"Fuck that," she mumbled under her breath, "radar says Teeny needs to be in hospital and radar is never wrong!"

She dialled Derrick's number instead.

"M'y'?" he answered, barely allowing the phone to ring.

"I'm taking her to hospital, I got a bad feeling I can't shake D.."

"I'm five minutes away, I'll drive you. Pack her a bag, I soon come."

Yet another thing Maya missed in Derrick, he never doubted her radar, he may have had intuition on lock, but she had the radar. Together they were formidable.

Maya, ran downstairs and opened the front door ajar in anticipation of Derrick's arrival, grabbed Teeny's duffle bag she had spied in the hallway, and quickly ran back up to cram as many necessities as possible into it. Within the promised five minutes, she heard her ex-husband padding up the stairs his lithely way, and glanced at Teeny's bedroom door to seek confirmation.

"Hey D.," she greeted as he entered, turning her back before he could answer, lest she her eyes confess just how much she needed him there for herself.

"Hey," he replied, walking straight over to Teeny's side.

"Teeny-Tiny? How you feeling babe?"

"Hey Daddy," she managed to murmur.

"Ready to go?" Derrick asked Maya, scooping his baby girl into his arms.

"Yeah all set." She followed him out the door and downstairs toward the car.

Maya opened the door and stepped into the back seat, and stretched out her arms to receive the bundle that was Teeny onto her lap. The drive from Maya's three-bedroom house in East Acton to Saint Mary's hospital in Paddington took about 15 minutes, the peak time rush hour was over as was the congestion-charging period. To get there, they had to pass Hammersmith Hospital also situated in East Acton, but paediatric emergencies were no longer accepted there. Nia had cussed for a straight hour on finding out the hard way when taking her seven year old son, afflicted with sickle cell anaemia for the emergency treatment of a crisis. Maya silently prayed over her daughter, in between whispering tender words of encouraging reassurance. The drive felt much longer than the quarter of an hour it supposedly took. The 'mummy radar' had eased back from the abdominal knots and heart palpitations, to the gnawing feeling that refused to desist.

"She's gonna be alright, M'y', you just stay strong for her back there," Derrick assured, as he glanced back at them through his rear-view mirror and caught Maya biting her lip, forehead creased in concentration.

"I know D.," she replied. "Just a twenty-four hour bug, that's all, probably fussing over nothing".

Her voice trailed off. There seemed hardly any point in trying to convince the intuit, that she was fine, when she barely managed to convince herself.

"This is about as close as I can get, but I'm gonna have to go park up properly. Can you manage her on your own for a minute?" Derrick asked, as he drove up to the entrance of Saint Mary's A&E.

"Yeah, I can handle it, I'll need you to help me carry her out though."

It was 9.37pm. There were a few people waiting to be seen at the A&E reception, most were there for the attention of superficial wounds, cuts and burns. To her relief, Teeny's age and status seemed to automatically warrant the attention Maya had braced herself to start raving like a deranged woman for. By the time Derrick had come up to meet her, a nurse was guiding them to a corner cubicle of the paediatrics A&E section. Between them, she and Teeny's father lay their bundle joy on the bed for observation.

"I'll be back in a second to take a few details from you, I'm just going to bleep the doctor," said the nurse in tone of professional sympathy that came with a healthy dose of comfort. She wore pale blue scrubs, and white pumps. Just below her left shoulder, her name badge read 'Rachael'. Beneath that was a blue Bic biro and another silver cased pen that peeped from the top of a triangular based pocket. Her dark brown, chin length hair was styled in a bob, that didn't quite obscure her large ears from view as intended. Her eyes were hazel pools of serenity, accented by a pleasant thin-lipped smile. Her presence seemed to slow time and calmly neutralize the hustle and bustle that was commonplace in her work environment. Panic had no choice but to adhere to her rationale that was not expressed as words, yet was clearly present in her sunny disposition.

Rachael returned with a high tech blood pressure monitor with a pulse meter attached, that she clipped onto Teeny's left index finger before wrapping the girl's right arm in the pressure cuff. After about sixty seconds or so, she wrote down the results on a log sheet. "The doctor has been paged; he'll be here shortly. I'll take down your daughter's details now if you don't mind."

Derrick stepped up to supply the necessary. "Destiny Kingsley… September 27th 1996…. About three hours ago?" He said, turning toward Maya for confirmation.

"Ye – yes. It was about then that she started complaining of a sore throat and saying she was tired… No, she was fine earlier, I mean she was quieter than usual after school, but I didn't read much into it. I mean, Teeny's quiet is still chatty, just..." Maya's arms lifelessly flopped to her side in surrender as she gave a disheartened sigh of exasperation in response to hearing herself rant.

Teeny had now been in a coma for four hours. It was three and a half hours since the doctor ordered a saline drip and bloods to be taken. Two hours and ten minutes since he requested she be administered an intravenous dose of penicillin, after checking with her parents for allergies. An hour since the doctor returned a third time, admittedly unable to provide any justification for their daughter's condition.

"We found evidence of the onset of a mild infection in her blood, nothing serious at all. Other than that and her being a little dehydrated, her observations read within acceptable parameters. We can find no apparent reason for your daughter's current state. I'd like to take a fresh sample of blood for re-testing though," the doctor had said.

Maya wondered if Derrick stepped in front of her and lightly touched her arm because he could sense how hard she fought to refrain from venting her frustration by slapping the doctor senseless. Instead she wearily climbed onto the bed on which her daughter lay. A couple of rogue tears dropped from her eye and landed on Teeny's cheek as she enveloped her body around her as best she could, on the narrow cot of a bed.

2

This Could Be Heaven

The sun shone brightly as if it had been challenged in a bet to see how many it could make seek shade. A few birds chirped happily. A black bird shrilled every two seconds as if it were the designated town crier of old, commanding that all should stop and listen to the important wisdom it had to impart. Teeny squirmed in response to something that plopped onto her face and opened her eyes in time to see another drop about to splash down. She squinted her eyes against the sun, and noted the long blade of grass that had just dropped the last of its morning dew down onto her cheek. She lay still and rotated her neck to look around, not wanting to sacrifice the comfort of her position to her curiosity. More grass on her left. To the right she felt the presence of another lying alongside her, it felt like someone under her mink blanket. She turned and was shocked to not see her mother, but a panther. Not the picture of the one on the blanket she so loved, but a real live panther! '*Don't panic*' she thought, but it was too late, she was panicking. Her heart felt as if it was going to jump out her chest and run off before she managed to command her legs to organise themselves to do the same.

"Don't be afraid dear, I wont hurt you, I'm here to look after you."

That voice; it sounded eerily familiar, but where did it come from? It seemed to originate from the direction of the panther that had by now risen to its feet.

"Destiny my sweet, please don't be afraid. It's me, Nana. We don't have much time together, so let's not waste it."

Teeny looked in disbelief, her breathing taking the form of shallow pants. She swallowed hard and rubbed her eyes. She obviously hadn't woken up yet.

"Yes you are awake, and no you are not dreaming… well technically your are… Well sort of, but right now you need to trust that it's me; Nana."

It sounded like her grandmother all right, but she had died a little under a year ago, and yet here was this panther not only talking, but also claiming to be her beloved Nana?

"What is this? Where am I? How are you talking? Panthers don't talk, why do you sound like my Nana?" she spluttered all at once.

"This is what would best be described as a kind of lucid dream, also known as a vision by those who prefer to term it as such. You are in what is known as the Abridged Dimension, a plateau where the planes of existence converge. In this place, time is non-existent and impervious to the expansion and contraction that occurs as the planes honour their regular cyclic journey of rotation. In this realm, your eyes truly see and your ears truly hear. There is no division of language across species, for we are not prone to the illusion of separation. We are all one. And of course panthers talk dear, just because your human ears chose not to hear and acknowledge their speech, it doesn't mean they are unable.

"I sound like your Nana, because I am the soul you associate with your grandmother, I'm merely in a different form to the one you are most familiar. I have always adored panthers, such beautiful creatures aren't they? My favourite animals just as much as they are yours you know. I thought it would be nice for you to be in the company of one. I know I would have jumped at the opportunity in your position, but suit yourself..." the panther sighed in response to the quizzical look that Teeny continued to lay on her. "Lets do this the boring human way if it pleases you more. Goodness, I had hoped you wouldn't have been so closed-minded. You really are getting old aren't you Missy? Shame, that."

The panther pushed back on her front paws as if to pounce, but instead, began to slowly change shape. Its silky black fur, became a long ankle-length black robe, its fore paws became the mocha brown hands of an old woman that peeked out from the sleeves. Meanwhile the panther's ears shifted from it's position on top of its head to become aligned behind either side of its face making way for the space between the previous position of its ears to become neat silver white cornrows that fell just below its shoulders. The snout retreated to become a smooth face, save the familiar characteristic wrinkles her granddaughter was accustomed to.

The woman who now took the place of the panther that previously lay in her place, stood upright and smiled at a horrified Teeny. Her legs had long since given up hopes of running and instead chose to buckle involuntarily into a position that left her sitting with her legs tucked away beneath her in hiding. All the remainder of her body seemed to be able to muster was a silent, albeit visible 'gulp' accented with tears that came from - she didn't know where. It was really her Nana; her beautiful Nana that she had missed so dearly. Or was it?

"You still need a little more to help for you accept this I see," her Nana offered, in the same gentle husky tone she had used whilst in the form of a panther, except this time the voice matched the person to whom it claimed to belong.

The tears that fell were in relief that the memory of her grandmother hadn't faded as much as she feared time threatened it would.

"My name is Modupe Olufunmilayo Oshodi. During my last incarnation I gave birth to four children, specifically your mother, Maya Abiola Oshodi, now known as Kingsley. You are my namesake, Destiny Abebi Modupe Kingsley. I've purposefully brought you here to pass on some wisdom that I can't seem to get through to your mother. You come from a bloodline of spiritually gifted individuals. Your father is a multi-gifted clairsentient; a universal empath and your mother is a clairvoyant, with an aptitude for precognition, retrognition and intuition. Unfortunately for the most part she seems to ignore her gifts, preferring as of late to attribute perception of her additional senses to coincidence, unless it concerns you.

"You have been born into very important era of change. The Piscean age, marking technology and invention, has made way to the Aquarian, representative of light and thought. This has triggered the birth of a new breed of children, which have been termed as Indigos, due to the colour that dominates their aura - their personal energy field. The offspring of the most recent incarnations of these children are termed as Crystals due to the higher potency concentration of Indigo qualities within them. You are one of these children in need of the nurturing guidance of conscious Indigo parents in order to assist you toward your... well your destiny, to balance the planet as it undergoes it's evolution. Gaia; your planet, better known to you as Earth, is experiencing what you might best understand as puberty, for lack of a better word. She is very delicate right now. Consider yourself along with all other Indigos and Crystals as her regulating hormones, oestrogen if you will. Are you still with me dear? Are you remembering yet?" Nana paused and awaited a response from her bewildered granddaughter.

“I - uh, I think so. Um no. Wait, what do you mean; am I remembering?” asked Teeny, “And how does all this explain why I’m here, or even how I got here. Oh my god am I dead?”

“Hush no, my dear! Please just listen, you can ask questions once I’ve told you the basics, but I assure you, you are very much alive. When I say remembering, what I mean is, you have known all this before. However, during your transition of incarnation into human form, your time in the womb resulting in birth, you entered, as all physical beings do, a mental form of stasis known as hyper-sleep. The primary function of hyper-sleep is to enable your soul essence to fully integrate into your human body vehicle. All the information you would ever need during your stay on Earth is by default, pre-encoded in the DNA of your human body, the majority of which is set in a kind of timed release system. The rest are triggered by key words, phrases and/or sensations. All of which are predetermined by yourself before embarking your journey to Earth. All answers are found within, but more often than not, humans tend to look everywhere other than this most obvious place of safekeeping.

“Many that stumble upon this information, whether accidentally or intentionally by way of meditation or lucid dreams, or those that simply manage to retain a fair amount of their memory, have tried to share this information in the form of books and other various form of teachings. The most widely misinterpreted of which, to this day the majority of Gaia’s population continue to mistake or manipulate to their own advantage in the form of religion and worship. Bless their cotton socks. Deep breaths dear, it helps to facilitate becoming one with this environment which would greatly speed up the process of regaining your memory of all that you once knew.”

Nana paused again to take her own advice and gesticulated by circling her arm at Teeny, inviting her to do the same before continuing. “Every Indigo and Crystal Soul counts. Indigos are dependent on Lightworkers; the support network, fore bearers, fore warners and guides of this important time. Likewise the Crystals are highly dependent on the Indigos whom with the benefit of their knowledge, personal experience and maturation of their abilities would raise them with a different set of moral codes and spiritual guidance. Thus stimulating the activation of the knowledge contained in their DNA, the unlocking of which has been previously neglected, ignored and even persecuted by humans of prior generations. I have brought you here because your mother, a third wave Indigo, has some how managed to fall back into a state of hyper-sleep, unwittingly dragging you and your father with her. We cannot have that. As I said every Indigo and Crystal counts, and we have already lost millions to drugs, crime, gang warfare, suicide, misdiagnosis such as insanity or attention deficit disorder, poor diet, the list goes on, but I'm sure you get the picture. As with all necessary change, resistance is the expected variable we must cater for. This is not a bad thing, just a polarity thing; a natural phenomenon that occurs in all dual-natured expressions of existence. Thus for every action…"

"There is an equal and opposite reaction!" Teeny concluded excitedly. "Wow, this is so cool, a few minutes ago I didn't have a clue what you were talking about, all these words - they are new to me, but I understand them in my head now. It's like hearing a bedtime story that was read to me when I was younger."

"That's right." Nana gave a smile of satisfaction. "You are remembering. Now all that I have to tell you will become easier to digest. The language, the words I speak to you, may initially sound confusing to your adolescent ears, but within my verse are words that are the key DNA triggers you chose before your incarnation, that you felt best suited to awaken you."

Somehow the term 'Indigo Child' seemed vaguely familiar. Teeny pondered on where she could have come across it, and found her attention being drawn to the memory of a short news segment. Within the brief report, parents had spoken of their children being gifted and able to recall past lives. A doctor argued that molly-coddling parents had coined the term and invented attributes to excuse their children's excessively delinquent behaviour.

"Indigo and Crystal Children represent the dawning of a new Earth. Synchronous to Gaia's evolution, her inhabitants are also evolving as a species. Indigos are pioneers paving the way for global rebirth, the first of which began incarnating approximately a century ago. Fifty years later saw the next generation of their kind, this time in greater numbers. It is this collective that are known as Lightworkers. The year 1970 was herald to the third wave that came in considerably larger figures. This group in particular bear a more aggressive warrior like nature as they actively tear down redundant structures and thought processes including, but not limited to governmental, educational and political institutions. They are passionate in their rebellious fight for change. Their belligerent disposition was necessary to successfully nullify expired methodologies. Having done so, these third, or gamma wave Indigos as they are also known, are now in their late twenties and early thirties and are not only maturing into positions of leadership, but are giving birth to a new wave of beings; the Crystals. These Crystal Souls began to incarnate from the year 2000, with a few arriving slightly earlier. What makes Indigos and Crystals so different to humans yet to evolve, are the spiritual gifts with which they are endowed. They vibrate on the frequency of the third-eye chakra, which facilitates psychic energies such as telepathy and clairvoyance and as such exhibit these and other abilities. In time all humans will transition to this stage of evolution. Post 1970 Indigos and new Crystal Souls are also unique in that they have never incarnated on Earth before," Teeny's grandmother concluded.

Nana neglected to mention there were exceptions to this rule, dictated by the fact that there were different classes of Indigo and Crystal children: Those who were indigenous humans, the first of their kind to emerge from the evolution process. Those who were Starseed coordinators specifically assigned to the planet to assist in the facilitation of the period of transition, and lastly those who were a combination of the two.

"Well wouldn't that make me an Indigo then? I mean; I was born before the year 2000," Teeny observed.

"Very good!" replied Nana. "You would be correct, except your soul is rare amongst other incarnations. Even so, Indigos can transpire to become Crystal if they so choose, by elevating their consciousness and submitting to the necessary emotional and physical transformation." She daintily lifted the part of her black robe that brushed her knees, between thumb and forefinger and with her head held elegantly high, she knelt to sit down beside Teeny, took her hand and breathed deep. Teeny instinctively closed her eyes and copied.

For the first time since her arrival to this strange place, she found herself able to relax and welcome the suns caress that had since removed the evidence of tears from her face. Without opening her eyes she could some how the sense the beauty around her that in her initial fear, her eyes had censored. She opened them now and gasped at the wonder of the wealth of colour, so picture perfect it caused her to muse whether this was how the biblical Garden of Eden might have looked. The grass beneath her was a lush radiant green, thick and soft that felt like a cushion beneath her. This quality of grass spread in every direction, broken only by flowers that appeared to grow wild, yet seemed to have been nurtured by love for how well pruned they looked. Little mounds rose in unpredictable intervals, some with more flowers of numerous variety and colour, but all in a bed of the same luscious carpet of grass she had awoken in. Plants grew in random patches with the same tell tale signs of tender loving care applied to their long leafy foliage.

Trees danced in the light breeze that gently swept through the clearing that surrounded the two souls. United by their Earthly memories of one another, they sat sharing a moment of peace and love communicated without speech. In the distance the young girl could hear water running and knew it to be a waterfall, tumbling down a cliff that looked dangerous with its spontaneous juts of rock that insisted the water take another route by separating into two and reuniting below its indignant, yet aesthetic obstruction.

Small woodland creatures habitually sniffed and tasted the air, ears twitching as if to listen for predators they had encountered in previous lives that had once sought them for sustenance. On one of the mounds, something that appeared to be a transparent panda sat quiet and still amidst the buzz of chatter.

"What's that? And what is it doing?" asked Teeny of her grandmother.

"He is a panda that answers to the title Chieko. He is resident to one of the higher realms known as Supreme Truth. He has attained much wisdom throughout his lifetimes and has found that which lies between the ever-shifting polarities of agreeable versus disagreeable and is preparing for ascension to the realm of the formless ones, the Etherean. He is in the process of surrender. The only reason we can see him at all is because of the convergence of the Abridged Dimension. As we speak he is experiencing events taking place on hundreds of dimensions simultaneously and becoming one with each of them. All realities and densities are superimposed, so if you look carefully, you may see many other similar apparitions floating by. They are inhabitants of other varying degrees of lower densities that are usually beyond our ability to perceive, due to the difference in frequency on which they vibrate. Likewise you may see those that resemble lifelike statues. They are beings of a higher density, a lower frequency oblivious to our presence. To those of them that are more aware, we on this frequency may appear like ghostly apparitions or cloudy wisps caught in the glimpse of the corner of an eye, usually dismissed as ones imagination."

"Is Chieko a grandfather to another Crystal child like me on Earth?" Teeny enquired.

"No dear," Nana chuckled, "he is beyond the need for offspring. He is not, and never has incarnated as a human. He has been many things, but he found his bliss whilst living as a panda over a millennia ago. He usually remains more or less formless in the ethers, but as I said, the convergence enables us to perceive him in a way our minds and eyes can comprehend."

"Okaaaay, maybe I'll just breathe some more shall I? Because that went way over my head!" Teeny admitted sheepishly.

"Never mind, that is not what I brought you here for anyway."

"Okay, so what uh – plane is it that we are on, and exactly how did you manage to bring me here? In English please Nana!"

Nana laughed and then sighed. "We are in the heart of the Mental Realm, the plane on which man and mind meet. It serves as a kind of bridge between the upper and lower planes. For the sake of simplicity, lets say there are seven major planes in all. Within each of the seven there are sub-planes, and within each of those are more sub-planes still, altogether loosely equating the sum total of seven, to the seventh power of seven. Now don't make the mistake of trying to illustrate in your minds eye, the planes as being stacked in a linear fashion. Like time, each coexist and bleed into and within one another and can impress upon persons, places and things in adjacent planes. The ability to discern these impressions is dependent on the level of awareness and sensitivity of the person, place or thing in question. This is how I managed to implant a harmless viral infection into you, initiating the rapid onset of a sequence of events that lead to you being brought to hospital. I altered the parameters of the virus to cause your body to simulate a fever intense enough to trigger your mother's intuitive response and seek immediate professional care.

"Meetings such as this usually require a more aggressive trigger such as a near death experience, but because of your age and natural willingness to follow your bliss, such tactics were unwarranted in your case. Even so, this meeting would never have been necessary at all, if only your mother would pay attention to the signs that have been guiding her. Your parent's divorce threw a spanner in the works of her heightened perception. In other words, she became very sad. So sad she could no longer hear or see the way she used to." Nana paused in reflection. Her own sadness evident in her eyes at the frustration of no longer being able to comfort her daughter through her trials. Hindsight was a regrettable wisdom.

"Hyper-sleep is usually initiated for the purpose of transition of the soul from one state of being to another. The most common method is through insemination of the soul into a human body vehicle via impregnation and gestation within a hospitable womb, leading to birth. The gestation period nurtures the development of the personalized human body vehicle, taking one third of genetic material from each parent. The final third is that of the souls unique identity that it retains life after life, which binds into the other two thirds. No matter how many times a soul reincarnates, each life will provide a new wealth of missions and experiences for it to complete, learn and evolve from. For the sake of the well being of your physical body i.e. adequate hydration amongst other things, it was essential to induce stasis within a controlled environment, hence the need to have you admitted to hospital. Once in the care of trained health professionals, the virus instructed your body to re-enter a state of hyper-sleep that the doctors are referring to as a coma."

"That was English?" asked Teeny, tilting her head and squinting her eyes expressing her mounting confusion. She wrinkled her nose in obvious disapproval of her Nana's explanation.

"Close your eyes and breathe deep dear child. All I have said will make perfect sense in a few seconds," instructed Nana. Teeny complied, her mouth slowly curling into a smile, accompanying a rhythmic nod that indicated she now understood.

That the Mental Realm was the connection between physical and non-physical existence made it so that any could access or communicate with upper realms via thought. Knowledge, wisdom and inspiration were all product of the simplistic method of access. Great thinkers were merely those who tended to relish in the addiction to information and a desire to know themselves and thus know All-Oneness, known to some simply as All, or Oneness. Devotion and determination were all that were necessary to access infinite awareness, but few were focused enough to truly comprehend and as such, unbounded information intimidated undisciplined minds. Corporeals loyal to the attainment of wisdom developed themselves in order to increase access efficiency. Some became skilled in the ability to request data, while others nurtured the talent for receiving it. Each method, an art form unto themselves, though best utilised together. Prayer was the art of the request, whilst meditation the art of clear reception and overstanding. Confusion was not an uncommon side effect of thought, as many requested, but failed to appropriately translate the response, and instead settled for the inaccuracy of their own interpretation above that which was supplied in abundance.

Teeny followed the path of a butterfly as it flew around the low hanging branches of a purple leaved cherry plum tree. For a moment she saw what appeared to be another butterfly enter her peripheral vision, she turned her attention to it only to lose sight of it altogether. She readily dismissed it before wondering if it had been an apparition like the ones her Nana had just told her of. She focused her attention in the area of the tree once again, determined to see something or at least convince herself that it was indeed nothing. She burrowed her forehead in concentration daring not to blink. She held her gaze so resolutely until her eyes began to smart and lose focus. Just as she approached unwilling surrender to the need to refresh her stare, she saw something. It seemed to resemble a puff of smoke. She reflexively rubbed her eyes in an attempt to clear her vision, but by the time she opened her eyes again it had disappeared.

Teeny slumped back onto her elbows in dejection. She had so badly wanted to see, and kicked herself for breaking her line of sight the way she had. What she saw, somehow reminded her of when she first woke up some mornings, vision blurred, impaired by sleep that had yet to be shaken off. She looked across at her Nana, who appeared to have her attention consumed by the butterfly that had now landed on a bluebell flower. Then suddenly she saw it again, this time more than just a puff of smoke, it was foggy impression of silhouette outline! Teeny sat up quickly, what she had seen had disappeared, but she could now see another, and another. They were everywhere, sparsely dotting the scenery at random intervals, sporadically fading in and out of view. Some appeared slightly denser than others, making them more readily visible, but all were little more than a ghostly fog. There were different shapes and sizes and each moved at different speeds, making it hard to grasp any discerning features. It seemed as if the less obscure variety moved with less haste than their wispier counter parts. Teeny smiled inwardly with satisfaction as if she had just passed some kind of elitist vision test. She didn't question her absence of fear at what she saw. She simply accepted the semi-present populace as being similar to persons she might have encountered during a visit to a park.

Teeny closed her eyes and breathed deeply in anticipation of a complicated response as she asked; "So Nana, why didn't you just tell me or Mummy these things when you were alive - I mean, in human form?"

"Because sweetie, back then, I didn't have a clue."

3

Man's Intuition

"M'y'. M'y', wake up!" Derrick gently shook Maya's shoulder, "wake up M'y'".

"Mmm, what?" she stirred.

"They're gonna move Teeny to a ward now. The nurse is saying we should go home and rest up."

"What? You mean leave Teeny alone? What if we aren't there when she wakes up?" Maya retorted, now fully alert. She carefully pushed her self up from around Teeny, as if to avoid disturbing her sleep. As she stretched, she looked around reacquainting herself to the cubicle and the situation at hand. Their sleeping beauty looked peaceful, blissfully ignorant of her parent's anxiety and doctors stupefaction over her untenable 'coma'.

Rachael poked her head around the curtains that had been drawn around the cubicle. "Mr and Mrs. Kingsley, a porter is on his way to transport your daughter to the 'A' ward. May I suggest you go home and get some rest, there really isn't much else you can do here just now. I assure you we will contact you of any significant change to her status."

"No way am I leaving my Teeny. She needs me, I'm not going anywhere!" Maya replied indignantly.

"Mrs. Kingsley, I promise you, Destiny will not be alone. Besides it is 3am, I'm afraid we can't permit you to stay on the ward out of visiting hours. Please, you need to get some rest. You can come back first thing in the morning," Rachael patiently coaxed, unflustered by Maya's emotional response.

Maya looked at Derrick who was showing signs of wear. He had maintained vigil whilst she had succumbed to a couple hours of much needed sleep beside Teeny.

"Come Maya, lets go, she's gonna be okay. Lemme get you home."

"Okay," she surrendered.

"It's late, I don't want to be worrying about you driving home like this. Stay the night."

It took the whole duration of the drive back home for Maya to gather the courage to request that her ex-husband get some rest back at what was once the family home they had purchased together. When he had requested a divorce, he had insisted she and Teeny remain there; he would be the one to move out. Maya could never fault him for lack of fairness and generosity. It was he that initiated maintenance payments that exceeded the courts assessment of how much a non-resident father should give. She didn't have to do a thing except lament over how much her mistake had cost their family.

Derrick paused in hesitation before accepting her offer. It had been two years since he last slept under the same roof with his ex-wife. The situation with Teeny made him feel a sense of responsibility for Maya's anxiety. He could feel her misplaced guilt and related to her feelings of helplessness. However, he refused to fall prey to any attempt she might possibly make to get him back. He still loved her; there was no question of that. He simply couldn't bear the heartache he felt when around her for extended periods of time. Should she make an advance on him, he doubted he would be able to resist. Maya was a rare combination of beauty, sexiness and determination. She wore her natural hair in short fine twists, that bounced when she threw back her head in uncontrollable fits of laughter and flopped back neatly into place when she fought to recompose herself. Her high dimpled cheeks rose like the sun, and her full African lips warmed his heart every time she smiled. Teeny's petite frame was an inheritance of Maya's small stature. Though she stood a shorter than average 5'4", she carried herself tall with her regal walk. Her skin was a flawless, silky pecan brown. He missed how he would trace his fingers along the contour of her bare arms and nuzzle into her neck when he would creep up behind her as she cooked or sat working on the computer.

Once home, Maya went to prepare the spare bedroom for Derrick to sleep in. He walked into the kitchen and put the kettle to boil. They could both benefit from the soothing properties of chamomile tea before retiring. By the time Maya had come downstairs her cup was set at the table placement opposite the one on which Derrick had sat himself. She cautiously sat down and picked up her mug.

"Thank you," she said, unable to look him in the eye. "I'm sorry." She felt deafened by the silence that echoed around them.

"For what?" Derrick queried.

"For everything, for this… I don't know. I swear she was fine one minute; next she's lying on the stairs, too weak to walk. I just don't know what… How could this happen? How can this be happening?" she sobbed.

Derrick's soul reached over and held her in his arms, but his body remained frozen in his seat. He wanted to comfort her, but he didn't dare allow himself to touch her. Instead he said in his most soothing voice; "M'y', this isn't your fault, even the doctors are at a loss for explanation. Look, I don't know how or when, but I know I can promise you we are going to have her back whole again. We just gotta stay strong and focused for her. Everything will be all right."

"You say that like you know something I don't. What makes you so sure? You said it yourself, not even the doctors have a clue," she sniffed.

"I don't know, I'm just… I'm just saying what you should be saying," he responded, head bowed. He seemed to be speaking to the tea he held cupped between his hands, fingers interlinking where they met on the print side of the mug. "You always know what to say and do at times like this, always know if there's reason to worry. I know you're scared, hell I am too, but there's something different about the way you have been throughout all this. There isn't something I know that you don't, there is something *you* know that I can feel. That is what makes me so sure."

Maya placed her elbow on the table and rested her forehead in her hand poised in thought for a few seconds taking in Derrick's words. She knew him well enough to trust his feelings, but sometimes he came out with cryptic comments that perplexed her and this was one of those times. "Okay, help me out. Explain," she said finally.

Derrick blew a gust of air from his nose in a nasal kind of sigh. "Cha, You know I don't have a clue how this ting works, I just know that's all. Should be you telling me, I thought this intuition stuff was supposed to be a women's ting anyway."

Maya scowled.

"Alright, alright! Shit!" he scowled back then closed his eyes and rolled his neck from left to right. Not even he knew why he ritually performed this action, but it somehow seemed to make him focus more on what he was feeling. If asked, he'd probably have dismissed it as simply a way to loosen any residual tension. He took a deep breath and tried to relax. He frowned and opened his eyes. He looked almost agitated.

"Well?" Maya demanded.

"I don't know, I feel it, but I don't know what it is. It's like its there, but it's not there," replied Derrick, uncomfortable with being put on the spot.

Maya knew better than to press him when he was like this, but she wanted to feel as sure as he that Teeny was going to be all right. She waited a few seconds before daring to nudge a little more. "D.?"

"M'y', look its as if there are two of you, one knows the answer, the other is just – I don't know! I just know I'm backing the part of you that knows what this is all about. Can we just drop it already, I'm tired as hell and my head is pounding aiight? I'm going to get some sleep, you should too." Derrick pushed back his chair and rose to his feet. "G'night Maya."

Maya threw herself onto bed and rolled onto her back. She was frustrated, pissed off and frustrated. '*There are two of you, one knows the answer.*' Ugh! What answer? And what did he mean there were two of her? Did the one that knew the answer know how to bring back her daughter? If that was the case, did Derrick hold her responsible for the fact that Teeny lay in a coma unnecessarily? She thrashed her arms onto her quilt in a mock tantrum, then rolled onto her side and closed her eyes. A few moments later she opened them again grabbed her pillow, and angrily thrust it between her thighs. How the hell could she be horny at a time like this? She blamed Derrick's presence two rooms down the hallway. Two years older than her, aged thirty-four, he oozed sex appeal that seemed to mature like a fine wine. He stood at 5'10" and wore a well-manicured beard that extended down the sides of his jaw line into a neatly trimmed goatee, which in turn framed a pair of sexy, full lips that would part in to an ever so cheeky smile. A feature his daughter had clearly inherited. Above his high cheekbones, small mid-set eyes hinted of an old soul whose depth and wisdom could have given birth to galaxies in universes unknown. Over the years his hair had gone from a flamboyant high top, to a laid back bald fade. "Maya hold it down and go to sleep!" she growled at herself. She grabbed the pillow and tossed it across the room.

Derrick and Maya had been in each other's lives, both separate and apart for fourteen years now. They had met at a poetry slam held in a club in Ladbroke Grove. He had come with a woman he had been dating, and she had been there with a couple of friends who had insisted she would simply, "float in the vibe". The master of ceremonies had called for anyone to come share his or her flow. Something must have stirred in Derrick to make him suddenly step to the microphone as he had done, because as soon as he got there, he looked almost as surprised as his girlfriend whose jaw had dropped, her face a picture of horror. This was obviously his first time, and his girlfriend didn't seem to have had a clue that he harboured a poetic side deep within. He had glanced over to his woman for support but she had slid down in her seat and shaded her forehead with her hand, already embarrassed to the point of having disassociated herself from him. Derrick looked to the floor and started to speak. The first words he uttered were an inaudible mumble. His nervous eyes fleeted across the crowd for a second before dropping back to the floor. He forced a cough into the side of his fist and tried again. The poem was deep. Women held their breath nodding to his every word, men hollered and whooped "Das right!" "Teach!" and "Tell 'em bro!" as he spoke apologetically for being the good man that every woman prayed for, yet being rejected for not being ‘thug enough’. His eyes never once left the floor, not even to receive his standing ovation. Instead he stepped off the stage seemingly oblivious to the pats on the back and cheers of “Gwan wit yo’ bad self!” and walked out of the club. The woman he left behind was now sitting upright, face aghast. She looked confused as if she may have lost something precious, but wasn’t sure how, what or when.

The affect his words had had on Maya was the exact opposite. As soon as he had stepped on the stage, she had leant forward placing her elbows on the table and cradled her chin in her fists and breathed the words, “Damn, that man is fine!” When he spoke, her body had trembled to a chill that ran down her spine. His poem had made her soul cry, as she felt his pain. She knew right then she wanted to be the one to pick up the pieces of his heart that he left shattered on the stage. When he had walked out the door, a strange loneliness overcame Maya that she couldn’t explain, her throat became dry and she felt breathless. Without thinking she jumped out of her seat, to the surprise of the company she had attended the evening with, and ran out after him. She frantically looked around running aimlessly down the street in no particular direction until she came to a road. She looked left and right then doubled over to rest her hands on her knees. She didn’t realise just how out of breath she had become. She stayed in her stooped position catching her breath before pulling herself up to walk back. Her heart almost jumped out her chest as she saw the stranger she had been chasing after, step out of the Cost Cutter store she had just passed only moments ago. She watched as he shoved his change into his jeans pocket and broke open a bottle of Snapple then suddenly found herself walking up to him. Still panting, she shoved a closed fist in front of him.

“Here. You left yours in the club back there.”

He looked at her through reddened eyes that held choked back emotion. He said nothing, but opened his hand to receive what she had to give. Maya dropped her hand in his and opened it to reveal nothing - her hand was empty.

Derrick looked in his hand, then back at her as if she was crazy. “Wha?” was all he could manage to say of his puzzlement.

Maya, still trying to compose herself from her sprint, placed one hand on her hip and with the other pointed back in the direction of the club. “You left your heart on the stage,” she gasped, “I thought I’d loan you mine while yours is on the mend.”

Derrick took a step back cocked his head to the side and said, “Lady are you high?” Then burst into laughter, looked up to the heavens and continued, “Damn, you really have a sense of humour!”

Maya slapped her thigh realising just how crazy she must have seemed. “Yup, you lost your heart, I just lost my mind, and any sense of self respect I may have had. Cue the ground opening to swallow me now puh-lease!” She paused as if waiting for the concrete to actually grant her shelter. “Okay, so the floor isn’t gonna help me out, so I’m just gonna – you know, walk away with the little shred of dignity I have left,” she said easing back and rotating into a slow deliberate about turn, that was more for the purpose of avoiding further embarrassment through Sod’s Law causing her to trip and fall on her face.

Maya finally fell asleep and was dreaming. The theme was the same recurring nightmare had been haunting her on and off for almost a year now

“Mummy!”

"Teeny? I'm coming for you baby, hold on!"

"Mummy!"

"Teeny baby, I'm here. Where are you?"

Usually it came roughly once or twice every three or four months. But lately, it had been at least once a week. The dream started and ended the same way every time. She would hear Teeny crying out, in a panic she would run to find her, but her vision was obscured by some kind of fog or mist. She'd run in the direction of Teeny's voice and just as it seemed she was close enough to reach out and touch her, she would stumble and fall, waking up without ever having seen her daughter's face. Every time she woke up from this dream she would run to Teeny's room to make sure she was okay and that the dream was just that and nothing more.

Maya woke up with a start, and like so many times before darted out of her room to check on Teeny. This time the bed was empty. It took a minute or so for Maya to recall the events of the last ten hours. She was actually living her nightmare. She walked toward the spare room where Derrick slept and stood outside the door, hesitant. She raised her fist to knock on the door then thought against it. Five minutes passed while she stood deliberating, but it could have easily been an eternity. Finally she held her breath, gently turned the door handle and poked her head inside. Derrick looked over his shoulder toward where she stood standing at the door.

"I'm sorry… I…" She hadn't for a second catered on him being awake. "I just – I didn't know you were awake, I just..."

"What's wrong, how come you're not sleeping?" Derrick interrupted. Maya fumbled for a good excuse, but could find none and had to settle for telling the truth.

"I was thinking about what you said, you know, earlier about my having the answer. And well, I think I kind of understand what you mean. It's like my conscious mind doesn't know, but my subconscious does right?"

"Yeah I guess," he yawned.

"Well, I was thinking you could do that thing you used to do. You know, where you connect with me and know what's on my mind?" She knew she was clutching at straws, but it still came as a shock to hear Derrick without hesitation issue her a point blank:

"No."

"W-what? Why?" her tone increased pitch by an octave in disbelief.

"Why?" said Derrick now sat upright with one knee drawn up to his chest and rested his elbow on it. "Because we don't have it like that no more, that's why. You called me and I came. While I'm here, I'll do everything I can to be there for Teeny, but not that! I'm not tryna walk down that road with you Maya. Bearing in mind the shit we've been through over the past couple of years, you should know better than to ask," he said angrily.

"I know it's intimate, but I'm not asking for us to get back together…matter o' fact, hold on… I called you? I never called you, you called me, and seeing as you're here and you're the one who said I had the answer, you might as swallow your pride and help me get it!" Maya was heated.

"Oh I should swallow my pride? Me – swallow my pride? I called you, because you were too proud to call me, even though you knew damn well you wanted to. If I had left it up to you, how long would it have been before I was told Teeny was sick?" Derrick was tired and no way was he in the mood for mind games.

"I'm sorry, you are trying to tell me I wanted to call you? You must really think you are all that, Derrick Kingsley."

"Damn right I'm all that, remember who you're talking to and what you just came here to ask me. You're literally asking me to pick your thoughts out of your head for you, but you don't believe I can feel when you call to me, but are too arrogant to pick up the phone? You want me to call - I call. I feel no way about going above and beyond the call of duty for my daughter, but connect with you like that? Not any more."

Maya knew she was beat, but Derrick's irate response gave her ammunition for one last desperate attempt. She folded her arms and said one word.

"Wuss!"

"What?" he was lost.

"I called you a wuss. It's okay; I get it. You're so scared of being that close to me, that you'd rather our daughter suffer. What do you think would happen when you hold me D.? If you are truly all that, you needn't worry about losing yourself. Anyways, it doesn't matter. I'll let you get back to sleep." She walked out and pulled his door shut behind her and went to her bedroom. "I'll give you till morning" she smirked to herself and walked back to her room.

Knowledge

"We have received word of a medical enigma in the vicinity of our 'prodigal son'. A young girl has succumbed to a coma of unlikely circumstances."

"An agent of the Initiate Class? N9ne Blood?"

"Unlikely that the child is N9ne, it is unprecedented that one be deployed in such close proximity to another. It is plausible that she may indeed be an Initiate."

"There has been confirmation?"

"Negative, but it would seem that the infamous Rachael has resurfaced. She was present during the child's administration."

"Maintain distance, but keep us informed. Rachael may be of the Nurturing Class, but past experience has taught that we should not mistake her pacific nature for weakness."

Dialogue between two of 'those who fear most'.

Location: Whitehall, London.

4

Gorillas Smoke Pipes

"Walk with me," Nana said, and rose to her feet with the same eloquence she had sat down. Teeny scrambled up alongside her.

"Where are we going?" she asked.

"Just for a walk, dear. Would you mind if I return to the form of a panther? It really is the best way to enjoy this place."

Teeny shook her head and stood back. Nana knelt on all fours and quickly resumed her previous form. Teeny watched this time with eyes that danced in a fascination that replaced the uneasiness she felt when watching her Nana's previous transfiguration. They walked through a thicket of trees until it thinned out and became a grassy riverbank. In the distance Teeny could now see the waterfall she had heard earlier.

On the other side of the river, Teeny saw a statue of a couple, arm in arm in apparent mid step. They looked like lovers taking a stroll that had some how been freeze-framed. Both were men, and seemed to have been engaged in an amusing conversation. One had his head tipped toward the other and wore an infectious smile. The other had his eyes wide and an arm raised as if to enhance on an animated tale he had been telling.

"Who are they?" Teeny enquired, wishing she could hear what the couple had been saying.

“Who dear?”

“Them, the two men over there,” she said pointing over at the immobile couple.

“Men? I don’t see any men.” Nana looked in the direction her granddaughter indicated. “Oh them!” Nana said looking about thirty feet from where Teeny had shown her. She slowly turned her head as if she was tracing the path that the statues might have walked had they not been frozen. She smiled. “That’s Cedric and Barney, they have just been reunited. Cedric experienced physical death about four months ago. Barney just yesterday. They have much to catch up on.” Nana laughed, “That Cedric, he is such a comedian, always has me in stitches.”

Teeny looked at the panther in confusion and wondered if in her felid form, her Nana could see and hear what she could not. She followed the direction her grandmother seemed to be looking in, and saw nothing. She shrugged her shoulders and instead looked further down the riverbank where something else caught her eye. A group of four; three against one, were in hand-to-hand combat, but for some strange reason they fought in slow motion. Two of the three aggressors were female fighting against another woman. Even the sound of the battle seem to trail behind as the impact of each blow dealt was silent, though a second or so later a noise that would have matched the point of contact echoed. The female that defended against the trio showed no signs of intimidation and effortlessly delivered a powerful kick to one of her attackers. Teeny’s mouth fell agape as she witnessed the recipient fly back slowly, even so having little time to brace herself against the imminent impact of her landing.

The spectacle she had unwittingly experienced was the opposite of the ghostly presences. These were residents of planes more dense than the ones on which the apparitions inhabited, thus their manifestation was more solid and discernable. Her Nana had experienced the scene a little differently however.

Cedric and Barney had been in full motion and she had laughed at hearing the sound of Barney's chuckle. The battle Teeny had seen in slow motion was nothing more than a blurry wisp of semi-presence that the little girl had recently struggled to make out.

While Teeny continued to marvel at the incredulous view, out of the corner of her eye, she saw the panther run off somewhere. She looked on a little longer before turning to see where her grandmother had gone. Her Nana had run to meet a huge silverback gorilla that lay basking in the sun. The beast stood up and gracefully bowed in acknowledgement of her approach. Nana greeted him by rubbing her head on his thigh. Teeny would have been forgiven for forgetting it was her Nana at all. She walked up to join them.

"Teeny, meet he who calls himself Imhotep," said Nana.

"Greetings little one," said Imhotep placing the pipe he held into his mouth freeing his right hand to offer it for her to shake.

Teeny cautiously reciprocated, only just managing to hold two of his giant fingers in her little hand. She couldn't help but stare to the point of abandon at the pipe Imhotep removed from his mouth allowing for the exhalation of thick smoke from his large mouth.

Teeny fought to contain herself before finally blurting, "Gorillas are allowed to smoke in heaven?"

"Hmph, from what catastrophic combination of genes did you just exist? Pusillanimous meets ignoramus?" retorted the Gorilla snidely.

"Oh don't you go there!" Nana chided.

Imhotep made a shape with is mouth that seemed to be a smile. "And how are you my dear Dupe?" he said stroking Nana's furry head.

"Ready to bite you if you insult my genes again!" Nana retorted and haughtily pushed her nose up in the air.

Imhotep gave a bass filled roar of laughter that vibrated through Teeny's chest.

"Okay, so I take it you were a man that used to love to smoke then?" Teeny asked meekly trying to redeem herself.

"Man? Me? Never!!" Imhotep spat. "The fascination with souls who feel the need to incarnate as such ignorantly savage beings is beyond me!"

"Ah – ah – ah, never say never," interrupted Nana, "I'm sure you too will fall prey to the enticements of humanity through your soul exchange"

"Ugh, don't remind me. The price one must pay for having superior intellect…" Imhotep lamented.

"Soul exchange? What is that?" asked Teeny.

"Well," said Nana deviously as if about to share a tasty morsel of gossip. She slinked a circle around the great silverback, relishing in the opportunity to get her own back, then cheekily lay at his feet. "A soul exchange is when two souls share the use of one body. The first volunteers to commandeer the human body vehicle for a set period of time agreed upon before incarnation. When the date arrives for the first soul to relinquish occupation of the body, it surrenders ownership to another who will live the years remaining until expiry. The exchange is a delicate process and is usually performed during the purposeful instigation of a deep stasis. An event is staged leading to the loss of consciousness of the human body vehicle, creating an environment suitable for the first soul to be extracted and the other to be inseminated. The event is usually one that appears to be life threatening and is sometimes coupled by the occurrence termed by humans as a near death experience. It's like a soul transplant, for which careful preparation is necessary for a seamless surgery. Likewise, each soul undergoes hyper-sleep so as to minimize the trauma such rapid transition might induce. The human body vehicle is encoded with the memories of its previous owner that carries over to the transplanted soul. Upon waking the new soul becomes one with it's host body.

"Others; friends, relatives and associates of the previous resident, would observe the most notable changes as a sudden new lease of life as if an epiphany had been experienced. The body seems to develop new preferences, ranging from dress style to awareness for ones health. Imhotep here has held knowledge of several cures to many physical ailments on Earth, but in his previous incarnations, humans remained ignorant to the wisdom he tried to impart."

Imhotep's soul exchange was the third example of those who were exception to the rule of Indigos having never before incarnated in human form on Earth that Nana hadn't mentioned in her earlier explanation to her granddaughter. They were indigenous souls who volunteered for the transplant process by donating their bodies at their end of their life expectancy for the use of coordinators. This was an amicable decision that benefited both parties. Coordinators who preferred, or did not feel the need to experience humanity so intimately spent minimal time in human form and the indigenous went on to reincarnate back on Earth in a new vessel just as they would have anyway. Insemination to one of these host bodies were often the explanation behind sudden miraculous cures of terminal diseases, and of tragic events which the average human would otherwise not have been expected to survive.

"Imagine that! I could sign in five languages and the most it got me was a bloody banana! Now I have to incarnate as the very epitome of ignorance that failed to recognize that the sun doesn't shine out their bloody arse!" Imhotep thumped his fist on the ground in annoyance.

Nana howled with laughter and beat one of her fore paws on top of the other. Teeny stifled a giggle.

"Aww it's not that bad Imhotep," soothed Nana. "Your experiences are nothing without having tried humanity for size."

"Pff! Says you!" Imhotep pouted. "If I must incarnate in the form of a human at the very least, I should be permitted to do so in the form of the superior of their lowly species! An autistic human body vehicle would be a more fitting shell, but nooooo! Their lesser human counterparts deem them as having a developmental disability. Idiots, the lot of them!! I know you are simply loving this aren't you?"

"Well, just a little. But then what do you expect when you insisted on insulting me so?" Nana answered.

Imhotep warmed to the autonomous nature of humans that were hence labelled autistic and attributed their reputation for 'living in their own world' to being a god-like quality that 'lesser humans' were unable to conceive. He reasoned that it was not they who were by impaired by limited ability for social interaction and communication, rather it was the rest of humanity that egotistically revered themselves as a measure for what was accepted by the majority as normal behaviour. Was it the autistic one's fault that everyone else was unable to communicate on a wavelength compatible to higher minds? Surely it was not difficult to perceive that the characteristic of repetitive behaviour was not restrictive or futile, but a micro-scaled perfect mimicry of the order with which All gave birth to universes. Did humans fail to note how closely the term autistic resembled the word artistic? If 'normal' humans were incapable of acknowledging such things, why should the god in human form concern himself with such tedious incarnations?

"Isn't this heaven deal supposed to be free of arguing and stuff?" Teeny butt in.

"Arguing? Who's arguing? And what's all this talk about heaven?" asked Imhotep.

"Oh, don't mind us dear, this is how we love to spend our time together. Winding each other up about our collective experiences. There is no animosity. On the contrary; I love old Imhotep and he loves me, in all my recollected lifetimes I don't think I have ever loved another more."

"Okayyy, just as place starts to make some form of sense, I find out my grandma is in love with a gorilla, now I've heard it all! Could things get any more weird?"

Nana and Imhotep looked at one another shook their heads and chimed, "Human!" then laughed.

"Oh Imhotep, I'm finally seeing it now, I mean I thought I saw it before, but now I really see what you meant. Human's really do miss the point entirely," Nana chuckled. "My dear child you are, but eleven Earth years old and already you have become so readily assimilated by the limited perceptions of humanity. Thank goodness I brought you here to remind you who you really are."

Teeny didn't know whether to be offended or curious.

"Little one," Imhotep softened the tone of his gruff voice to address her, "different laws apply on different planes of existence. The three lowermost Realms: Impulse, Physical and Spiritual are predominantly, though not exclusively governed by physical laws. The Mental Realm is of course governed by Mind, hence the term; mind over matter. Beyond the Mental there are three other realms, Supreme Truth, Supreme Reality and Alloneness. Only souls who have evolved to a point of completely shedding the physical can reside within Truth, but even then, to elevate beyond Truth they must grow out of the need of a soul. The soul itself is another form of vehicle similar to that of the human body and as such, must be relinquished in order to access Reality where the Etherean reside. In that realm there is no 'me', 'you' or 'I'. All move, think and perceive as one. The uppermost realm is the return to a state of Oneness with All.

"To be in love does not imply there is a wish to procreate or copulate. Love is simply a peaceful surrender, a willingness to shed the illusion of separation and yield to the ultimate desire to become One with. That I love your Nana, is to say I would happily acquiesce in All with a soul who's purest intent I have come to respect and adore. Such a concept is not suited to the lower realms, as the essence of its true meaning would be lost in translation. The Mental Realm however is synonymous with the heart chakra, the openness of which is readily able to comprehend.

"The closest translation I can offer would be to say that the purest expression of love is found in the relinquishing of fear; the shedding of the ego and the opening of ones heart to the extent that all that remains is the quintessence of the soul. In that state, that which binds us to the illusion of all that is physical dissipates, leaving a clear path along which euphoria in all its abundance becomes accessible. Humans are able to temporarily indulge in this sensation under certain conditions, the most commonly practised one being at the point of climactic sex. They refer to this sentiment as an orgasm. It takes only a single experience for many to become addicted to this feeling and spend the rest of their lives trying to recapture it through random acts of promiscuity.

"A strong factor many neglect to take into consideration is that of compatibility. Compatibility increases the possibility for achieving the state of Supreme Oneness or to put it simply, nirvana. Even so there are varying degrees of compatibility: physical, mental, spiritual being the main ones. Some are souls are attuned enough to recognise and acknowledge another who bears close semblance to their measure of perfection, the ideal compliment to their incarnation. These matched souls may chose to become travelling companions with whom they journey on their mutual quest to rediscover All. Sometimes they may encounter one another in more than one lifetime. On occasion they may actually even recognise each other. Either way, these companions are known as soul mates or twin souls due to their apparent similarities. That is not to say that each soul only has one mate or twin. Do not fall for the same misinterpretation made by the majority and confuse the word *soul* for its homonym *sole*. "

"Don't forget to relax and breathe deep my love," Nana advised with a wink.

Teeny breathed.

5

Broken Hearts

Maya stood leant up against the kitchen counter waiting for the kettle to boil. It was quarter to six in the morning. She had never made it back to sleep after her altercation with Derrick. She had tried, but so many thoughts blazed through her mind. The dream seemed to be what currently held centre focus. What did it mean? Had this dream been a warning? Preparation for what Teeny was going through now? Guilt clouded over her and she mentally kicked herself for the millionth time over the affair that made Derrick so reluctant to make prolonged physical contact with her.

Back when they were a couple, they had been inseparable. Their relationship had never gotten stale or fallen into a rut, as she had heard friends, clients and colleagues complain of in her line of work as a therapist. They had never left their 'honeymoon period' and everyday was another in which they found joy in being with each other. Sure they had had their share of hard times, but they were external pressures. Like the times one of them had been out of a job and the other had to work extra hours to make ends meet, or how when childcare was hard to find on those ridiculously inconvenient teacher training days, Teeny's school had once every other term. For Maya and Derrick however, these things were causes that had the effect of bringing them closer over the years as they harmonised and honed in their unwritten 'I got ya back' decree. If anything, the only major source of contention they had was over Teeny's favourite hobby, skateboarding.

Maya had thought it cute when Teeny begged for a skateboard at the age for four after seeing her cousin riding his. After a few months of persistent pleading, Derrick had obliged and started teaching her the basic kick-push motion and how to turn left and right. Little Miss Fearless soon mastered these fundamentals as well as the tic tac, and before long was demanding her father teach her how to do ollies, nollies and kick-flips. Her father, not wanting to leave himself open to embarrassment by attempting a demonstration for his daughter, chose an alternative route of distraction and started plying her with DVDs, magazines, hoodies and all other paraphernalia synonymous with the world of skateboarding. The most recent being a Tony Hawk: Project 8 game for her X-box 360. In the meantime as Teeny struggled to copy the stunts taught by her cousin and the DVDs, Maya found herself tending to new scrapes and bruises in areas of Teeny's body that knee, elbow and wrist pads couldn't protect. As for the helmet, no matter how many times she had demanded her daughter wear it, she always came back home from a trip to the ramps without it. Apparently wearing protection that could prevent Teeny from "cracking her skull open" simply wasn't "cool" enough. Worse still, skateboarding on the weekends was no longer enough to satiate Teeny's need to "kill herself".

A couple of times a week Elias, Teeny's fifteen year old cousin, would detour on his way to the park from his home in White City to call on her to accompany him. If there was one thing to be said of skateboarding, with it was a kinship that was oblivious to age, colour and gender. Despite the age gap, Teeny had Elias' respect and they often spent their free time together rolling to some place or another. Over the years, Derrick had sided his little angel and encouraged Maya to come see just how good she had gotten. It had taken until Teeny was eight years old before Maya reluctantly followed them to the skateboard park in Westbourne Grove. Never again! Maya was sure she would have heart attack as she watched the dare devil stunts that Teeny effortlessly performed. She was good yes, - okay so she was excellent, but every move that took the skateboard away from parallel ground had Maya wincing and squealing in horror.

Right now, Maya needed for Derrick to do his magic. He had a knack for knowing exactly what was on her mind, that for some reason became more potent when he cradled her in his arms as they relaxed. They came to make a game of it and instead of asking "How was your day", she'd run to him folding his arms around her and say "Tell me how my day was". Derrick would shift his head from side to side, take a deep breath and proceed to tell her who should be fired for causing her brain disturbance that day and they'd fall about giggling. He was almost always spot on. It wasn't all one sided; in the mornings as he prepared himself for work, he'd call out for predictions of what his day had in store for him from the bathroom;

"Maya, is Walter gonna be in a bad mood today?" Walter was Derrick's boss.

Maya would pause a few moments before saying; "Nah, he's happy, his wife gave him a lil sumthin last night!"

"Go Walter!" Derrick would holler back in approval. Some days Teeny would add something along the lines of:

"Mum, Dad, take your umbrellas it's gonna rain hard today, you'll be sorry if you listen to that weatherman!" or "Daddy, your car is thirsty, she needs some water!"

Since Derrick had left, coming home was no longer like coming home at all. Hello and Goodbye were greetings rarely used in their household. It was always “Welcome home”, “Home soon!” or “Come home soon/safe”. They didn’t need to be in their house for their adopted greetings to be applicable. Home was wherever they were together.

Derrick stirred upstairs.

Maya’s heart pounded as she heard him enter the bathroom. “Calm down,” she ordered and decided to occupy herself with making scrambled eggs on toast for them both.

By the time Derrick had come downstairs, breakfast was on the table.

“G’ mawning,” she welcomed, gesturing for him to sit down.

He looked at her searching for a motive, but found none and so sat down to eat. He was famished; he hadn’t found time to eat the night before. “Apology accepted,” he said, obviously in a mood, crabby from lack of sleep.

“Apology for what?” Maya asked.

“For calling me a wuss,” he responded without bothering to looking up from his plate.

That had been the cue she had been waiting for to bring up her request again. This time she had the fall back option of attributing her persistence on the fact that it was *he* that had yet to drop the issue.

“Oh that,” she said, feigning forgetfulness. “I’m sorry, that was uncalled for. It’s just…” Maya paused deliberately before continuing, “well it’s just this whole Teeny thing has me really wound up. And you saying I knew the answer, I just hoped you could help me get at it. The thought of Teeny just lying there is tearing me up inside,” she sighed. “Look, I understand why you don’t want to, and I know the way I approached you was inappropriate. But I’ve been having nightmares,” she bowed her head and waited for him to take the bait.

“What nightmares?”

She had him.

“I’ve been having them for a while now, but over the past month they have been getting worse, scarier, all of them are about Teeny,” she admitted truthfully, and proceeded to tell him about them.

It wasn’t hard to convey her upset over them. That was genuine. She noted the way he shifted uncomfortably in his seat. There was an air of thoughtful silence as she finalised her embellished recount. Derrick finally conceded. He had witnessed too many of Maya’s dreams come to pass for him to ignore this one. He pushed back his chair.

“Okay, lets do this,” he sighed, as he stood up, obviously unhappy about it.

He opened his arms for Maya to take position in them. She got up and walked toward him, turning to nestle in his arms, and all at once became overwhelmed. Her mind raced and her body tingled for being ‘home’ again, albeit as a temporary resident.

“Relax,” Derrick ordered, the command as much for himself as it was for her.

He initiated his typical ritual and let out a deep breath, at which Maya bit her lip trying hard not to enjoy the memory of how well their bodies fit one another. She pondered on how she could have been so stupid to throw it all away. Those damn braids! She cursed, recalling the night that led to her demise. She jumped as Derrick suddenly thrust her from his arms.

“What the fuck?” he demanded.

“Wh-what?” Maya stuttered.

“How you gonna show me that. Is this some kind of sick joke?” Derrick bellowed back.

“I don’t understand; what are you talking about?” Maya shook nervously.

“You know what! How you gonna rub that shit in my face. That’s bitch low Maya. Bitch fucking low!”

“Derrick, what happened, please?”

“What happened? You spreading your fucking legs to that nigga is what happened. You ask me to help you find the answer for Teeny and all that’s really going on in your mind is your night spent fucking him? Fuck you Maya! Fuck you!”

Derrick was pacing around the kitchen hysterically. Maya was speechless and mentally turned the clock back a few minutes, searching for evidence in a replay trying to figure what brought this on.

“Oh my god Derrick, no its not what you think I swear, I wasn’t thinking of him like that… Oh shit! I was thinking how I lost you and… Oh Derrick I didn’t mean… I wasn’t trying to rub it in your face. I was just…. Baby I’m sorry, I’m so sorry… I…”

“Baby? Baby? Fuck you, about Baby! I ain’t your baby!” Derrick had entered selective hearing mode usually only reserved for when he watched football.

He was in a rage unlike any Maya had ever witnessed. This was worse than the day he had called her from his hotel to bid her sweet dreams the night she of her mistake. Back then he had stopped in mid sentence and quietly asked Maya what was wrong, why did she ‘feel’ different, then he asked her what had changed. Nothing more had been said before he silently hung up the phone. He just knew. When he had come back home he was withdrawn and shut her out. She couldn’t do anything to make him listen back then either, but this was so much worse. Never in his life had he ever shouted or sworn at her as he did this morning.

"Derrick please listen, that man - he meant nothing to me, I made a mistake. Please Derrick I wasn't trying to hurt you. I didn't mean for you to see that."

Whenever Derrick 'felt' things he described them as images that came into his head along with a feeling as if he was there in a front row seat at a movie, except he could 'feel' the emotions and physical sensations of the characters as if they were his. Maya couldn't even begin to imagine what he had just experienced through her undisciplined mind's rerun of her regret.

"It was one mistake, a bad one I know but…"

"See, here's the thing, all these years you have clean missed the point. It wasn't the fact that you fucked another man that messed us up. It's what made it happen that tears me apart."

"D., he was nothing, he meant nothing."

"And that is exactly my point!" Derrick said, and weakly collapsed into the chair.

Maya stood immobilised in silence.

She finally sat back down across from Derrick and waited for him to continue. He remained silent trying to find the words to vocalise his pain, looking to the left of her at nothing in particular.

"We had a good thing Maya. I've never been tempted once because of how good we had it. Nothing out there could compare, nothing out there was worth loosing you over. Women are all around but I don't see them, because I had you. My boys'd be talking about the next arse they were tryna lay, but they weren't happy like I was. My search ended the night I stopped looking and you found me. All my life I've fought the odds to have the best and it was paying off. With you, that 'nice guys finish last' bullshit didn't drop. I got a phat job, my own home, a nice ride and beautiful woman to share it all with. From where I was standing, I thought we were good. The sex was good right? Or was that just my imagination?"

"No D., it was perfect."

"I just got promoted to Senior Networking Consultant, running my own department and I'm thinking life couldn't get any better. I keep wondering what I missed, what I did wrong, and Maya, I swear I don't know. What did I do to push you away like that? What did I do to make you give our life, my love the middle finger like that? I need to know Maya, I need to understand, because two years after the fact, I still can't breath for the way you knocked the wind outta me."

Derrick now looked in Maya's eyes demanding an answer. She broke his gaze and averted her sight to trace a pattern the natural wood of the dining table at which they sat, made. She couldn't bear to look at him; the unsatisfactory frolics of one night had terminated the gestation of universes, and the age-old wisdom in his eyes had been replaced by confusion and pain and she was the cause of it.

"I'm sorry," she offered once again, but knew that word had long since become moot. "I know it makes no difference. What I did was wrong. I wish you could find it in your heart to forgive me. But to be honest, I can't even imagine ever being able to forgive myself. I hurt you, I hurt you real bad, and you so deserve better. But I swear to you it was nothing you did. You are and always have been a good man, the best thing to ever happen to me. I know you don't wanna hear it; but even as I was with him, I couldn't begin to fathom how it happened. It's as if I just lost my mind and something else took over…"

"And before you knew it your thong was round your ankles and your arse was riding his dick? You're right, I don't wanna hear it Maya," Derrick spat. "You know what hurts most? What hurts more than everything, is you not only broke my heart, you broke my spirit Maya. Can you understand that? Do you even care? You keep apologising about that night, but you have never considered the fact that the reason I left is because what you did took everything that made me the man I was become a joke. I became a fool for believing that it was possible to break the stereotype of the black family. You know the one where the man is a playa and a hustler that disrespects his woman, the man that has three baby mammas and another illegitimate child on the way, the man that spends all his money on weed, clubs and bling. The man whose main jump off is a woman that places priority on getting her nails 'did' over paying the rent or buying books to help encourage her child to read. I'm the sucker who overlooks them fine booty shakers, and boasts how naturally beautiful his wife is and reminisces the four most important days of his life as being the day he met her, the day he proposed to her, the day he married her and the day she gave birth to their baby girl. *That* is what you fucking did!

"Everything I've worked so hard for to become the best I man I knew how to be, your actions that night said otherwise. I'm not good enough; but that's all I know how to be. I don't know how to be anything else. And that leaves me with nothing. I'm empty now, there's nothing left. No life, no love, no purpose. The very sight of you makes my soul jump for joy and my stomach turn in disgust. I've had to cuss out some of my people for trying to make me feel better by putting you down, all because I can't stand to have a bad word said about you. I don't know how to be around them or you. I'm alone and it scares the hell out of me. I've lost my best friend and my lover and not even she can tell me why." A tear escaped Derrick's eye. Maya felt hot with shame. There was nothing she could say. The guilt she had been nursing the past two years had fallen way short of all the pain the love of her life had just confessed. He was right; she had missed the point entirely.

The ex-couple drove in silence to the hospital and sombrely walked to Teeny's new location. On the door of her room a sign read:

PROTECTIVE ISOLATION

Visitors/Staff to Report to Nurse-in-Charge before Entering Room

ANYONE WITH COUGHS, COLD OR SORE THROAT SHOULD <u>NOT</u> ENTER THE ROOM

Before entering room: Remove white coat…

Maya could read no more, she turned her head away as if to negate the sadness the notice stirred in her. She glanced at Derrick to see his response, either he didn't see it or chose not to acknowledge it. She had a feeling it was the latter.

Beyond the door, Teeny's condition remained unchanged. Maya had brought a book to read to Teeny, but felt too sick and ashamed to read it in front of Derrick. They awkwardly passed an hour avoiding eye contact, and instead performed distractions like plumping up Teeny's pillows, smoothing imaginary creases in her mink blanket that she still lay tucked in, and filling and sipping cups of water. Finally Derrick answered a page from work and excused himself to attend to a server that had gone down. He kissed Teeny's cheek and headed for the door. Maya sighed and permitted herself to dare breathe normally again when she thought he had made good distance between them on his exit. She kissed Teeny's forehead, curled up beside her daughter once again and fell asleep.

6

No Such Thing as Aliens!

“Soooo seeing as you kind of know everything and you talk about being human like we are just these big old snail shell housey things, does that mean aliens really exist?” Teeny asked eagerly.

Nana looked at Imhotep, unsure of how quite to respond to a question that she herself didn’t know how to answer. He shook his head and squinted his eyes in obvious confusion unable to ascertain what she meant. He looked away as if in thought, while he sought clarification by merging with the Realm for explanation of the word that he was at a loss for the definition of. The term ‘alien’ was new to him and inspired a curiosity he had not experienced for a few centuries.

“Ahh! I see,” exclaimed Imhotep. “Pff. What a ridiculous notion, there are no such things!” he guffawed dismissively.

“Oh,” replied Teeny disappointedly.

Imhotep answered honestly from the perspective of one who had incarnated into various life forms thousands of times over, across copious planets, within a multitude of galaxies. As far as he was concerned, every incarnation no matter how physically dissimilar were all beings that were part and parcel of the incalculable expressions of All. And yet Teeny’s downhearted response caused him to wonder. Could it be that her reference to aliens was in regard as to whether or not the universe was inhabited by life forms other than those indigenous to Earth? Preposterous! He knew humans were ignorant, but surely it could not be that they were so obnoxious as to believe they were the only form of intelligent life in the galaxies abound? That they considered themselves intelligent at all still caused him to snort the air in laughter so hard, he was sure that if he passed the thought whilst in physical form he might cause himself damage. Obviously there could be no such thing as aliens if in fact nothing was foreign in All!

"I wish I could be a panther!" sighed Teeny moving on from one mournful subject to another.

"Oh, but you can dear," replied the panther that was Nana.

"Really? How?" Teeny's eyes widened.

"It's simply a matter of asking with the expectation for it to be so. That is the way of the universe, we needn't want for anything. Do you know what your name - Abebi means? It means, 'We called her and she came'. Your very existence was due to a need that had to be fulfilled."

Teeny laughed, "Or maybe Mum and Dad got busy and I came along for the ride."

"Is that what you think? That children are born out of the haphazard consequence of a quickie?"

Nana stood up, padded over to where Teeny stood on the edge of the riverbank to take a closer look through her cat eyes at her grandchild.

"Well not always, I mean sometimes children are wanted, but sometimes they come by accident," reasoned Teeny, suddenly feeling anxious.

"Oh really? Well with that kind of thinking you wont ever be able to become a panther or anything else any time soon for that matter. Child you better sit down again because I'm about to school you!" The softness of Nana's tone seemed to take on a stern quality.

Teeny quickly sat down, not wanting to agitate the great felid that stood before her.

"First of all, there is no such thing as coincidence or accidents, so whatever you have come to believe about such events; let it go. It doesn't serve you." Nana began. "The universe is like a big ole pick 'n' mix dispenser that is activated by thought energy. At the time your parents '*got busy*' as you like to put it, they were in love. They came together to form a union that was an expression of an attraction, heightened by rareness in compatibility that led to them reaching a point of experiencing the pure Oneness that Imhotep described. At this wondrous point, your mother formed a thought that was echoed by your father. The thought was, how amazing it would be to create a child in such a state of perfect bliss. This thought shifted the chemical balance in the region of your mother's uterus creating an environment that not only welcomed, but also facilitated the perfect sperm that your father's soul had pre-selected to win the race to her anticipating ovum. The penetration of that ovum was effortless for that determined sperm. The zygote that resulted became the perfect vehicle for your eager soul to unite and bond with. The night your parents 'got busy', set into motion a chain of events, the result of which was your physical incarnation on Earth."

Teeny listened intently, she was sincerely interested in all she was being taught, though was unable to resist internalising her upset. It was unfair the way her grandmother penalised her for lack of knowledge on all this new information. Even if she had indeed known all of this before, she could hardly be blamed for not knowing it now. This kind of subject matter was hardly likely to be covered in her school curriculum. Then she wondered if indeed it had, during one of those times she had fallen asleep as her teacher droned about something that caused her to zone out. At least that would explain why hearing it taught to her now sounded distant remnants of a dream she had long forgotten. When she hadn't been reduced to discreet snores, she would find entertainment in imaginary worlds where she fought battles against arch nemeses, but somehow, here and now was engagingly different. Even if she was dreaming, thus far it was an edutaining albeit occasionally discourteous one, that enrolled her into granting this lesson her undivided attention. She decided it was one she owed it to herself to remember when she woke up back in her world.

"Thought is that which impregnates the Source of all things causing it to yield to the silent requests of all that reside within. When two people come together in union, whether consented or otherwise, all it takes is for a single thought before, during or within seventy-two hours of intercourse to set in motion the conception of a baby. That thought may be something as idle as, '*I hope I don't get pregnant*', it matters not. If the prolonged emphasis is placed on the thought, it will manifest. The universe doesn't discern between, 'I want' or 'I don't want', it will simply respond to the emotion that accompanies the thought. The term 'emotion' translates best as 'energy in motion'. The more emotion placed on the thought, the more momentum is given to manifestation of it into the physical. Thoughts are ethereal in nature, but with increased potency through repetitious enforcement, become crystallized and channels are created, the harmonious deployment of which allow them to materialize.

"There is no such thing as good luck or bad luck, in fact there is no such thing as good and bad period. There just IS. On planes such as the one you have come from there are duplicitous natures or polarities, which personify as opposing genders. A by-product of these two natures was the theory of "as above, so below".

This was correct and acceptable, but keeping in line with this theory would mean that there became that which is incorrect and unacceptable. Language and history took this simple concept and made it complicated by dubbing one polarity positive and the other negative, one good and one bad, one lucky, the other unlucky. Then came the ridiculous notion that one must choose between the two. Which of course is impossible because there is no two; only one crudely composed of two, or more in some cases. So called good and bad are variables that are only such, according to the interpretation of those it affects. For example: creation is generally accepted by dual natured beings as being good and destruction as bad, however in order for something to be created, something must first be destroyed. Creation is merely destruction that takes place in an order in that is customary as being performed in an organised or visibly conceivable manner, yet even so, for something to be created, something had to be altered from its original structure. To those that reside within the confines of the structure, their world has just been torn apart. To those that benefit from the new creation it is called progression. Instead of the words good and bad or positive and negative; agreeable and disagreeable are favoured terminologies as it explains the concept of duality with accurate simplicity. To be agreeable is to comply without question, to be disagreeable is to not be in favour with, and to raise objection.

"Essentially, you chose yourself. You are called forth the moment your father impregnates your mother. You are chosen if you step to the plate and be who you were born to be, and do so to the best of your ability. Sounds easy, but notice how many people succumb to fear and settle, or are too lazy to make the effort. Some people only ever live to please others despite how it kills their soul to do so. I'm sure you recognize many around you that fall into these categories. That leaves very few to do the jobs of many."

Teeny contemplated on this for a moment then asked: "Well how does that explain miscarriages, abortions and still births? Why would a soul choose to incarnate into a life that will end early or painfully?"

Imhotep piped in to answer, "For one of two simple reasons: to experience or to balance karma. You do know what karma is don't you?"

"Of course, that's the name of Ludacris' daughter. I'm joking, I'm joking!" Teeny hastily added on seeing her Nana throw a paw over her head in shame and Imhotep's teeth clench down painfully around the mouthpiece of his pipe. "I know what karma is okay, I do watch The Avatar you know!"

"Ugh, heaven help us," Nana cried.

Imhotep raised an eyebrow and nodded in approval. "Good, it's working then," he said.

"Huh?" asked Teeny.

"You mentioned The Avatar, I assume by that you were referring to The Legend of Aang? That show is a manifestation of the thoughts of Crystal Children. They collectively requested to be reminded the reason why they were here. They knew there were answers, but not necessarily the questions with which to inquire, and absent or sleeping Indigos were unable to teach them. The universe responded by inspiring or spiritually introducing if you will, the idea for the show in the minds and hearts of those most perfect to execute the assignment. Don't tell me you thought it was just a chance idea the writers happened to accidentally stumble across? I suppose you think Naruto is just a nifty piece of animation too no doubt," Imhotep scowled and looked over at Nana who stared back as bewildered as Teeny. "You're genes!"

A sheepish "Touché," was all Nana could respond with.

The truth was so blatant, it was easy to dismiss unless consciously acknowledged. Over the years cartoons had gone from being dominated by animated adults battling for a better tomorrow, to small groups of unsuspecting children thrown together to complete missions. The first of these cartoons seemed to surface during the 1980's, in which teens and/or adolescents began to be represented as unsung heroes. Often they held a responsibility for defeating greedy or destructive adults in a quest to save the world or to some how assist in protecting humanity from self-destruction. Their missions were often spiritually inspired or developed to embody similar connotations. The popularity of violently slapstick, to fluffy moral abiding animals, declined. Where animals once replaced the role of humans, children travelled alongside them, able to communicate as friends. Another interesting aspect of these children was that as well as talents that varied from parental style leadership to technological affinity, their greatest gift was their loyalty, sincerity and unwavering determination. Their level of intelligence, awareness, common sense and empathy often surpassed adults that boasted high IQ's and held positions of influential responsibility.

"Anyway, where was I?" asked Imhotep rhetorically as he thoughtfully stroked his pipe. "Oh yes, experience and karma. All souls are on a journey of enlightenment toward the destination of returning to the perfect state of Oneness with All. The route of which requires that they satisfy the curiosity that caused them to instigate the simulation of what it is to be an individual separate from All. Of course, All is just that. One can never truly be separate from it, hence the simulation that we call Illusion. Each soul's journey is unique, the determination of which are experience and karma. There are souls whose only desire is to experience the sensation of being born - to mature in the confines of a womb and eventually travel down the birth canal of its host. Once they have indulged in this experience, they have completed that particular journey and thus abort themselves shedding the body so that they may move on to proceed with their voyage, curiosity satiated. Karma comes into the equation through the soul becoming so attached to it's physical incarnation that it forgets that the body is merely a vehicle and instead becomes trapped within Illusion, believing it to be the definitive reality.

"Guilt and regret are forms of energy that upon death, become determining factors for the following incarnation. Despite them not being constituents of the soul in its purest expression, they are forms of energy nonetheless. Energy cannot be destroyed, only temporarily contained or redirected, thus this residual nervous energy must go somewhere, usually in the form of excess baggage the soul carries on into its next life in an attempt to rectify or at least balance the equation, that of which led to the sensation in the first place. Thus a person's current experiences are subconscious predeterminations of their interpretation of past events. In short, the differentiation between karma and experience is the way in which the soul translated marked events that became time references of an education they felt the need to repeat. It is highly likely that aborted foetus contained the soul of a woman of a recent life that could not go further in their journey without fulfilling a perverse need for retribution."

Nana proceeded to answer Teeny on why 'the good die young' explaining that it was because they were so good at being who they were that they died. They were souls that favoured short incarnations, or temporary assignments as those in accord with the Mental Realm preferred to term them. They would incarnate on Earth specifically to inspire, motivate and mobilise progress in ways that were sometimes so subtle, many would not notice until they left the Earth plane. On successful completion of their undertaking they would exit promptly to move onto their next mission or experience. They were well aware of their life expectancy, which often ended so abruptly it would shock those they came to affect. In fact they would often choose the approximate time of their departure before agreeing to their assignment. Likewise, those that lived long lives were souls whose preference were for long term assignments. The exception was for those who returned to balance karma. Longer lives increased their opportunity to gain absolution from that which bound them. Even so, those who initially incarnated for lengthy periods could find themselves exiting prematurely if instead of leaning toward the nature that would free them, they ventured so far off course that the possibility for liberation became no longer obtainable within the initially set time frame. In other words, nothing they did with the remainder of their incarnation could restore the balance they had incarnated for in the hopes of achieving.

Physical

"For the love of Him not even you, shall not break me! We are married and I love you with all my heart, but my first vows were to my Lord and Saviour Jesus Christ; I serve him before all others. In his name I find strength and rebuke your lies and blasphemous ways. You are possessed, allowing the devil to work through you. Without a doubt, you are being used as his agent, yet he does not love you, but I do, and so does The Heavenly Father. Know that my God is a powerful merciful God, thus he sent his only begotten son to die for our sins. For all the lies you speak, a ticket to hell has surely been reserved. I will pray for you. Pray that you guard your tongue and find humility, enough to open your heart and accept Jesus as your one true means of salvation. He is your only hope. The blood of Jesus washes white, come and be cleansed by the Lamb of God. The path you are choosing is not a good one. I am scared for you, but I have faith that even you can be saved, it is not too late. I beg you, from my heart I beg you, repent for your sins and become born again and made whole."

Modupe's (Nana) last words to David Oshodi

Location: London Heathrow Airport – August 14th 1981

7

A Friend In Need

Derrick couldn't help feeling relieved at having being called into work on this particular Saturday morning. He stroked the casing of the server he had been called to attend to.

"Thank heaven for logical shit that makes sense," he muttered and got down to work.

His position at Systech Corp. was his dream job. Computers were a lot more straight forward and common sense than people. No lies or confusion. If there were a problem, a computer wouldn't hesitate to let you know in the form of error messages or bleep codes. People however, were complicated. That he was able to perceive them the way he did didn't make any more sense of the way they made the simplest things become difficult. People said one thing, but ninety percent of the time meant something completely different. They hid their truth behind a façade of slick words; fashion sense, designer labels, fake smiles, overly pretentious personas and other customised false fronts. He however, viewed the world through simple bold Arial Black type faced letters that spelt single words that seemed to hover above the heads of those in denial of their own truths: Liar, Hurt, Frustrated, Weak, Sad, Lonely, Egomaniacal, Lazy. Who was he to judge? He no doubt had his own that probably read: ALONE. He loved his own company; he had always been at peace enough with himself not to fear it. The value he placed on his solitude served to refine an appreciation of the beauty of sharing his soul with another. And those he did share it with, were precious to him.

Derrick's personality emulated the traits of his preferred operating system, Linux Fedora Core: - a versatile, user-friendly distribution of the prominent Red Hat variety, with a welcoming and attractive graphical user interface. The first choice for many whom after one too many system crashes, viruses and critical errors, sought more than the misleading reputation its globally dominant counterpart could offer. The server soon responded to his attention by whirring to life, confirming POST; Power on self-test, and settling back into a rhythmic hum. As he exited the server room he bumped into Paul, a network administrator under his authority.

"You're here? Why'd they call me in if you were working the shift?"

"'Sup Slick-Rick? Yeah I was gonna see to it, but I was dealing with a cable break somewhere on the top floor. I coulda well and handled it when I got done. The secondary server was fine to take over for a few, but you know Walter, he don't need a reason to freak out and have a panic fit. He wanted it done, like yesterday," replied Paul.

"Yeah, I heard that. Well look, I'm done here, so I'm out. You cool?"

"Yeah I'm good, say 'Hey' to the wife and kid for me."

"Yyyyup," Derrick drawled as he turned to leave. Paul's last comment felt like a cruel joke at his expense.

***

Maya woke up and propped herself on her elbow. She stared at Teeny's face that looked no different to when she slept; she even looked peaceful, except she wasn't sleeping. Maya stroked her face, and gently played with the baby hairs that lined her forehead. She pulled herself up and rotated to sit on the edge of the bed, shoulders hunched, head hung low.

"Mrs. Kingsley, how are you bearing up?"

Maya looked up at the door to find the nurse who had tended to Teeny in A&E the night before. She looked different in civilian clothing.

"Oh, hi – uh…"

"Rachael," the nurse intervened.

"Rachael, yes."

"Just finishing my shift now," Rachael volunteered as she entered the room, ignoring Maya's obvious reluctance to entertain a chat. "I just came up to check on Destiny. I did promise she'd be well looked after," she beamed.

"Thank you Rachael, you've been so wonderful. Oh and… I'm sorry, I didn't mean to be rude last night," said Maya, suddenly recalling her outburst.

"Oh, never you mind, it's already forgotten. She's going to be alright you know," assured Rachael.

Maya let out a brief laugh. "You sound like her father," she said tilting her head back gesturing to Teeny, before resuming her head hung low stance.

"Your husband is a wise man, you should listen to him. He knows what he's talking about."

"Yeah, well he's not my husband any more," said Maya surprised at herself for so openly talking to the nurse that less than twenty-four hours ago was a stranger to her.

Rachael paused thinking how best to unobtrusively offer a sincere line of hope to a rapidly sinking Maya. She walked up to her, gently placed a warm hand on her chin and raised it as if to politely insist Maya look her in the eyes. "Humpty Dumpty may not have been able to be put back together again, but your family will."

Maya stared at Rachael, too surprised to question her bold action. Rachael's serene eyes seemed to enchant her into a feeling a calm she hadn't experienced in some time. The endearing wrinkles around her fifty-four-year-old eyes, reminded her of her mother who had worked as a midwife when she was alive. Maya broke her gaze and pulled away, suddenly feeling self-conscious. She cleared her throat, sniffed and swallowed as if to recompose herself. "Yes, well... If only that were possible," she said.

"Don't worry, you'll see," Rachael responded, then abruptly turned and left the room.

Maya gathered herself together, whispered "I love you baby" into Teeny's ear, kissed her on the cheek and left soon after.

A few moments after Maya's departure, Rachael returned to Teeny's room and closed the door behind her. She pulled down blinds and tiptoed over to Teeny's side. She took a few deliberate breaths and raised her hands, palms face down above her body hovering them up and down before suspending them about a foot above Teeny's chest and abdomen.

"My, you do have a beautifully strong aura, I can see why your Nana believed you to be ready. Some argued your incarnation to be too young, but your reputation made for strong defence," she smiled and pushed her hands down an inch and 'plugged in' before closing her eyes and proceeded to give Teeny Reiki healing energy to supplement her body whilst on her journey. Rachael radiated her focus for approximately twenty minutes before pulling aside the mink blanket that covered her friend's granddaughter. One by one she gently massaged each of

Teeny's limbs down to her toes and fingertips encouraging circulation. She flexed the little girl's arms and legs each to a count of thirty. It was her aim to reduce the potential for bedsores as well as to deter the onset of muscular atrophy. At the sound of doctor's voices nearby, she quickly threw the blanket back over her patient, uttered a goodbye with a promise to return, and exited the room.

Maya stood waiting at the bus stop for a number seven to take her home. She had a little shopping to do that she would have really preferred not to have to contend with. She deliberated on whether to go continue waiting for a bus or walk to the Somerfields supermarket situated a little further down along Edgware Road from where she stood. She opted for a third option and rummaged around her handbag for her phone. She keyed in Nia's number and waited for it to ring.

"Hello?"

"Hey Nia, how you doing?"

"Maya, I was just this minute thinking about you girl!" Nia chirped.

She always sounded vibrant and lively, her voice a perfect expression of her personality. Maya attributed it to her profession as a fitness instructor, "it's all them endorphins that keeps you so damn high, make me tired just looking at you," she'd tell her friend of ten years. They had met at a toddler's playgroup that Maya had sworn never to find herself attending. She had no need for such 'mother's meetings', but she had actually enjoyed it, having met Nia who had only recently started taking Alysha. They immediately took to one another in the form of rejecting the facility for not wanting to be having other mothers 'up in their business'. Before long they stopped taking their daughters there, and instead arranged play dates at various parks or in each other's homes. From there they had started doing their shopping together, calling for a chat a couple of evenings a week and before they knew it they were like 'bench and batty'.

"You up for a visit?" Maya asked.

"Sure thing, in fact why don't I come down to you? I have the evening to myself, Morris has taken our two for a movie treat," said Nia excitedly.

"Cool, I'm not home right now though, I'm just coming out from St. Mary's. Teeny's in a coma and I just needed someone to talk to," Maya quietly responded.

"What! How? But her and Alysha just walked home together yesterday. Oh my god she didn't fall off her skateboard?" Nia's voice became panicked as if the news she was hearing was about her own daughter. "You know what, I'm getting in my car now Maya, just hold tight. I'm gonna put down for a second and call you from my mobile once I got my Bluetooth on, ya hear? Hold tight!" Nia hung up.

Maya breathed a sigh of relief. Nia was perfect in situations like these; she had gained much practice with her son, Cory. Nia was a no-nonsense, 'don't tes' me' woman, who may as well have been a doctor herself for all she had learnt about medicine. She chose to remain well informed of her son's health and often gave medical staff a run for their money for the way she cross examined their every move. One too many horror stories of how sickle cell patients were treated in various hospital led her to put her foot down and declare, "Hell no - not my child!" For the most part, all the preventative measures she raised and taught her son by were successful for keeping him healthy, but at age seven, he sometimes rebelled against "being treated special", and would occasionally find himself suffering a severe pain episode that required hospital admission.

Maya's phone rang.

"I'm on my way, 'bout another ten minutes. Fill me in." Nia urged.

"Oh Maya," Nia sighed for the fourth time and hugged her friend for the fifth. They had returned to Teeny's side for a while, before she insisted on at least helping Maya with her shopping. They slowly shuffled down the freezer aisle more focused on their conversation than the various ice creams and frozen desserts. "I'm with Derrick, she's gonna be okay. Just be patient, she's a tough little thing that one. As for the whole other thing with D.," Nia shook her head, "Maya, I don't know what to tell you. He's a good man hurting. To this day it still don't sit right you two being apart. You're like the trophy family everyone wishes they could have. Call me an optimist, I'll put money on it, you will be getting it together again. You are like two parts of the same whole, like the Earth and the moon."

Nia had said the same thing religiously since Derrick first left his and Maya's home. Where some would witness a marriage, shake their head and say 'I give it six months…' similarly when Derrick and Maya had divorced, Nia had said matter of factly; "It'll never last".

"Hmph, Rachael reckons we'll be getting together again too. I'd sure love to know which planet you both come from," said Maya, smiling weakly as she shook her head.

"Rachael?" Nia tried to place the name, without success.

"The A&E nurse," Maya replied, still thoughtful.

"Ahh, well there you go then, anyone who agrees with me knows what they are talking about!" said Nia snapping her fingers in approval.

They drove back to Maya's, ordered in some Chinese and talked for a couple of hours before Nia had to leave.

Maya looked at the clock, and then at her watch to confirm it was indeed as late as 11.32pm. She thought about phoning Derrick, then remembered what he said and grabbed the phone to call him, before he had the opportunity to put her to shame.

"Maya." Derrick answered blankly.

"Hello Derrick." She felt awkward, and fought to think of something to say. "How was work?" She kicked herself.

"Fine. I went to see Teeny a few hours ago, still no change," he answered just as blankly.

"Yeah, I spent most of the day there." Well at least he's talking to me at all, she thought. "Look D., I'm…"

"Yeah, I know. Let's just leave it aiight?"

There was an eternal silence that the ticking clock on the wall above the modern fireplace claimed to have only lasted a mere five seconds. Maya pushed her hand into the left back pocket of her jeans and sidled toward the pictures that lined the mantelpiece. She picked up the one of Derrick holding her from behind, kissing her temple. The image in the photograph epitomised happiness that now seemed to be a distant memory.

"I'm sorry," she said finally. "I know you don't want to hear it, but I have to say it again. Because you were right, I didn't have a clue how just how much I hurt you. I was so focused on the physical act of my unfaithfulness, that I didn't ever give thought to what it did to the part of you I love most. Looking back I realise how selfish I have been, hoping that soon enough you could forgive the unforgivable."

"M'y'..." Derrick tried to interrupt, but she continued firmly.

"I'm not saying this to try to win you back. For the first time I get it, I really get it. It's time to move on. The way I've been acting since that night has been me still being selfish, not wanting to let you go, hoping I could make it up to you somehow. But I can't make up for what I've done. I fucked up. I monumentally fucked up, and I continued to insult you every time I begged your forgiveness and every time I begged for a second chance. Since that day I have schemed, plotted and planned. I've used every low down method that has earned women notoriety for being manipulative, in my persistent attempts to get you back. In doing so I've fallen far from being the woman you once loved. I look at myself and I see the woman you left in the club that day we met; unappreciative of the beautiful soul I had been blessed to have touch my mine. I've become the one who broke the heart I so wanted to be able to breathe faith back into. I'm so sorry Derrick, not only for what I've done to you, but for myself and other sisters like me who totally miss the point and fail to see, acknowledge and support true soul brothers that work hard and love hard, only to fall prey to the bitch like me, who in a single thoughtless act, tears it all to shreds, totally oblivious to the devastation she leaves on a brothers soul. I know even now I'm still clean missing the point, but I have to say from the heart. I'm sorry. I hope one day we can at least be friends again."

Another long silence; this time a mutually thoughtful one. Derrick could hear the ticking of the clock that Maya stood beneath. He played over her words; she had struck a chord. She had finally gotten it, not all of it, not even close to all of it, but with the little she had got, she was sincere and he felt and appreciated it. Her overdue apology left him tired as if he had been waiting up night after night to hear it so he might one day sleep again. Now he had heard it, all he wanted to do was close his eyes and surrender to the fatigue that incessantly tugged on his spirit, entrancing his body into the lull of unconscious peace.

"Goodnight Maya," he said, and hung up the phone.

Their divorce was finally official.

8

Chasing Waterfalls

"Nana, can we go closer to the waterfall? It's so beautiful," asked Teeny looking longingly at the mesmerizing spectacle.

"Sure, lets go," Nana replied.

The company of three walked along the bank towards the waterfall until the grassy terrain became a stony one. They descended along the curvature of the bank, till the waters edge lapped on their bare feet. The stones became rocks and Teeny could feel the spray of the waterfall on her face even at the distance that lay before them. They were still about fifty feet away, the spray intensified with every step. Teeny opened her mouth and stuck out her tongue the same way she did every time it rained. By now, twenty feet away, she was soaked through to her skin.

"Nana!" she shouted over the sound of crashing waters.

Imhotep seeing her alarm picked her up and placed the little girl on his back and continued walking toward the waterfall. Teeny screamed in fear of being crushed by the pressure. Nana and Imhotep were walking right into it! She lay sprawled across the giant gorilla's back gripping onto his fur for dear life. Before long they were standing in the water, the torrent of which felt profound, but in its mercy did not crush them. Teeny uncontrollably gasped over and over again. It reminded her of when she tried to look straight up into the shower when it was on full power at home. She screamed again, this time in excitement and delight and raised a hand to catch the water. Suddenly the trio emerged on the other side of the fall in a dimly lit cavern. Imhotep lifted Teeny from his shoulders and placed her back on the ground. He gestured toward a rock that slowly altered form to resemble a chair. Teeny walked over to it and ran her fingers across its seat before sitting down. She was still dripping and gasping through a huge grin. Within the rocky sanctuary, her awareness was drawn to how the occurrences of wispy apparitions appeared to increase in regularity. Still she felt no discomfort by their presence, on the contrary, they were some how almost a comfort, whilst adding to her swelling awe.

"Wow! Wait till I tell Alysha about this!!" she exclaimed.

"There'll be nothing to tell dear," said Nana, looking at the floor at the grass that suddenly grew effortlessly beneath their feet.

Imhotep walked over to a mound that seemed to form in unison of the steps he took toward it. As he sat on it, the light increased and the roof of the cavern became a clear night sky, lit by hundreds of stars that were strangely bright.

"You'll be lucky to remember up to ten percent of what you have experienced here," Nana continued, "like I said before, I called you here for a specific reason, the reason is the part of all this that you will remember when you re-awaken in your body vehicle."

Nana looked at Imhotep and nodded in approval. "Nice décor," she commented.

"Why thank you Dupe," he replied, and pulled out his pipe from nowhere in particular and placed it back in his mouth. He looked at Teeny, who was still dripping, then at Nana. "Pray tell, there seems to be something wrong with your genes. Why is she wet?"

Teeny looked at him and her Nana incredulously and for the first time, came to realise they were both as dry as if she had been the only one who entered the water.

"Teeny my love, you seem to believe you are wet, but you are not currently in your physical body. Think yourself dry dear."

Teeny thought about her Nana's logic. As it slowly began to make sense, she too became dry, her hair, her clothes, her hands, feet, every part of her dehydrated until she returned to her previous state before having entered the water. "How – cool – is that!" she cried.

Imhotep rolled his eyes and turned his attention to a portion of grass that lay between them. The grass disappeared, and in its place an uneven circle of earth formed, then a pile of logs that lit up and became fuel for a small fire.

Teeny looked at him. "You did that?" she asked eyes widening.

"He did all of this. Your chair, the grass, the roof," Nana quickly answered, before Imhotep could give a snotty reply.

"Can you do that Nana?" Teeny asked sitting forward in her seat.

"Uh, no. Unfortunately I'm still too attached to the physical to be able to fully utilise my mind without being limited by the confines of my human conditioning. I can only do small things I can wrap my head around." Nana said wistfully.

"That's what you mean when you keep talking about me being too human isn't it?" Teeny asked rhetorically. She sat deliberating on all that she had learnt and experienced since she arrived in the Mental Realm. She closed her eyes and breathed as she pondered. Finally she opened her eyes. "Nana, I need to remember. I need to know who I am and what I'm supposed to do."

Imhotep tilted his head, giving a discreet smile of satisfaction. Teeny was a fast learner, with an insatiable hunger to know more. This was good sign; there was hope.

"You actually haven't forgotten that much because you are already doing an excellent job of being who you are meant to be best," said Nana.

"I don't understand, there is nothing special about me, I haven't done anything impressive. I mean, Mummy says I'm a handful - that I have a death wish. Even you used to say I was out of control. I get sent to sit outside the school office for talking too much and disrupting the class, though in my defence, I'll say that's better than falling asleep. The only thing I'm really good at is skateboarding. Oh and computers, Daddy's taught me a lot about that. I'm gonna be the worlds greatest hacker, just you wait and see. I'll break down old systems and make information free to everyone. The will be no more secrets!" said Teeny.

Imhotep and Nana glanced at each other in knowing approval.

"I know what I said when I was alive. Forgive me; I was human. I didn't know much about anything back then." Nana walked up to Teeny and placed her front paws on her lap and looked in her granddaughter's eyes. Her voice softened. "Though I said it once when I was alive, I never said it enough. You, Destiny Kingsley, are a most beautiful soul with everything going for you and I love you so dearly. You were never out of control; you were simply BEing. It was our fear that labelled you a handful. You knew what we had forgotten. We told you off and disciplined you harshly for the way you used to talk back and question our authority. Looking back, the questions you asked were reasonable, but we had forgotten how best to answer.

I remember you once asking me as I tucked you into bed, where your prayers went. Instead of taking the time to answer, I simply said good night. Truth was, I didn't know and I couldn't be bothered to even try attempting to explain according to what I believed I knew. I knew my answer could not satisfy you, because deep down it didn't satisfy me. It's the little things like that that has contributed to your memory becoming impaired." Nana paused and dropped her head. Then looked up at Teeny again and asked, "Tell me something, what is your attraction to skateboarding?"

"Why? What's that got to do with anything?" asked Teeny in surprise.

"Everything. Tell me," said Nana.

"I don't know. I just love it. It's the one thing I do best I guess," shrugged Teeny.

"No Teeny, think!" Nana urged.

Teeny threw up her hands in surrender and allowed them to flop down as she shook her head and shrugged again. "Skateboarding is… it's like flying. Yeah. It's like I'm flying through the air and no one can stop me. I'm free, no one can tell me what I can't do and if they try; I kick-flip, I grind or even just ollie down a bunch of stairs and show them otherwise. Nothing is impossible when I'm rolling, I can float in the air and touch my own sky. Sure gravity is gonna pull me back to Earth, but not even she can stop me from flying. When I'm in the air, I kiss the sky with a 360 or a christ air and my heart is free. It's the best feeling in the world, just being able to fly and I can't get enough."

"That sounds like an amazing feeling," sighed Nana.

"It is," Teeny sighed in return. "Almost like being here," she added as an after-thought.

"It would seem that skateboarding is the method by which you stay connected with All; it is your spirit's joy," said Imhotep thoughtfully.

"In order that I help you understand the importance of who you are, there are a few things I need to explain," Nana commenced. "The awakening of a soul as it incarnates onto the planet, through birth or exchange is much like waking up from a dream. The more traumatic the awakening, the harder it is to recall the dream. From the time of birth, a child begins to collect and assimilate data to assist them in their life mission. A child knows exactly what they want, but requires guidance in order to successfully achieve it. Unfortunately guidance is often absent and instead most parents attempt to fashion their children to conform to their beliefs and standards, which are often quite hypocritical in the first place. This makes it harder for the child to remember who they are, as from birth they are taught to be other than who they were born to become. Then you have parents that give birth, but the neglect is on a whole different level. The parents are so self absorbed or lazy, that the child is often left to raise themselves from a young age. No boundaries are set, and again, guidance is null and void."

Nana removed her paws from Teeny's lap and walked to sit by the crackling fire. She appeared to be gazing at the smoke. Teeny thought she saw a sadness flicker in the slow blink of her Nana's eyes, but then what did that look like in the eyes of a panther? Teeny stared at her grandmother, patiently waiting for her to continue, but Nana was lost in an internal collision of sadness, regret and frustration.

Imhotep watched them both. He sympathized with Nana's struggle, the love he had for her caused him silent grief. Precious time passed as his friend fell deep into a place he was unable to catch her. It was imperative that Teeny remembered; the most he could do now was to not allow her to fall prey to her grandmother's fate. He resumed from where Nana left off. "For the most part, children know what they need and will demand it the best way they know how. What they need is not necessarily known in words on a conscious level. It may be difficult for them to articulate, thus they do so in action, hence the term 'acting out'." He was none too familiar with children; they were far removed from his area of expertise. He paused, seeking guidance from the Realm for adequate explanation. "They perform actions that are out of character in order to gain the attention of one they assume can give them the missing element they seek to complete their equation. The vital guidance that parents are meant to give a child that would prevent memory degradation is simple, whilst at the same time difficult, if the parent themselves have lost their way. Children need to be taught balance - cause and effect. This fundamental concept is best understood by a child who is secure, and is allowed to BE. The problem is adults tend to be oblivious to the level of a child's awareness. From the womb they are already learning and preparing for the environment beyond the belly of their mother. They learn through emotion, sound and sensation. If a mother is depressed during pregnancy, so to will the child be predisposed to depression.

"Though the memory of their destiny becomes vague over time, a child will still subconsciously prepare for its future by finding joy in things that adults consider to merely be hobbies," he continued. "In actuality, they are gathering experience in the use, or administration of the unique tools they have chosen to support and maintain paths they have clearly seen they will walk. A child may pester a parent with constant requests for a computer, or in your case, a skateboard. Your chosen tool reminds you to be fearless and persevering, to rise to challenges, and also of the feeling of Oneness. This feeling keeps your charkas clear, aligned and able to flow. This is why you rarely fall ill. Like an Indigo, you question authority and offer alternatives to dated systems of thinking, your love of computers nurtures your ability to solve problems using logic and skill. On top of all this you have Indigo parents whose love for one another has kept their heart chakras open and as a result kept them in tune with their abilities, where in sleeping Indigos, they have lain dormant through social conditioning."

The average incarnation failed to see the wisdom their soul tried gently to guide them toward. Soul stirrings, the inner guidance of All, found in the form in countless media formats worldwide. Even religious devotees missed the message of their own scriptures that prophesied warning against forgetfulness. A phrase often quoted cited that, though many were called, few are chosen. Those that feared most insisted that it referred to them, chosen by royal lineage, creed or denominational god above all others. Then there were those whose fear or ignorance deemed themselves unworthy to be chosen at all. Fear being that which it was, lied to both followers of its path. It was the individual that made the choice for themselves. The true definition of being a chosen one was simply to BE; epitomize the beauty of ones present (gifted) incarnation, living to fulfilment by being the best version of that which one was naturally born to be.

"Essentially Teeny, your mission is; no matter how hard and it will be hard, DON'T FORGET TO BE!" Nana's was now staring intently into her genes' eyes; her voice had reclaimed its stern authoritative quality.

Teeny knew well enough to pay close attention and heed her warning.

"Don't allow anyone or anything to determine who you should become, or encourage you to be other than you feel happy to BE. Don't fall prey to peers who pressure you to follow into their definition of cool. Misery loves company and it will come in many forms to befriend you and have you lose your way. Do what you love and love what you do. This will keep you immune from forgetting to BE.

"Remember when you first came here, I told you that resistance is the expected variable that must be catered for. Well in terms of retention of ones memory to BE, the variable is fear, which is the opposite of love. Of course when fear dominates the region of the heart, the chakra closes, cutting off the vital connection between the upper and lower planes and chakras. Fear is more readily taught over cause and effect. It starts off innocently enough, for example in the form of parents trying to protect their children from harm. But then it becomes a tactic of manipulation to instil compliance to expired social structures that serve to benefit the few who fear most. Worse still, in the present era of human civilization, misery yields a good profit. Sickness, depression and loneliness equate to more wealth for these dominant authorities. Nobody, and I mean *nobody* is born without potential for greatness. The difference is whether or not they acknowledge it, and actively work toward it. The work both starts and finishes in the mind.

"The event that took place that led to your parents divorce was the responsibility of both of your parents. Fear entered their hearts and became manifest. That same fear must not take you with them."

It was Teeny's turn to stare thoughtfully into the flames that danced as if inspired by the possibilities all that had been spoken of posed. How could such simplicity become so distorted? "Nana, what is the event that made my parents divorce? What happened that was so bad?"

Nana broke her gaze and looked at the ground. "I'm sure that information isn't necessary for your mission," she quietly replied.

"Uh, excuse me? They are my parents, and I have lost my father, my family because of it. I mean yeah, Daddy's still there, he comes to see me during the week and I stay with him most weekends, but it's not enough - not for either of us, and I think I have the right to know why!" Teeny wailed.

"I'm sure you do honey, but I really don't think it's for your ears to hear, at the very least not from me," Nana responded, still looking down.

"Not for my ears? Not for my… I cannot believe you just said that! Not after all the things you've just taught me. Here, in this place, I've learnt about sex and orgasms and a whole bunch of other stuff that no adult would ever dream to teach me about. Didn't you say that I knew of all of these things before I was born? Pick an adult, any adult, drop me in front of them and let me tell them everything I have learnt since I have been in this Realm. They probably wouldn't have a clue, not without having come here to remember. You brought me here to teach me how to do my bit to save my Indigo family so we can BE, but suddenly my ears are too young to hear it? Because that is what you're telling me right; that I'm too young to know? Man you talk about me being too human? Well not only are you too human, you're… you're too grown! Teeny turned her back and folded her arms in a huff. She was sulking.

"Well she got you there Dupe," Imhotep chirped.

"I can handle this!" Nana snapped.

Imhotep mimicked a smirk, shrugged his shoulders and pulled on his pipe. Nana walked up to Teeny and placed a paw on her shoulder that was immediately shaken off by the obstinate girl.

"You're right, I'm sorry," said Nana. "I am too human, it's the reason I am unable to ascend. I have to reincarnate because I simply have too much to both relearn and unlearn. I'm treating you like a child, and forgetting that your soul and the wisdom it has collected is infinite."

"Yeah, that's right. In all my incarnations, I'm probably older than you!" Teeny cheekily added over her shoulder.

Nana paused in thought. "You know, you just might be," she agreed, surprised at her granddaughters quick deduction.

Teeny turned back to look at the panther, "So does that mean you're gonna tell me then?" she said suddenly switching from her sulky pose to one of eye-wide anticipation.

"No, that is not what I brought you here for. That is something you'll have to ask your parents," said Nana, torn between her present form as an unbiased soul and her previous life as a mother and grandmother.

"Been there, done that. They just go quiet, give me some lame 'it's an adult thing' type of speech, or they change the conversation. It's the only time I don't like them - when they think I'm just a dumb little kid. One minute it's, 'you're only ten years old, you're too young', then it's, 'you're almost eleven years old Teeny, grow up!' And I'm the one who gets called a handful? Do you grown ups even know how hard you are to please?" Teeny threw herself to resume her sulky stance with her back to her Nana.

"I'm beginning to like this character, can't pull the wool over her eyes," Imhotep nodded and raised his pipe in the air in agreement.

Nana shot a look at the great ape and bared her fangs at him threateningly. His comments were definitely not welcome or funny. Imhotep did a playful jiggle in his seat - he was having fun even if no one else was.

Teeny turned around and leapt from her seat. "I am sooo lame!" she cried. "What am I asking you for, when I can just think the question and the answer will come. I mean this is the Mental Realm where all thoughts, knowledge and wisdom reside right? Ha!"

"No Teeny, that really wouldn't be appropriate, you mustn't…" scrambled Nana.

Imhotep slapped his thigh and gave a roar of laughter. "By N9ne the blighter has got it! Good on you!" he boomed.

"This wasn't supposed to happen and you are not helping," Nana growled.

"Oh yes I am, I'm in full encouragement of her expanding her horizons and she has just taken a step outside of the containment of her limited human perception. Within a few hours of being here, she has figured what it took you months to work out. Now *that* is the essence of N9ne. Good on you Teeny, there is hope for you yet!" said an excited Imhotep.

But Teeny wasn't listening. She had her eyes closed and was taking long, deep, slow breaths.

"My mother had an affair?" Teeny yelled suddenly, her eyes were now open, but squinted in disgust.

"Teeny, it's not what you think," said Nana quickly, "your mother..."

"How can it not be what I think? My mother had an affair! I'm not stupid you know. I do know what that is. She cheated on my Daddy with another man! It's just like how I've seen it happen in Eastenders. No wonder why he left! I wish I left with him, how could she be so mean and selfish? I hate her!" Teeny was near hysterical with anger.

"Destiny Kingsley that is enough! Sit down, shut up and listen!" Nana roared.

Teeny fell back into her seat in shock. Hearing the roar of a panther scared her into silence.

“First of all, the word ‘hate’ is never to pass your lips again in this lifetime or any other. You know nothing of what it is to hate, heaven forbid you ever will. Do I make myself clear?”

Teeny could manage nothing more than a blinked response; she was still stunned.

“Secondly,” Nana said, her voice a little calmer for having Teeny’s attention. “Did you not hear Imhotep compliment you a few minutes ago? Well you just went from thinking beyond the confines of the human mind, to exemplifying the species’ ignorance at is worst. Had you been listening to what I had spoken of earlier, you would remember that I said there is no good and bad. Yes your mother cheated on your father, and in all fairness, back when I was incarnate, my initial reaction was to be angry at what I judged as being her stupidity too. But like you, I took one piece of a puzzle and felt I saw the big picture and believe me Teeny, this picture is huge.” The panther paused and sighed. “Imhotep tried to explain before, that what happened was the responsibility of both your parents. Perhaps now would be as good a time as any to elaborate.

“In your father, your mother had something amazing that she hadn’t seen anywhere else. Being a psychotherapist, day in day out she hears her clients talk of the pain of their marriage in some shape or form. Outside of work she hears the same thing from all of her friends, and even sees it on the television when she finds time to relax in front of it. She is living her perfect existence in a world that says such a thing does not exist, or is at least, not meant to last. She feared how she would ever cope without your father in her life.

“Likewise in your mother, your father found happiness in a world that deems him unworthy of becoming anything more than a played out thug, a world that tells him that no matter how well he does, despite the fact he chooses to be more than the typical stereotype of a young black male, he will still finish last. Of all his achievements, the one he prides himself on most is the love he shares with his wife and family, and he feared what would become of him if he were to lose it. Fear is a powerful emotion. Remember what I said about the word emotion? Fear is a nervous energy that seeks to gain momentum. Like a parasitic virus it seeks a host to feed off. The host's belief in it makes it stronger and eventually becomes an effective instrument of contagion used to spread its infection. Your parents were so in love, and so happy that they believed it to be too good to be true. Instead of living for the present day, they worried for a future that need never happen. They worried that what they had, might some how come to an end.

"The universe doesn't distinguish between what you say or think you want or don't want; it will provide for you what you focus your thoughts on most. What the universe receives is the vibration of the person, place or thing that emphasis is predominantly placed on. If one declares 'I wish never to be sick', the emotion that is stressed upon through thought and visualisation is interpreted to the core characteristic: *sick.* This happens because even though the thinker is stating a desire not to be ill, in saying so, thought and thus energy is placed on the word 'sick'. For a moment, no matter how brief, the thinker mentally determines what the word means to them. The thought is faster than the speed of light and is often never consciously acknowledged, but that split second of contemplation is enough to contribute toward a cause, that will manifest at some point in time as an effect, if further emphasis is placed on it through repetition. So 'sick' is exactly what one gets. The dominant thought is what is processed and then made potent via the most efficient tool of delivery - anyone or anything willing to play host. In the case of your parents, their thoughts crystallised to become the perfect opportunity for their own demise. Even the man, with whom your mother cheated on your father, is not to be viewed with animosity. He was merely the perfect vehicle through which your parents' 'wish' was transported. Thus the fear energy was channelled, until such time as your parents are ready and willing to neutralise and immobilise it through confrontation, understanding and forgiveness."

Teeny slumped. Nana was making more sense than she cared to admit. She reflected back to when her world was perfect, her family happy and together. The fear her grandmother spoke of, even she had felt it. She had just never known what it was. It wasn't something tangible, one could never quite put a finger on it, but it was there. It was like a subtle force, a kind of friction. She had experienced it many times on the vert ramps in the park, as she was about to descend with the intent of doing a 360 on the other end. It was a tiny feeling that spoke inaudible words. A more apt description for this entity was that it was like a thief that operated in the shadows. It came discreetly, and often left almost as soon as it arrived as if to avoid detection. Within a heartbeat it came and stole a breath, a bite into her spirit causing her to doubt. It happened so fast that when she tried to question it, it had already long gone and left her wondering what she had been thinking. That was the way it worked. However, it didn't only steal a breath, it stole an essential part of a memory. The memory that she had performed this feat hundreds of times before and had no reason to question whether she could do it again. The way she responded to this feeling was to face it head on and even go as far as to add a cocky variation to her stunt; her way of affirming that she was more powerful than anything that dared to presume otherwise.

She'd felt it in her home too, she saw it in her mother's eyes whenever her father came to pick her up on a Friday evening or Saturday morning. Her mother tried to hide it by fussing unnecessarily on things like picking out invisible fluff from Teeny's hair or smoothing down the lapels of her jacket for the umpteenth time, or even going back and forth to the kitchen in between making tea she had no intention of drinking.

She recognised it in her father also. He'd jingle his car keys and look at his wristwatch or the clock on his mobile phone as if to demonstrate that he was in a hurry and needed to leave. He'd look around at nothing in particular, but if his eyes fell on the pictures on the mantle, he would become even more shifty as if looking at them sent a shock wave of pain through him making it uncomfortable to sit or even stand still. He'd pull at his ear, rub on his moustache then shove his hands into pockets and start shifting his weight from one leg to another, until Teeny finally freed him from his torture with her readiness to leave. Her parents were afraid to be around each other, around anything that reminded them of how much they had lost. They were afraid that they would hurt forever without the other to hold and assure that it was just a bad dream and everything was really going to be okay.

"There are two kinds of rollers you know," Teeny said finally, "there are those who skate on the street and don't need ramps or parks to do stunts. The whole world is a park, and every obstacle makes life interesting, even the ones that get you in trouble, because there are so many cool ways to get over it, under it or around it. The only limitation is your own imagination, and because it's fun, you never give up, just to be able to catch and hold that feeling of achievement for as long as you can make it last. Then there are those that prefer ramps or other custom made objects to skateboard on. Their way is fun too, but after a time everything that can be done, gets done and it's not so much of a challenge any more. All there is is to improve or perfect what you already know how to do." Teeny gazed into the fire, her voice sounding distant whilst she reflected. "Mum and Dad were street rollers you know? Then its likc they fell, but instead of getting back up to try again, they dusted themselves off and walked away. But they still wanna roll, I know it - they know it. They're both acting like skateboarding didn't ever mean the world to them and it's not worth trying to fly once more in case they fall again." Teeny bit her lip and looked at her Nana. "I can't imagine living in a world where I couldn't be around what I love most about it. This kind of thing is so much easier to watch on Eastenders; it's not so cool when it's happening for real."

"I cannot believe you are comparing the deterioration of your parents marriage to the stupidity you insist on watching on Eastenders!" Nana growled through gritted teeth. "Just you wait, I'll send both your mother and father a dream to make them throw that blasted television away, or at the very least ban you from watching that over dramatised nonsense."

"You wouldn't!" Teeny gasped.

"Oh, but I would. I mean, look at you. I'm trying to explain something serious to you and for a split second you actually sound like you are getting it and then you bring up bloody Eastenders! If it's not that, you are referring to some other television show or hippety hop music celebrity. The very idea!" Nana choked.

"Ah well, The Avatar is actually very educational…" Imhotep intervened.

"Oh if you think you can convince me that Eastenders is the product of Indigo and Crystal children, you have another thing coming. Besides, right about now, I'm not talking to you!" Nana snarled.

"Well the fact remains, it taught your genes here what an affair was, that's all I'm saying," said Imhotep who playfully mimicked the sealing of his lips with his thumb and forefinger then tossing an imaginary zipper over his shoulder.

“The point I’m trying to make, is that fear is what was ultimately responsible for what happened between your parents,” said Nana. “Fear, like anything in small doses, is harmless. In fact it can even be beneficial in terms of keeping us safe from danger. But when it is fed into, it grows exponentially, yet with such lowly cunning, that it hides within the subconscious of he or she that gave birth to the thought. Like any energy, it is indiscriminate and seeks an outlet to avail itself for discharge into another form. It surfaces shrewdly in various ways, sometimes in the form of varying degrees of paranoia, or as blatant yet inexplicable self-sabotage. Worse still, it is highly contagious and camouflages itself within ones intellect, rationalising why such and such is impossible, dangerous or will lead to failure and therefore should not be attempted. It’s mobility is assisted by its trusted ally - ego, that verifies all falsehoods and conveniently provides examples of others who have succumbed to it and manifested their own worst nightmares, affirming why one shouldn’t try to be more than who or what they currently are.

“A popular and accurate acronym for fear is ‘False Evidence Appearing Real’. And that is exactly what it implants into the hearts and minds of unsuspecting beings. The subservience to this disagreeable energy is not restricted to one species, or plane of existence. It’s only worthy adversary is its opposite; love. As such, it seeks to preserve its existence by first eliminating its competition. Hope and its allegiances are quashed as it perpetrates the illusion of loneliness and isolation,” she concluded ruefully.

From the perspective of her current state of awareness, Nana had gained much insight through her external reflection of her first hand experience as a mortal. Truly the extent to which fear and doubt had hindered progression could be seen in humans who considered themselves helpless participants born in to a life not of their choosing. She mused on how it was a common misconception on Earth that humans had little say over their existence to the extent of the establishment of hierarchal segregation. Such belief was exemplified throughout the species in the form of societies, races or even genders claiming to superiority over their counterparts. An extremist demonstration of which was the 'big brother' society commandeered by those who feared most, unwittingly playing host to the personification of resistance to overdue change.

Imhotep picked up his imaginary zipper and unfastened his mouth. "So Destiny, how does one defeat this indestructible energy?"

Teeny looked at Imhotep as if he had asked a stupid question, then furrowed her eyebrows in determination. "You trick it. You play it out in your head and think of the worst that could possibly happen. Usually it's actually not that bad when compared to the best possible outcome. Then you remember the passion you feel for what you love, think of how truly beautiful and worthwhile would be to own that feeling and know you are the one responsible for creating it. Then you stop thinking altogether and face the fear and do it anyway. You take your right to be the happiest person in the world and laugh in the face of fear as you do. Or at least that's what I do." Teeny paused in thought before continuing. "I mean, thinking is good, but if you think too long and hard you miss that perfect moment and facing the fear becomes that little bit harder."

"Bravo! Simply delightful! I take it back, with your genes weren't so foul after all. I think she's just about ready for the next step," said Imhotep proudly.

"Indeed," agreed Nana with matching pride. Choosing to receive the great ape's derogatory comment as a compliment.

"Ready for what?" Teeny asked. "I mean okay, so I get it, fear was to blame for what Mum did, but that's not likely to bring my family back to the way it was."

"Your being brought here was to put into motion part of a double edged sword effect. The objective was not only to educate you, but also to encourage your parents to enter into a dialogue that forced them to face a fear equally as great as the one they had of losing each other. Together they now must face the possibility of losing you. Of course you will be returned to them without harm, but the prospect of such a loss is causing them to pay attention and focus on what is important. When all logic is absent, the only thing left to turn to, is what lies within."

"Or insanity," piped in Imhotep.

"My genealogy will prevail." Nana responded confidently, then continued in her address to Teeny, "Your parents are one, for them to truly look within, they need each other, and trust will of course be a major factor. Even so, you will have to be the one to see the plan to its successful end on you're return."

"What?" wailed Teeny. "Why me? Didn't you hear me before? I'm too young to know what I'm talking about when it comes to 'big people's business'. For me to find out why they split up, I've had to be put in a coma!"

"I know it may sound a little daunting," soothed Nana, "but I cannot be the one to do it. I am unable to cater for all the variables that may occur, whereas you can. You have a better chance of succeeding through your ability to improvise. Besides, that hard-headed daughter of mine isn't paying me any mind. I've sent her numerous dreams. I've even gone as far as sending one so plain and simple and repeating it over and over for the past year and still she misses the point. You are the one person who they care enough about to listen to, and believe me, after this scare, they will listen. Any other adult may unintentionally personalise the issue and approach the subject from an angle of fear and make things worse. It has to be you."

"Truth in all its simplicity is best administered from the mouth of babes," affirmed Imhotep. "Thus far, having children teach other children has worked extremely well in alpha simulations deployed through passive methods of education, as you so keenly discerned. It is now time for the beta phase. Select Indigo children have been chosen to ensure the awakening of others like themselves as well as playing mentor to the first and second wave Crystals. You are one of those selected to herald the awakening."

Teeny opened her mouth to speak, then closed it, then opened it again, eyes squinted, eyebrows arched. She had questions, but didn't know where to begin. The most pressing one she had at that moment was, had she just heard right? She closed her mouth, stuck her tongue out the corner and held her head in contemplation. Suddenly her parent's words didn't feel so insulting after all. She slowly started nodding then pointed to herself, her nod gaining momentum. "I'm only ten years old, I'm too young. I'm the one with the death wish remember?"

"Your age and experience are beneficial, you are quick, intelligent, resourceful and Crystal through and through," said Imhotep.

"But before I came here I didn't know anything about Indigo and Crystals and all that. I don't know about empaths, clairaudients, telepaths, precognitive abilities, telekinesis, none of it."

Nana and Imhotep looked at one another, then back at Teeny.

"Teeny," said Nana, "neither of us mentioned clairaudients, telepaths or telekinesis."

“Yes you did, you…” Teeny trailed off. No sooner had she tried to deny it, she realised they were right. “Well, what are they then and how did I know to even say those things?”

“I think by now, it would be reasonable to request that you attempt to seek the answer within the data pool expanse that is this realm and tell us what you know; what you remember of these things. Time to remove the floatation aids and allow you to experience what it is to swim in the deep end,” Imhotep said softly.

9

And Life Goes On

It was a Monday morning and Maya could barely bring herself to prepare for work. She could easily re-schedule her appointments and take the day off, but if she did, she might just do so indefinitely. Besides, she needed a distraction. Work was as good as any; it might do her good to hear other people's problems. Her occupation as a psychotherapist always reminded her that no matter what she was going through, she had much to be thankful for.

Sunday had gone so by so quickly, she had to check several times to be sure she hadn't simply missed a day some how. She had gone to visit Teeny and read, prayed, hugged and cried over her body that remained indifferent to the world around her. Elias had phoned for his cousin, wondering why he hadn't seen her at the verts. She had talked at length to Nia. The only thing she hadn't done, despite wanting so badly to, was seen or spoken to Derrick. This time it wasn't ego that stopped her, it was acknowledgement of the fact that he deserved some time to himself.

An hour later she reluctantly stepped into her pearl blue, five-door Audi A2 and drove to her workplace.

“Good morning Mrs. Kingsley, your nine o’clock called to say she’ll be about five minutes late,” chimed Leah, her receptionist.

Maya threw a glance at the clock behind reception. It read 8.50am

“Good, just enough time for a coffee, lord knows I need one,” said Maya walking towards her office.

“There’s one on your desk.”

Maya paused to turn and look at the young Asian woman. Everyday her bubbly demeanour brought lustre to the building that freshly cut flowers and daylight bulbs failed to employ. Her efficiency was unparalleled and yet she continued to go above and beyond the call of duty. In truth, she was as much a partner to the company as Maya herself.

“I’m sorry Leah, I’m being so rude. Thank you - it’s much appreciated. And good morning.” She tugged down on the handle of her office door and let herself in.

“Come in,” replied Maya in answer to the knock at her door.

“Your 9 o’clock,” said Leah as she ushered in a tall corporate looking white woman, whose hair was pulled tightly in an immaculate bun.

The woman clicked her way to the couch on Prada heels, the shoes of which matched a tan brown pencil suit. Maya forced a smile and gestured toward the couch. She discreetly pressed play on her Dictaphone, and took the seat beside the chaise lounge as the woman neatly folded her matching coat and placed it the end of the seat as delicately as though she were handling a baby. She sat down and smoothed her skirt and patted her hair so gently Maya could have sworn she never even touched it.

“How was your weekend Sarah?” She always started her sessions so casually that by the time it was over, most of her clients would say exclaim, 'Is that it?' Majority found her by way of recommendation, many of them through the woman that sat before her now. Maya was renown for her ability to quickly ascertain the root of most issues in such a manner, that despite no longer needing further meetings, it wasn't unusual for her clients to book her for a chat just so they could off load the week's stress to the one and only best friend they sworn they had found in her.

After having caught her husband in a compromising position with Richard, her masseuse, Sarah had spent the last two years visiting Maya. She was well over the whole drama surrounding her husband and his new found love, but enjoyed her therapist's confidential, forthright, non-judgemental conversation to the point of her treasuring each meeting like a reunion with an old friend. The official excuse for continuing their fortnightly meetings was, "prevention is far better than cure, darling". She'd even bring a bottle of champagne to drink as she lamented over the incompetence of her accountant or the how the gardener had planted roses on the east side of her garden instead of the west. She'd complete her coat folding, skirt smoothing, and hair patting ritual., then light a chamomile cigarette before finally relaxing into the session.

In the past Maya experienced problems with ending Sarah's weekly sessions in a timely manner, as she would throw up her hands and say, "But we only just started talking, darling! Don't worry about the next person, they can wait, I'll pay for another two hours, it's not a problem."

Maya listened and jotted on her pad, and as Sarah droned about the complexities of her life, whilst sipping intermittently from her glass flute. She inserted timely gasps of "uh huh" "no!" and "she/he didn't!" Usually she'd look forward to Sarah's sessions for an update on her life saga, but today her mind was elsewhere. Fortunately Sarah had to rush off to a board meeting, and so didn't pout at Maya for more of her time as their 'reunion' drew to a close. When Maya looked down to examine her notes she was surprised to find doodles of broken hearts, and squares that spiralled into themselves, each lesser square, crashing into the lines of its predecessor.

"What a hypocrite," she sighed. "Looks like I'm the one in need of therapy." She stood up, walked to over to her desk and picked up the phone to buzz the receptionist. "Hey, uh something's come up, can you reschedule today's appointments for next week please? Thanks Leah."

She grabbed her brief case, slung her coat over her forearm and went to the hospital to see Teeny.

Maya sat by Teeny's side, wondering if she felt any pain. She had long since cleared the fever, but doctors remained stupefied over her condition. She held her daughters hand and stroked her cheek.

"Daddy says you're gonna be just fine and we know he's always right don't we? Elias sends his love, he said to say the crew would 'kiss the sky for you,' whatever that means. I called your school again today, everyone's routing for you there too."

Maya didn't know what else to say, she felt guilty for supposedly having the answer, yet not knowing what it was. She turned on hearing a knock at the door. It was Rachael.

"Greetings Mrs. Kingsley. How's our girl doing then?" she said brightly.

"No change, I feel so helpless," Maya said earnestly.

Rachael bustled in with a large backpack on her right shoulder and checked the readings on the blood pressure monitor.

"Mrs Kingsley," Rachael hesitated, before continuing, "forgive me for being forward, but I just came to cover a shift, only to find the person turned up after all. I've been coaxed into standing in on another and was about to go for a coffee while I wait to start. Would you care to join me? Nothing fancy mind you - just the hospital canteen. I make a good shoulder to lean on," she smiled.

Maya thought for a second. "You know what, I could really do with a coffee right about now."

"Rachael, do you mind if I ask you something?" said Maya as they walked toward a vacant table after paying for their coffees and snacks.

"Sure go ahead, Mrs Kingsley," Rachael replied, throwing a blueberry she just picked from her muffin into her mouth.

"Call me Maya please. When we last spoke, you seemed so confident that Teeny would be fine. How can you possibly know this, when even the doctors seem less than hopeful? I know they say otherwise, but I can see it in their eyes. They don't have a clue what they are dealing with."

"Every situation presents a choice and I choose to be an optimist. I've seen many so called miracles in my line of work. Over the years I've come to find that the one variable that turns doctors' theories, or lack of, on their head is the human spirit, and the place that it is usually strongest, is in children. Children are the most robust little creatures, even in the face of the harshest environments. They are survivors," said Rachael, still eating tiny clumps of muffin picked between thumb and forefinger.

"Yes, but how do you know? How do you stay optimistic in situations like this? Don't you ever sometimes feel scared to hope in case it's all in vain?" Maya gripped the edge of the table with her hands as she leaned in to whisper her fears, scared that someone else might hear her.

"Nope, never," said Rachael fumbling at a stubborn blueberry. "It's hard to feel any less than complete confidence when you look around and realise exactly what we are all a part of. A microcosm of the most beautiful kind, and when you put it all into perspective and realise that even she herself is but a baby. You can't help but feel hope."

"I'm sorry, you've lost me," said Maya. She kicked herself for having an emotional leak in the presence of this strange woman before her. "I should get back to Teeny, I guess I just needed a little hope, I don't know what I was thinking. I'm sorry."

"I know," said Rachael. She dusted of her hands to the side of her empty muffin case and folded her arms on the table. "Hope is exactly what I'm trying to give you Maya. I know what you are going through is extremely difficult. You feel alone, frustrated and pretty much useless. As for what I was saying, I was referring to Gaia, Earth. She is a baby, but look at the beauty and efficiency with which she provides for us. On a smaller scale we ourselves are mini self-contained planets; perfect replicas of Gaia, but in a human form. Imagine if you can, a planet hurtling through the solar system at amazing speeds whilst maintaining a host of parasitic life forms in a multitude of perfectly balanced environments and ecosystems. We in our infinite wisdom believe her to be our servant, but we are merely fundamental elements of her physical make up. Like the bacteria we find in our own bodies, we are akin to her good and bad bacteria. Some of us poison her others of us heal her. We bicker, argue and go to war, much like her immune system does with viral threats to her body in an effort to protect. Overall she may be in bad shape, but she is still alive and kicking. We know this because so too are we. Yet, we represent the bodily functions of a being that is essentially an adolescent who happens to be dealing with the onset of puberty. If a baby can survive all that, and Teeny is made of the same stuff she is, she's going to be just fine."

Maya couldn't help her fascination with Rachael's far-fetched theory. She was ashamed to admit that this woman's crazy logic was for some reason, making sense. Or maybe it was simply that her desperation to share in the same confidence that Derrick, Nia and Rachael had in Teeny's recovery, led her to welcome any offer of rationalization, no matter how bizarre. "Isn't Earth like a billion years old? How did you come to the conclusion that she is going through puberty?" she asked incredulously.

"Well, essentially she is. It's all in the breathing," Rachael replied, matter of factly. "Every being breathes right? Well so does Gaia. Trees don't just serve to provide us oxygen, they are Gaia's bronchioles. In our bodies, we define the branches that extend from the main bronchi as bronchial trees, the job of which is to infiltrate the lungs and deliver air to the alveoli responsible for transference of gases, namely oxygen and carbon dioxide. Alveoli are to us what leaves are to trees. When we inhale, we take oxygen into our lungs, and on exhalation, we release carbon dioxide. Isn't that what Gaia does, but on a larger scale? Except of course in her case we term it photosynthesis and respiration. At night, we retire, shed our clothes and go to bed. Gaia does the same every winter. We mimic her every expression of life on a scale so minuscule that we fail to see it and dismiss her as being little more than some oversized habitable rock. But even rocks are living entities capable of maintaining their own ecosystems. Notice something else too; look how Gaia blossoms when in the perfect balance of love and positive intent or TLC if you like. Is it any wonder that she is most beautiful in regions where there is less collective stress? There are no coincidences Maya, just like Gaia, your little girl is undergoing a miraculous transformation. I don't doubt it for a second. All she needs is a little time, patience and the continuing support of all around her."

Maya gave short whistle of overwhelmed satisfaction and awe. She was speechless. She couldn't help but find herself swayed by the simplicity of such common-sense logic. "I - I never thought, I mean, you make it sound so simple, its – its…" she stammered.

"It is simple isn't it? Child's-play really. That's were I get my optimism, from the simplicity of life. It assures me that everything is going to be okay. In the end it always is, even when it appears not to be, it still is. We are just not privy to the bigger picture yet is all. Take for example, earthquakes, landslides, volcanic eruptions and other so called natural disasters – growth spurts, greasy skin and burst pimples. Just like your average teen," Rachael grinned.

Maya laughed. "Wow, I love the way look at the world. Thank you."

"Ah, what are we here for if, not to add our pennies worth to the equation?" Rachael replied modestly."

"No, really. Thank you. I feel so much lighter, and very encouraged. From the start, Teeny's father was confident too. When I tried to ask him why, all he could say was he could see that I knew the answer. It gave him hope. I, on the other hand felt all the more lost for hearing that." Maya hung her head in shame. "If I do know, it's hiding deep in my subconscious and I just don't know how to get it out. I feel so guilty seeing my baby lying there and I just don't know what I'm supposed to do. All I know is I can't lose her." She looked up at Rachael and pursed her lips. "Got a smart answer for that one up that sleeve of yours?" She bowed her head and took a sip of her coffee. It had gotten cold.

"Hmm well, seems to me if your subconscious is harbouring the answer, the most likely course of action would be to ask it to give it to you."

"What?" said Maya jerking her head and squinting an accusatory left eye at the woman who sat across from her.

Rachael seemed to be more focused on the meticulous folds she worked into the wrapper that previously surrounded her muffin.

"Ask for a dream," she said in a totally nonchalant manner. "Before you go to bed, ask your inner wisdom to provide you a dream that would give you the answer to the predicament at hand." Rachael suddenly fished a watch from her top pocket, glanced at it, and shoved it back. "I'm really sorry, but you'll have to excuse me. I have another shift starting in five minutes. I have to go. Good luck Mrs. Kingsley… uh Maya." She leapt from her seat, threw her rucksack onto her shoulder and shuffled off.

Maya barely noticed, she was lost in deep thought.

UNDERSTANDING

"I for one am at a loss for explanation. While the circumstance of Destiny Kingsley's sudden coma is not unique, the cause of such phenomena remains elusive."

"It certainly is a conundrum. Blood tests return results minus abnormality."

"Meanwhile EEG scans confirm heightened levels of brain activity, yet no response to external stimuli has been recorded. Curious. Essentially, the lights are on, but nobody's home."

"How often does one get to say that and mean it?"

"Hmm, not much else we can do other than to wait and see how this pans out."

"Agreed, let's just keep a close eye on that cerebral activity. I notice results have been recorded in the patients notes every six hours, from now on, make it four."

Dialogue between Registrar and Senior House Officer, accompanied by a student doctor trio.

Location: Protective Isolation, ICU. Familiarised as 'Teeny's Room'.

10

The Uncelebrated Nice Guy

It was a Sunday afternoon and the weather was as overcast as Derrick's mood. Grey clouds teased those who dared to venture from shelter without umbrellas, releasing intermittent light showers across the South East of England. He thought of visiting his daughter, but after two months without sign of change, his confidence was beginning to wane. That he felt so doubtful left him feeling guilty and frustrated at himself, as if he had let her down somehow. He needed to believe Teeny was not lost to him, but today was a day, that for all his exhaustion, he was weak. He could do little more than wallow in self-pity at the tight-fisted portion life had served him.

He glanced over at the alarm clock that sat on his bedside table. The time was 12.14, but still he lay in bed, immobilised by depression. Torn between a desire express his anger through a blind rage, a reckless drive, or a simple release of the dam that held back unmanly tears of painful emotion. For the moment, staying put in his bed seemed to be the least detrimental option.

He looked over to the side of the bed that should have belonged to Maya, holding her essence, bringing comfort to his soul even without her being physically present. How on Earth did this life befall him? He had done everything by the book. Well, more or less. Okay well, at least since the age of twenty or so onwards. He had been a good student at school and strived to earn good grades. He'd gone on to do the same at college and university, during which he worked part time jobs to support himself. All the while staying focused, trying his best to keep his eyes on the prize. But the prize was akin to a moving target that seemed to respond to his ambitions by telling him he was asking for too much.

His dream for success didn't include the desire to be rich and famous or to have an entourage of adoring women. What he wanted was the kind of success that was even more rare. He wanted a life free of debt, to raise a strong supportive family, the freedom to be a good man and not be penalised for it. Just to be a nice guy and live a simple life without having to defend his decision to go against the life predetermined for him by society's stereotypes and prejudices. Instead the path he had chosen equated to a ceaseless struggle, a life of bad luck and heartache. His preference to respect women, to not sell drugs and to take pride in his history as a black man as well as the future of his people, deemed him less likely to succeed. His preference toward clothes that fit and knowledge of how to utilise a belt made him less intimidating and manly to his thug brothers to whom empowerment meant calling one another 'nigga'. Derrick never could fathom how the meaning of the word supposedly changed according to which race uttered it. He sighed and kicked a foot out from under the covers as if to prove to himself he had every intention of getting up. He didn't always feel so disillusioned, but today was one of those days. One on which he felt too weak to be strong.

To women, Derrick was too good to be true. Apparently the fact that he didn't abuse, beat, or pimp them in some way or another, proved to be an enigma for many. The fact that he had to "work late tonight", actually meant he was out earning his wage, confounded them. The house he owned could have only been by way of an inheritance and of course his Mercedes was simply a loan, an insurance perk, while his Golf was getting fixed. If all of the above didn't diminish his chances, it was the fact that his home was immaculate; he could cook, and even put an outfit together without the accent of contrasting trainers and an oversized pendant.

Of all the hardship life had dealt him, he had never in his life felt the pain he felt now. Not even the pain of his broken marriage could compare to the way his soul agonised over his baby girl. He had never known helplessness like this. With any other obstacle he faced, he simply needed to try harder or find an alternative angle from which to approach the problem. He would somehow keep himself in motion by reflexively swinging one foot in front of the other in robotic style compliance. Trusting that as long as he kept moving in the direction of hope, he'd get there, wherever 'there' was. Yet the situation with Teeny was different. He kept up the appearance of being a strong father of unwavering faith. He'd diligently visit, sometimes up to twice a day, talking to her, reading her magazines, and as of late a book. They were now on the last chapter of 'The Ankh Akademy' by Marvin Ellis, but as he came to the end, his heart sank even further. The young heroes of the story would live to see the impending sequel, while his little heroine still showed no signs of change. What pained him even more, was that to date, doctors could provide no explanation as to how his daughter came to warrant such a fate.

He missed Maya. His friend's attempts to help him "get over her already," had had little effect. In fact, the couple of dates he had been on for the sake of appeasing others, had done exactly the opposite. It made him miss her even more. The women were appealing; very accomplished and attractive, but they definitely weren't Maya. The time he spent with them was little more than a temporary distraction. After sleeping with them he felt as if he had fornicated and ended the courtship soon after. The second woman was none too pleased to hear his "it's not you, it's me", speech. She flew off the handle, screaming words to the effect of: "Don't give me that tired bullshit! I've used that line a thousand fucking times, and now you're tryna use that shit on me? Nigga you must have lost your damn mind!" At which point he hadn't bothered to say another word, and simply walked out of the park they had been walking through, ignoring the abuse she screamed at the top her deceptively powerful lungs.

Maya was too much of a woman to make such a public spectacle of herself and she despised the 'N' word as much as he did. Maya… Since their break up he had made a habit of secretly checking up on her some evenings after work. He couldn't help wanting to know if she had gotten home safely. Or at least that's what he told himself. Truth be told, he just wanted to feel close to his family. Now he found himself doing the same, outside hospital visiting hours with Teeny.

Maya… He closed his eyes and imagined the way she would instinctively find his arm and wrap herself in it as she slept soundly beside him. Shit! Once again his body lustfully responded thoughts of her naked body wrapped in his. Ten months without sex led his body to need little to no stimulus at all to encourage a hard on. He kicked off the covers, swung his other leg out of bed, and kissed his teeth as he reluctantly got up to take a shower.

11

The Mentanet

Teeny closed her eyes in deliberation as she tried to search for answers. Within her mind she saw what appeared to be space. Clusters of stars that resembled galaxies in the way they swirled. What was this, where was she? She thought. Instantly the answer availed itself to her. She was in a holographic style environment that was a universal library of sorts, the essence of the Mental Realm as translated to her in a way that suited her level of comprehension. '*It's like an interactive encyclopaedia*,' she thought to herself. '*No, no its... Oh wow, it's like being in the Internet! An intuitive galactic sized Internet of thought, knowledge and wisdom.*'

"*Yes.*" was the affirmation she received, though she was unsure how. It wasn't a voice that said yes. Rather a feeling of such clarity it was almost audible, a pleasant wave that pulsed through her body.

A beautiful cloud of what appeared to be fuchsia-coloured gaseous ribbons lay ahead of her. '*What is that?*' Teeny wondered. Like before the answer became clear.

"*Inspiration.*"

Someone somewhere; no a collective group of minds were tuned into the Mental Realm and were finding inspiration in the company of one another. It was a school, her school! It was a whole school assembly! Within the cloud there was a particularly potent spike of pink-navy colour. Teeny suddenly realised she was flying, no more like drifting toward the nebulous cloud. She had to know what it was.

"*Toby Kwele.*" was the response.

'*Toby Kwele? Even here that idiot is off key!*' she thought, oblivious to the momentum she had gained in her initial drift toward the direction of the gaseous mass.

Toby Kwele was Teeny's playground nemesis. Ever since he started attending her school, he had been a thorn in her side. During a race she ran with a couple of friends, Toby claimed to have witnessed her trying so hard that she kicked her own rear with her feet. He had never tired of humiliating her whenever he caught sight of her, which was all too often as far as she was concerned. To make matters worse, he was a roller too. Before he became a pupil at her school, she had seen him on several occasions at the various skateboard parks she and Elias would frequent. Back then he had never bothered her, but now... now she struggled to refrain from picking a fight with him. Wasn't ignoring a bully meant to be the best way to make them stop? She could surely testify to who ever came up with that solution that it did not work! Aside from his annoyingly cocky attitude, the fact that Toby wore dark sunglasses to school everyday was simply too much. Who did he think he was, acting like he was so cool? She refused to admit that part of her disturbance was attributed to having been sent to sit outside the head mistress' office for her obstinate endeavour to sit through class wearing her favourite blue tinted shades.

Teeny didn't share a class with Toby. Though they were the same age, the times of the year they had been born meant that by default he was allocated to the year above her. Even so, it was common knowledge that he was the one student who teachers didn't penalise for such perpetration of "unruly dress code".

Why did he warrant exemption? He was no more a model student than she, considering he spent more time in remedial classes than any other student in the school.

"Focus Teeny," she heard Imhotep urge. "What is an empath? What is telekinesis and clairaudience?"

"Oh yeah – yeah. Sorry," muttered Teeny, eyes still closed. '*So easy to get carried away in here',* she thought. '*Calair-au-di-ence. Emmm-pathhh. Te-le-kin-ee-sis.'* She mentally drew out the words insistently beckoning herself from the wondrous distractions of infinite data.

No sooner had she focused on seeking the words, than she found herself gagging against the tidal wave of information that swept over her. The 'toe' with which she had tested the waters of the Realm no longer fathomed any tangible surface. Instead she found herself hyperventilating from the shock of being mentally tossed around like a leaf in a typhoon. From beyond her union with the Realm, she heard her grandmother's diced cries of "maybe… too much… not ready… too young". She could barely feel her own body, and wondered if it was responding to the data rush in the same way as her mind did now. She felt sick with nausea, but the little she could make out of her grandmother's words was enough to ignite her flammable determination. She forced herself to breath, but seemed to choke on her own bile. She thought she felt her own fingers grip her neck in response to her inability to breath. '*I have no physical body here; it's all in my mind.*' Teeny grasped for the logic of recently administered wisdom to help her overcome. She had no body, yet she felt eyes weep in frustration and fear. The semblance of galaxies seemed to play on fast forward as comets flew past her at dreadful speeds, unfamiliar planets shot around the stars of their bi and tri-solar systems. She herself seemed to be a vehicle of some sort and hurtled past moons, nebulae, and swirling vortices that urged her to come close. She threw her hands in front of her as if to brace for impact, but no appendages showed themselves. She stiffly urged her memory of her 'neck' to permit her 'head' to look down against the *g*-force and saw no torso, legs or arms. *'I have no physical body here!'* Truth became reality as she embraced the concept as fact and all at once everything became still. Silent. Calm. Black. An impenetrable darkness blanketed her, but she indignantly refuted fear and thus felt none. There was no thing to fear. She mentally sobbed and surrendered to the serenity, and all at once became lost, then nothing...

"*It is not time little one.*"

Teeny awoke, surprised and wondering when she had even slept. What happened? Where was she?

"*Oneness.*"

The answer came as a multitude of voices that spoke as one. It sounded like the crashing of waves, the explosion of volcanoes, the lull of a gentle summer breeze, birds chattering and bees buzzing all at once, and yet she heard it not with her ears.

"*It is not time little one,*" the mighty voice repeated. The beauty of its tone was captivating, harmonious and tranquil. There was nothing to fear.

Teeny found her bodiless form erected and placed lightly back at the shoreline of the Realm, her 'toes' firmly on the beach of lapping data waves. Her view panoramic of an ocean of infinite awareness resembling a display with multi-channel screening, and suddenly she remembered her objective:

"Empath stems from the word empathy, which is defined as the ability to perceive and relate to the emotions of another," began Teeny. She kept her eyes closed as she verbally delivered the explanations requested of her. "However the term empath refers to a person gifted with an extremely high range of sensitivity enabling them to not only perceive and relate, but actually directly experience the emotional, physical, mental and even spiritual state of another is if it were their own. They are able to perceive the subtle vibrations that accompany thought and feeling and resonate on the same frequency, facilitating them to act as a conduit for such energies. There are different varieties of empath. There are those that are more attuned to specific expressions of empathy, the most common being emotional, physical and mental, then there are others who are sensitive to more rare forms such as molecular, environmental, crystal etcetera. It is not unusual for an empath to exhibit an aptitude for perception in more than one form. Neither is it unheard of for one to be attuned to several. Those with a high sensitivity to multiple variations are known as universal empaths.

"A derivative variant of empathic sensitivity is that of telepathy; the capacity for non-verbal communication, via transference of thought wave frequencies. Some are more suited to sending, others to receiving and few to both. Empathic tendencies have more often only ever been explored in the area of being a superhero ability of cartoon or science fiction characters. However humans born with these abilities may reluctantly receive their natural gift as being less than impressive, as the intimate way in which they relate to their others may cause pain or discomfort until such a time that they become disciplined and thus skilled in the management of their gift. Many empaths remain completely unaware of their abilities even to the point of complete dismissal or addressing themselves as simply being 'sensitive'. Yet the extent of their sensitivity can be disruptive as it may cause them to avoid situations involving more than a few people at a time and even determine the kind of programmes they watch on television for the sake of reducing the likelihood of encountering overly stimulating situations. Unskilled empaths are usually in a state of 'always on' and involuntarily more often than voluntarily in-tune with the frequency of others. Empaths have a naturally deep sense of knowing, as they are able to see beyond the external façade and discern the truth behind the lie, even if innocently told by one oblivious to not living their truth. Whereas the average mortal experiences the world around them through five senses, the empaths highly receptive range of perception allows them to experience the world through what some may describe as a sixth.

"As with all those governed by the laws of duality, empaths are not only able to receive vibrational energy, but also send it. This is epitomised through another common trait found within empathic persons by way of their natural ability to heal, but their talents do not end there, as many mistakenly believe. The flip-side of empathy, the sending nature, enables them to affect and influence others by tuning in to the alternate polarity of their attributes, switching from being receivers, to broadcasters. This of course leads to morality issues, as they are able to form intimate connections to people with or without their knowledge and or consent. Though moral codes are difficult to implement within those who are unskilled or yet to even realise that they are indeed empaths…" Teeny gasped and opened her eyes. "That's why Daddy gets those headaches! He's feeling people. I mean, he knows he does, but he doesn't know why or how. He can do it on purpose if he concentrates, so I guess that means he's like a semi-skilled empath or something."

Imhotep closed his eyes and nodded his head in approval. "Continue. Telekinesis. Focus," he ordered.

Teeny closed her eyes once again. Within her mind's eye she saw her father sitting on the brown leather sofa in his living room. He held his head in hands, massaging his temples with his fingertips. Frowning in obvious discomfort. She watched as he suddenly dove for the phone and desperately tapped a number into the keypad. He spoke into the phone moments later an eventually hung up. He stood up and staggered toward the direction of his bathroom and fumbled frantically in the cabinet for pain relief and swallowed a couple tablets unassisted by water before passing out on the floor.

"Daddy!" Teeny cried.

"Focus Teeny," urged Imhotep once again.

"Daddy's hurting, he's on the floor," the little girl insisted, disturbed by what she had witnessed.

"No Teeny. He's not on the floor, he's at his place of employment. What you are seeing is in response to your thinking about the pain your father has suffered in relation to empathic sensory overload. What you are witnessing is past tense," explained Imhotep.

"I didn't know he hurt that bad - he never told us," said Teeny still visibly distressed.

"Your father is a universal empath dear, he is receptive to a wider range of frequencies than those attuned to just one or two forms of empathy. Since your parents divorce he has been in an 'always on' state. Being with your mother grounded him, keeping him focused enough to 'switch off' and find respite at will. I assure you Teeny, at this very moment he is rounding up his day at work, soon to be on his way to see you," said Nana.

"Promise?"

"Promise," Nana assured. "Now focus my love. Think telekinesis."

Teeny complied. This time she found her answer.

"Telekinesis, also known as psycho-kinesis, refers to the ability to influence matter by way of none other than mental manipulation. The power of the mind is utilised to affect objects causing them to move, or alter their current state… Wow, for real? That's so cool!" Teeny exclaimed her eyes still closed. In her mind's eye, she saw examples she found herself readily able to relate too. Images of one of her favourite cartoon characters, the familiarity of which served to further illustrate definition of the word. A playback of Jean Gray of the X-Men wielding her telekinetic ability caused her to smile. It humoured her to think of something as trivial as a cartoon being used to educate advanced knowledge. She chortled at seeing on of the eldest of three sisters in popular television series, demonstrating her power to move objects mentally at will.

Teeny had always loved watching programmes that centred on heroines with superhuman abilities. Perhaps it was because of the way such images affected her subconscious memory and reprogrammed her toward the recollection of a time that she was once whom she now longingly wished to be. Surely persons capable of such feats were nothing more than the idle fantasies of an over imaginative mind? She dismissed the notion and drew her attention to the talent known as clairaudience.

Navigating through the information became a little easier. The young girl wilfully attained information on the last term she had been requested to find the meaning of, without hindrance. This time she didn't even need to close her eyes. Instead she hung her head in concentration, staring at nothing in particular. Clairaudience described the ability of humans to hear clearly, though in a manner independent of physical auditory processing. This form of heightened perception did not necessarily refer to the reception of actual sound waves - rather it encompassed the hearing of impressions received beyond the limitations of the material ear. Clairaudients were persons possessing the ability to not only hear sounds relayed by speech, tones, and other forms of noise undetectable by the average human, they also heard thoughts and voices of non-corporeal beings. This made them readily receptive to communications from higher frequency life forms that eluded even sophisticated recording equipment. Those gifted with clear hearing described incidences of such transmissions being revealed as distinguishable mental dialogue that was not attributed to their own personal thought. Through this method, the clairaudient could receive higher guidance and even tap directly into the Mental Realm, and hear information without having to utilise the combined practice of meditation and prayer. Such persons gained information without formal learning and often only sought prescribed reference on what they learnt to gain further clarity of what they had already come to know. Clairaudients further described the information they received as absolute; it was not something they could enter into mental debate with, though it was possible to engage two-way dialogue. This was how they were able to distinguish such communications as being authentic and not of product of their own random ponderings.

Teeny looked down at the space between her feet replaying the information she had just gathered. She thought about how Imhotep had decorated the cavern. “Te-le-kin-ee-sis,” she repeated to herself softly. “I like that word.”

She smiled and thought how beautiful the flowers looked in the clearing that she had awoken in earlier and mused on how nice it would be if there were a few in the midst of their current location. She noticed a tiny distortion in the ground in front of her and poked at it with her finger. From the small warp, a plant shoot pushed through and rapidly became one of the flowers she had been thinking of. She sprang to her feet and leapt aside almost falling over her Nana. Her heart jumped at the sound of a loud and deliberate clapping of hands, which she turned to locate where it came from.

It was Imhotep.

“Bravo, you’ve done extremely well, I think we can safely assume her ready to know more,” he said.

“I think so,” said Nana, in amazement.

“Me? I- I did that?” asked Teeny.

“Indeed,” he affirmed.

Teeny walked over to the flower and cautiously reached out to touch it. She gasped in awe and replanted herself back in her chair still staring in disbelief at the white lily before her.

“Do it again,” ordered Imhotep.

“I - I don’t know if I can,” said Teeny.

“Course you can. Do it again!” he repeated.

Teeny looked over at the far end of the cavern and within moments manifested a mentally generated rendition of a rainbow.

12

"Please hang up and try again"

Maya found herself parking up her car in the driveway, barely conscious of how she had made it from the hospital to her home. She had been running on empty for some time how. Her daily attendance at work was merely the adherence to the pre-programmed response of an automaton. Though she was present only in body, only out of obligation did her mind tagged along for the ride. She continued to arrive at her office on time to sort through the dissatisfied minds of her clients with the same level of professionalism. Nowadays though, her heart just wasn't in it. There was a time that she felt lucky for not having to endure the problems her clients paid her to find the remedy for, now she envied the simplicity of their lives. For example, she so felt she could handle the panic faced by the evenings last client, Courtney Bingham. The implications of falling in love with her lesbian lover, who also happened to be her boss's daughter, sounded a welcome substitute for dealing with a comatose eleven year old. Teeny had slept through her birthday, deaf to the pleas of her mother's wishes for her to awaken.

She felt more alone now, than she been at the death of her mother. How she longed to hear her preach that healing would be her daughter's portion, "in Jesus' name". She missed her mother's irrelevant bible quotes that she seemed to have memorised for every situation. Right about now, she was sure they would have carried her through this "test of faith". But her mother was gone, and she had never known her father. He had died before she had been old enough to form any lasting memories of him.

Nia had been wonderfully supportive as always and called on her regularly. It was just that Maya couldn't help feeling like she had drenched her shoulder and bent her ear enough to fill an invisible quota for the next five years at least.

She had taken Rachael's advice and requested for a dream, only to receive an automated message that effectively told her to wait on hold. Her dream was infuriatingly simple and equally frustrating: She'd walk up the stairs and into Teeny's room and there would be a number written in large print on her 'message board'. It read 0945171207. In her dream, the first time she dialled the number she received a tone that indicated the line was busy. Half excited, half surprised, she had called again. This time she heard what sounded like her mother's voice reciting what she recognized to be one of her favourite biblical quotes.

"*Trust in the LORD with all thine heart; and lean not unto thine own understanding. In all thy ways acknowledge him, and he shall direct thy paths.*"

She chose to receive the dream as confirmation that Teeny would be returned to her, but she was less than impressed. Upon waking she went to her daughter's room to chalk the number on The Wall.

Maya kicked off her shoes in the hallway and walked to the kitchen, wincing at the contrasting temperature of the tiled floor on her warm feet. She grabbed a banana from the fridge and went to perform her new nightly ritual. Since the day Teeny fell into the coma, she spent night after night on the Internet searching for cases similar to her daughter's. She found references to shingles, chickenpox, diabetes mellitus and even a West Nile virus, all leading to comas. She had yet to come across the symptoms that matched what her baby girl had experienced. Doctors had reiterated that the virus Teeny entered the hospital with was minor, barely worth mentioning. It had cleared within twenty-four hours. In that sense, she had been right in her silent *'just a twenty-four hour bug, that's all'* chant.

Maya peeled her supper and powered on her computer, ready to launch the Internet. Her determination to find the answer she supposedly knew, meant she no longer had time to cook herself a proper meal. As of late, her nightly ritual included stopping to rest her eyes a little, only to find herself waking up hours later curled up on the sofa still fully dressed.

She looked over to the right of her where Derrick's computer once sat adjacent to hers, and coughed away the lump that threatened to form in her throat. The ex-couple once worked side by side, whilst they exchanged news about their work projects. Her no frills computer catered for the purpose of processing her client's notes for filing, paling in comparison to Derrick's powerfully high spec. terminal. He had built and customised it himself, loading it with multiple boot options of three Linux distributions: Fedora Core 4, Debian and Slackware. Maya found each as intimidating as the other. Teeny on the other hand, under the tutelage of her father, had become more familiar with open source software than its extortionate, globally recognized counterparts. She missed overhearing their nonsensical discussions over why Derrick was not yet prepared to upgrade his current Fedora version to the latest 'FC7'.

Maya wished she could split herself in two and receive the kind of advice that she was paid to give. To be able to lie on the consultation couch and play therapist to herself. She neglected to acknowledge that her wish to be counselled had been granted in the form of Rachael. Since their chat in the hospital canteen that day, they had somehow made a habit of bumping into one another. They crossed paths in Teeny's room, in the car park, in the hospital shop, even in the ladies' room. The chatty nurse always made time to talk. It was their conversations that kept her sane. Rachael had encouraged Maya to massage her daughter's body during every visit as well as read her words of wisdom and empowerment. For Teeny's sake, she did so diligently. It helped her feel just the tiniest bit useful and instilled an equal amount of hope. At times she wondered if that was the nurse's intention. Either way, she welcomed her words of support and encouragement. Hope was all she had now. It was the next best thing to falling asleep to thoughts of lying in the security of Derrick's arms.

MENTAL

"Born fair of face, the perfect guise of a merciless heart. She is dispatched when a mission must be completed by any means necessary. She brings fear into the hearts of men, freezing it cold with her ruthless temperament and yet she is wise. Wise enough to know what you know not. Scholars bow their heads in shame; they are lowly illiterates by comparison. Should she prophesise the time as nigh, kiss your children and bid your family farewell, for on her own she can destroy universes. A beauty to behold when favoured, but a ferocious beast when angered, one would do well to appeal to her compassion on bended knee. She is your both your keeper and annihilator, sing her praises loud that she may hear and be sedated into sympathy and choose to bestow love on your kin."

Desmond (Desi) Kingsley, Street Preacher

Location: White City Estate

13

Nana's Regrets

"Nana, " said Teeny, "did you know when you were going to die?"

Nana sighed deeply and sat down. For the third time she underwent the process of transfiguration and returned to human form. Still seated she swung her legs around, stretched, and then folded them to sit cross-legged facing Teeny.

"Yes, I guess I did know," Nana said thoughtfully. "I wasn't aware enough to acknowledge the signs, but deep down, I knew."

"Signs? What signs?" asked Teeny crawling down onto the grass, mimicking her grandmother's position.

"Little things. Things that made me question if I was losing my mind," said Nana, slowly recollecting her last human days. "I'd hear children playing in the middle of the night in my living room. I'd get up out of bed to go tell them off, and they wouldn't be there. I'd go to make breakfast and between entering the kitchen and walking to the kettle, I'd see your grandfather as a young man, holding your uncle in his arms when he was a baby. Then I'd suddenly find myself deafened by the kettle whistling, but I'd have no recollection of having put it on. It was as if I had gone back in time for a split second and relived a moment of my past. I would set out to go do my shopping and when I opened my front door I'd see flowers, grass, trees. I didn't know it back then, but what I was seeing was this place. I didn't tell anyone, because I was proud, I didn't want anyone to worry or think I was going senile. Then the daydreams, they were so vivid. Like one time I dreamt of your grandfather; he was smiling and telling me it's okay, that it was time to let go and come back home. Next thing I knew I'd be in the your mother's living room where she was trying to break up a fight between you and Alysha's brother. You were screaming at him to let go of something he had taken from your room with out permission. It took a while but things began to start making sense. I wasn't going crazy at all. I was slowly departing from the Spiritual Plane and was acclimatizing to the Mental. I had begun a process of transition. I was being born, but to do so I had to die. I was scared and I didn't want to go. Then I started to remember. I wasn't this body, neither was I this person. It was time to leave it behind and move on. But then I became upset because I was happy being alive, no sooner had I had that thought, you know what I realised? I realised I wasn't happy. I wasn't happy at all. I had too many things I had to do. Too many things I had to say, places I had to go and I regretted just how much I had wasted my life, but it was too late. I had agreed long before I was born that this would be my time, and all at once everything became so clear. Everything made perfect sense." Nana clenched her mouth and shook her head.

Teeny's eyes were wide, her body leant forward so as not to miss a single word. Only when she let out a gust of breath did she realise she had been holding it all throughout her grandmother's speech. "Nana, why weren't you happy?"

Nana looked at Teeny and smiled. "You know, when I was alive, I thought I was happy. I had raised four wonderfully successful children, and I had three beautiful grandchildren. I loved my job as a midwife. I owned my own home and unlike many black women my age, I could drive. I didn't start till late, but I could do it and I felt so free. Life was good. But I look back and realise that I spent my life worried and angry. I didn't class it as worrying, because everyone worries don't they? Likewise everyone gets a little angry once in a while. I worried about being overweight, I worried about what other people thought of me, of my children, of my grandchildren. I worried I wasn't good enough. Did I say I worried about being overweight? Hmm, if I knew I was going to die that day I would have slapped an extra dollop of mayo in the tuna sandwich I had for lunch. I would have given low calorie and diet this and that the middle finger and eaten pizza with extra cheese with side dip of full fat Heinz mayonnaise to boot. Then I would have washed it down with an extra thick strawberry milkshake because you know what? As I died and everything became clear, I realised that just as your grandfather had always said, I was perfect. I wasn't overweight. Well, maybe to the likes of those glossy magazines and catwalk queens I was, but Teeny, I was the most beautiful person I could have ever known, but I was never interested in loving me or knowing and being who I was meant to BE. Do you know the reason why some people are bigger than others? I don't mean as in big because you don't know when to stop stuffing your face big, or too lazy to get up and get a life big. I mean those eat right, live right exercise right, but still can't lose the weight."

"No, why?" Teeny breathed.

"They are big because their size is relative to their mission. They are the perfect weight to hold the size of the aura they radiate. You sometimes hear the term 'larger than life' used to describe the energy some people naturally exude. Well, they are literally, larger than life. Their auras are bright and encompassing. You can't help but feel good when you are around them. But not every physical being is able to carry such an aura. So their body mass is a little larger than what narrow-minded Earth residents feel comfortable to accept. They bring emotional balance the planet, for all the pain and negativity that some choose to wallow in; there are others who have to bear the weight for them. Literally. When was the last time you saw a person happy because they were on a diet? Those people are actually shedding their responsibility they had long before chose to accept in bringing balance to Earth. They have fallen prey to Illusion and are trying desperately to become other than who they were so perfectly meant to be. Now by my saying all this, I'm not implying that slim people can't carry the same amount of energy, far from it. They can, but to do so, they have to be stronger than the average human. They are very powerful indeed. Just like when you focus a great energy onto a small point. What I'm trying to say is, the vehicle we come in, at it's optimal health is the one most perfect for the mission we came to complete, the lesson we came to learn or experience we came to gain."

Nana let out a weak sigh and drifted to the recess of her mind where her regrets resided. Of the many that haunted her, there was one that continued to plague her most. At the time she had insisted was for the good of all, only to later find she had missed an opportunity for redemption from years of sadness. Twenty-five years after the death of her husband, she had met a man at a colleague's sixtieth birthday celebration. After exchanging pleasantries and accounts of how they had come to befriend their host, he had asked her to dance. The dance led to several more and eventually he had escorted her home. Once there, they stayed in his car just talking about everything and nothing until the morning hours. The man had been a divorcee, a father of two adult children, and had established himself in business of import and export. He had planned to return to Ghana, his country of origin, to live out his retirement. Modupe had been shocked and overwhelmed when only two weeks after having met, he requested that she share his life with him. As much as she had enjoyed his company, as perfect a gentleman he had been, as attracted to him as she had felt, she declined. She had no feasible explanation as to why she couldn't go. Each one she submitted was redundant. Her children were grown up, her career as a midwife would be welcomed with appreciation, should she decide to work. His financial security made it optional and he had made it very clear that he would support either way. But she was scared, no terrified of allowing herself to love again. She stopped answering his calls that begged for explanation as to why she suddenly shut him out.

On one of his numerous messages he had left on her answer machine, he had even offered to abandon his plans to emigrate and solicited her hand in marriage. At that point she picked up the phone and verbally abused him for being a liar full of fake promises. She told him to stay away from her and never darken her door again. She had hidden behind the shroud of her religion, rebuking him for living a life of servitude to Caesar instead of the one true Lord Jesus Christ. She condemned him to hell for trying to bribe her soul away from grace. Her fear of abandonment had been such that she refused to commit to a relationship ever again. The truth was, she had fallen in love with him, and ever since the day she abused him she had wished for a second chance. Instead she had chosen to break his heart and just for good measure, hers too. Even if she couldn't turn back the clock and pack her bags to follow her true desire, she would give the world if only to be granted one night of wild reckless abandon with him. In that night she would willingly give him her all.

Nana caught herself and cleared her throat before continuing as if to deny her elusive moment of dreamy reflection. "That is one of my bigger regrets, but I have so many other little ones too. I wish I hadn't been so judgemental, I wish I hadn't shunned friends because they weren't the good, blessed Christians I thought everyone should be. And oh the times I ignorantly prayed that another's soul should find salvation in the name of Jesus. I cringe to think just how ignorant I was. I was such a fool. I was the one who needed saving. All the money I spent on those blasted Sunday hats!" Nana closed her eyes and slapped her forehead in shame. "My god I was such a pompous fool. The times I spent nagging at your grandfather, for silly things that didn't matter like squeezing the toothpaste in the middle, leaving the toilet seat up, putting his feet up on the table... No wonder he left me. Even then, he tried to tell me. He tried so hard, but I knew better. I knew it all back then and no one could tell me otherwise." Nana held her hand to her heart and gave another deep sigh. Cascades of silent tears fell from her eyes.

"You know something? Until I died, I never realised that he didn't leave me at all. He loved me. He tried to tell me so many things, but I dismissed it as nonsense. He told me there were things we had to do and he needed for us to do them together. He kept telling me I was asleep and he wished I could see what he saw. When I'd diet, straighten my hair, and bleach that scar on my knee that I hated so much, he'd say that perfection could not be improved upon, and ask why I never opened my eyes when I looked in the mirror. Then one day he said there was something he had to do. He said he knew I wouldn't understand it, but he had to do what he came to do. He said he wasn't leaving me, and hoped I could forgive him, but he had to join the military. I was sure he had lost his mind. There was no war, there was no drafting going on. I was certain he was seeing another woman. But sure enough he wrote me letters and sent me pictures. He explained that he needed to complete his education so he would be disciplined in the future. He needed guidance and the only place he could think to find it was the army. You must understand, we were twenty-five years old, had three children and one on the way and he was talking about needing the army! I was livid. Every letter he wrote talked about how much he loved and missed me and I just tore them up in anger.

"He'd visit when he had leave, but our time was spent arguing, or rather I argued and he tried to talk to me about things that made no sense. Whenever he left again he'd kiss me on my forehead and say, 'I wish you'd remember'. Well, as I died, I remembered all right. I remembered." Nana paused to catch her breath. "I had already spent so much of my life angry and bitter at him. I blamed him for every hardship I experienced as a single mother. I blamed him because I could never trust any man again after him. I blamed him because I was lonely. But you know what my biggest regret was? It was that I never once knew how to love him the way he loved me. I never supported him; I was selfish and could only think of how alone I was. I never once stopped, not even for a second, to realise that not only was everything he ever tried to tell me the truth, but also the fact that I couldn't remember, left him lonelier than I ever was. I was a terrible partner. Simply awful."

Nana looked over at Imhotep and bit her lip. The great gorilla gave an affirmative nod, entrusting the remainder of Teeny's reawakening to her.

Imhotep slowly dematerialised into the ethers.

"Teeny," Nana continued, "your grandfather was a good man, the best any woman could ever wish for. He was honest, sincere, generous, loving, a bit of a rebel. In all honesty, I never really suffered as a single mother, not the way some women do. All of my anger was based on a story I told myself to justify my feelings of abandonment. All the money he earned, he sent it to our family and he wrote me every week without fail, but after a few years I stopped writing him back. Less than a year later, he died out there, shot in an exchange of friendly fire. I was told that as he died, he insisted on dictating one last letter to me. It was full of nonsense about if I stopped trying to die, I would then start to live and that when I chose to live, I would remember. Then there were words that made no sense. Words like, stasis, hyper sleep, and other incoherent ramblings. He asked me to remind him, he said it was too important to forget."

"I wish I met him." Teeny said quietly, then her eyes lit up again. "Nana, I can meet him here right? Oh – but he's probably got a new life now. Bummer!"

Nana took Teeny's hand into hers, and rubbed the back of it gently with her thumb.

"Teeny," said Nana, "he is here. He's been here with us all along."

Teeny jumped up and looked toward Imhotep, but saw only the mound on which he had sat.

"Imhotep! Where is he? It's him isn't it? He's my grandfather!" cried Teeny.

"No Teeny," said Nana, who also stood up. "Imhotep has never been human, remember?" Nana looked intently into Teeny's eyes. She reached up and stroked her hair then leant in and kissed her forehead. "David Afolabi Oshodi, I remember now. I'm sorry it took me so long," Nana whispered softly.

The little girl stared back at her grandmother quizzically, and then gradually understood the implications of her words. Teeny and shook her head, then turned and walked away head bowed in contemplation. She paced for a few moments then spun to face Nana.

"See, that's not possible! You said that the current incarnation on Earth is the first for all Indigos. If what you are saying were true, that would mean this is my second. How do you explain that?" cried Teeny.

"I also said that some souls prefer to do temporary assignments. I didn't elaborate as far as explaining that there are very rare exceptions like yours, where a soul incarnates, but instead of living out his full life he distributes his expected span across two incarnations within the time frame of what one life could have spent. You are a Star-seed, planted on Earth to perform a specific function. You are living the second part of the same mission, hence the need to remain in the same genetic line. You reincarnated through the daughter you never had the opportunity to get to know. You knew you wouldn't miss her, because you were to return through her and share her life from a different physical reference.

"Indigos have a strong innate warrior nature. You sought to nurture yours in the army, where not only would you find guidance and discipline, but you would also find yourself in a Masonic order that could teach you the things you desperately needed to remember. However your function was to become mentor, guide and protector of other Indigos and future Crystals and Rainbows. As I had explained before, so many Indigos lost their way and the manner in which we chose to make up for the loss was to allow a few select beings to incarnate as Indigos, gather necessary data for successful re-implantation and resume their lives a generation or so later. The process was experimental, and possibly dangerous, but you were one of a few who volunteered for the assignment. Your Earth parent's bond made them the perfect facilitators for you to incarnate through, enabling the retention of a higher than average percentage of your memory intact. However, fear tipped the balance and led to losing the family that were best suited to providing an environment that would assist in piecing together your memory and continuing your mission. Your memory should have been complete at the end of puberty, the onset of which your genes were to experience at the age of twelve. The duration of your pubescent maturation has been programmed to last exactly three years. Enough time for you to become one with who you were meant to be, ready to help sustain the process that humans have been labelling 'The End of the World', due to take place in 2012."

Teeny looked at her Nana, jaw agape. Then looked down at herself. She slowly lifted the hem of the grey, long-sleeved t-shirt she wore and reached her hand under and up to her chest. She rubbed on the fist-sized area of darker pigmentation that marred the otherwise even skin tone of her chest. The birthmark located an inch to the left of her heart had always been a source of irritation. Vanity that became more of an issue as she grew into the awareness of her body, caused her to upset over its conspicuousness. It also perplexed her that neither of her parents could discern whom in her family line she could have inherited it from. At night when she lay down to sleep, it would itch her and she'd rub on it similarly to how she instinctively found herself doing now.

The sound of a gunshot suddenly echoed through the cavern and Teeny lurched forward falling to her knees. She pulled out her hand to find it covered in blood that rolled down her fingers, trailed down her hand and coursed onto her forearm. She looked up to her Nana for explanation but her vision seemed to blur. She could no longer see in front of her. She tried to speak, but blood spattered from her mouth instead of words. Everything was becoming dark; she could almost swear she saw a light coming toward her in the shape of her grandmother.

Teeny found herself transported to a different place and time, her sight cleared to reveal an all terrain transport she drove along a dry dirt track road. But she was now he - David, the man of her previous human incarnation. He and his fellow soldiers had been on their way back to their base after a gruelling two weeks of field training exercises. Together the comrades laughed at fantasies of a cold beer and kicking up their feet to a large screen view of 'the beautiful game' known simply as football, and other small luxuries that made life worthwhile. Simplistic dreams kept them focused on the future. Dreams of home cooking, sex and even the nagging of significant others.

An explosion suddenly interrupted their banter. Protocol had David jamming his foot on the brakes and his team of six, comprised of his buddy in the front and four others in the back of the roofless reconnaissance vehicle, scrambling out to assume defensive positions. The thunderous sound of the detonation left them one sense down and below par as it deafened them. He glanced around him for signs of attack, as well as to ascertain the locations of his men. He hand gestured to the two he could see behind him to fan out to the right, and seek cover from the trees that lined their path. None saw sign of any aggressors to bear responsibility for the discharge, and yet a bullet ricocheted off the front of their vehicle. David heard nothing, his ears were still in recovery, but he saw the spark of contact made as the cartridge skimmed the edge of the bonnet. A few seconds passed and he could discern trickles of sound easing it's way back into his sensory range. All of his team were shouting confirmation or instruction, it seemed he was one of the last to regain his hearing. He heard a couple of shots fired, but something was amiss. He stood up from where he remained crouched behind the driver door for protection. He looked around and saw nothing, no attackers, vigilantes or soldiers, no one. Just the open dirt road. The explosion was a distraction, but from what?

"There's nobody out there, it's a rouse! Search the perimeter! I wanna know what the fuck is going on!" David shouted.

"That explosion seemed pretty real to me!" someone countered.

"He's right, there is no one," shouted back his cabin buddy, who had already ventured ahead of the vehicle.

A couple more nervous shots were fired in response to the swaying of the trees. David lowered his M16 rifle and sprinted toward the soldier ahead whose face abruptly dropped in a picture of horror. He stopped in his tracks in and wondered why his ears seemed to fail him again. He could not hear the words his partner seemed to shout in his direction and instead he followed his eyes down to his own torso. Blood? He touched the red fluid that stained his chest and spread freely onto his fingers. He stared at it, oblivious to having fallen to his knees in response to the how they buckled beneath him. Pain. A spontaneous rush of pain that coincided with the realisation that he had just been shot from the back, the projectile having exited cleanly from his front. His vision blurred and he found himself lain on the dirt. He blinked his eyes a few times as he fought against a gentle tugging that seemed to come from within.

"*Zauba-ah, it is time*," whispered a low voice within his head.

"Man down, man down!" screamed another in panic. "Hold on bro, just hold on! Where's the fucking medic?"

"Cover us, Tank. Mole, find and kill the son of a bitch that fired! Where's the god-damn medic?"

"It was friendly fire, Doc shot him."

"Oh shit, oh shit, oh shit!"

"Snap out of it Doc, we need you. Get it together."

"Quick, letter… My wife, I need to get a letter to my wife," David spluttered.

Nana ran to Teeny's side and cradled her head in her arms.

"This wasn't supposed to happen! This wasn't supposed to happen!" she screamed. "Imhotep! Imhotep! What's happening? Imhotep!!"

Imhotep rematerialized beside them and looked at Teeny. He tipped his head forward and to the side as if he was listening for something.

"This soul is well, have patience," he said unnerved by the cacophony before him. He touched Nana's shoulder. "All is as planned, but you are young, still too bound to the physical to overstand."

"My wife, I need to get a letter to my wife," Teeny gasped. "Tell her she needs to stop trying to die - that she might remember what it is she supposed to live for. Tell her she was born perfect; her incarnation is as it was meant to be. It was her job to remember, so I wouldn't forget. I will be back… Stasis… There are no guarantees… I need to remember, it is her job to remind me - her purpose, she was meant to be my guardian so she could remind me. I mustn't forget. I cannot forget. Hyper sleep… Look for the sign. This sign." Teeny thumped her wound and coughed, then spat more blood. "Destiny will be my new home."

Teeny collapsed and stopped moving, eyes still open. Her body transfigured slowly to become the man of her previous incarnation, dressed in the familiar army fatigue uniform down to the hole of the bullet wound that had pierced his chest from behind.

"Imhotep!" Nana wailed, "he's stopped breathing! He's not breathing! Oh my god I failed. I was supposed to wake him up and I failed!"

Imhotep stroked Nana's head tenderly. "She, not he, remember? Modupe, all is as it is meant to be, give her time. Do you so quickly forget that there is no death? How could she possibly die, when here, she has no physical form? She has simply ceased mimicry of all apparent functions and become One. She is remembering the best way she knows how. She is reliving the last moments of the first half of her incarnation. You know they all respond to this part of the process differently. You have completed your mission well. It is soon time for you to return also."

The young man's eyes slowly refocused, and as they did, the blood that saturated his face and chest, dissipated along with the puncture the reminiscent bullet had made. He sat up, then slowly rose to his feet and looked down at his form, then at Nana and Imhotep.

"I remember," said Teeny.

14

God Comes To Visit

Yesterday had been one of Derrick's better days. He had spent the evening with friends. Although he had done so with initial reluctance, his could find no reason worthy enough of rejecting the hand-delivered invite to his soul brother's first anniversary. None of their circle of friends had thought he would make it so far, in fact, bets had been made that his wife would plea for divorce within six months. By some miraculous feat, umpteen arguments, a couple of weeks on Derrick's sofa and an alleged affair that Jonathan insisted he could neither confirm or deny, finally totalled twelve months of marital 'bliss'. In keeping with his pre-marital playa he had secretly planned for his boys to meet at a gentleman's club, the night preceding his triumphant anniversary. His wife had callously threatened that if he dared forget, there would be no place on Earth he could hide. She would hunt him down, make a trophy of his dick and present it to his parents as consolation for loss of their son's life.

"After the year of hell you put me through, it can only be fair that I send you there to join me," she had said with a look so stern and void of emotion, he had believed her.

As his friends had pointed out after month six, he had finally met his match - it was time to settle down.

It had been nice for the attention to be focused on Jonathan's haphazard marriage. After psyching himself up for it throughout the day, Derrick had relaxed and enjoyed an evening of rambunctious brothers cutting loose and hanging out. He had even indulged in a couple of lap dances much to everyone's delight. He was cheered heartily as he mopped his brow and sucked in air through his teeth whilst he tucked in a five-pound note into the white lace thong of one of the dancers that tended to him personally. The excitement and laughter of the group made for a more pleasant energy to be empathically immersed in. It made him feel high, granting him temporary immunity from his troubles.

The morning after wasn't as dreadful as Derrick thought it might have been. To his disappointment, the souvenir hangover was mild in comparison to the sensation of empathic sensory overload. He had been looking for an excuse to justify taking a day off. Not for any particular reason other than to immerse himself in a day of nothingness. With hindsight, he was glad he hadn't skipped work. Lately it had been surprisingly satisfying, as if he could do no wrong. He had the magic touch and the sun shone so brightly out his arse, that even Walter had acknowledged him on a job well done in regards to a notoriously difficult client. He'd been able to leave on time for a change, and spent the remainder of Friday's evening by Teeny's side. As usual he chatted to her dormant body as if she was alert and listening, even pausing for where she might have answered.

"I see my little bro's been looking out for you, this place is beginning to look like your room at home. Yeah, Elias is good people, he misses you a lot you know. He came by me last weekend, and well, we kind of had an argument. I guess he's just a bit stressed or something. He was talking about how Uncle Desmond wanted me to come visit, he's got something he needs to talk to me about. Cha, I really don't have the time or patience for that man right about now, I don't know how Eli puts up with that mess. Maybe it's finally getting to him." Derrick paused to stroke his beard in reflection, suddenly feeling guilty for not being more receptive or at least supportive of Elias' attempt to reach out. "Maybe he's beginning to see why Uncle Desi and me don't talk," he whispered, feeling even worse for taking note of just how much of a responsibility his younger brother had on his fifteen year old shoulders.

Elias' maturity was as deceiving as was his peach fuzz goatee and the two inches he stood above Derrick. "Anyhow little man said something that made me think," he continued thoughtfully, "well actually he said a lot of things before he stormed out. He said that he wished he knew what it was you were doing that was taking so long. Said he thought you'd be back by now, even joked that I should ground you for staying out after curfew. Yeah I know, he got jokes for real, but it got me wondering. Your body is here, you're alive and breathing, but *you* aren't here. So where are *you*? I mean, you gotta be somewhere right? Are you lost? Do you need help finding your way home? I know it's silly, but I'm thinking maybe if I do that thing, you know - connect with you. Maybe I could show you the way back." Derrick sighed for hearing his own words. Even to him it sounded completely ludicrous. "Okay you know what, I'm gonna stop talking and just do it. I mean, what's the worst that can happen right?"

Derrick stood up, clasped his hands together, stretched out his arms in front of him to release residual tension, and sat back down. He gently slipped an arm under her neck as if to cradle his baby girl, and with his other arm he took her left hand into his. Finally he closed his eyes and rolled his head from side to side, but even that didn't stop his body trembling with anxiety. He breathed audibly. A few moments later he jumped up in terror. His chest felt as if it was on fire, burning from within. He reflexively withdrew his hold on his daughter and fell to the ground, moaning in agony of the sharp pain in his chest. As he rolled on the floor, he thought he heard someone shout something at him, a name, *Imhotep*. He tried to open his eyes to confront the person who he felt grab at him, long enough only to acknowledge that he was mistaken - he writhed in pain alone. Derrick closed his eyes against the blinding light that flooded his vision. He mentally cursed at the irony of conveniently experiencing what he swore was a heart attack, in a hospital at a time where there was no one to help him.

"*Imhotep! Imhotep!*"

The horrifying shrieks deafened his ears. What in the world? He continued to wheeze for a moment as he fought for breath then as suddenly as it had started, his 'heart attack' ended. He slowly stood up, shakily grabbing the arm of the chair for assistance. He gave a long, loud kiss of his teeth and dejectedly sank back into his seat and strained for composure. What had he been thinking? Teeny was in a coma for gods sake! Yet there he was falling about on the floor having some kind of empathic seizure. Derrick flicked on his teeth with his thumbnail, looking at his daughter who lay indifferent to the failure of his attempt to reach her. *Imhotep*; *One who comes in peace,* he thought, recalling the translation a thirst of curiosity for Egyptian history he had years before attempted to quench, then kissed his teeth again.

"Fucking idiot! Get it together you're losing it. One good day and you suddenly think you're god or something."

Derrick grabbed his jacket and left, head hung low in humiliation that superseded disappointment. In his haste to exit from the shame of his godly enactment, he neglected to hear Teeny's utterance as she affirmed her recollection. Similarly, the hour and a half that had elapsed during his 'momentary' connection with her motionless form eluded him.

15

The Middle Man

It was 8.45pm and Elias was feeling low. He sat outside his Uncle's flat, reluctant to let himself in. He'd been avoiding his Uncle for pretty much most of the week. He checked up on him when he knew he'd be asleep, but he wasn't ready to deliver the news of Derrick's rejection of his invitation to talk. He thought about going to stay at his parents', but quickly dismissed the idea after mentally playing out a quick scenario of his mother demanding why he was coming in so late. He'd already stayed over at his brother's on Sunday and Maya's on Monday. Tuesday and Wednesday he stayed at his parents, but had gotten in at a decent time, making him impervious to interrogation.

On Thursday, he'd slept at the hospital. Rachael had taken pity on him and turned a blind eye to his presence in Teeny's room. He sighed and ran his fingers across his freshly braided hair that Maya had done for him during his overnight stay. At the sight of a police car approaching he flicked up his skateboard with his foot, caught it by the trucks and braced himself to face the music of his Uncle's ranting. Upon quick perusal on entering the two bedroom flat, he found had worried needlessly. His Uncle wasn't home, though the television and all the lights had been left on. Typical. Elias left the small screen on and ignored the urge to clear up the mess he found in the kitchen and living room. If he left everything and locked himself away in his room, his Uncle was more likely to assume he had slept out again. No doubt Desi was somewhere local, probably sitting one of the walls of White City Estate favoured by his street kin. Elias could almost hear him recounting false heroics of how he chose to remain “under the radar”, in a clever attempt to “thwart the Illuminati’s plan”. How he purposely smoked marijuana to hide his brain patterns from their detection and prevent their discovery that he was in fact a god. Desi insisted that the Illuminati desired the superior knowledge he kept so they could manipulate it for their cause.

Derrick had fallen out with his uncle when at Teeny’s naming ceremony, he had started screaming that he had seen her face at the gates of hell. He went on to animatedly insist that Zauba-ah having arrived was surely a sign that the end was nigh. Eight years later he had been diagnosed as having Bipolar II. Around that time, Derrick and Elias’ parents were constantly stressed at the behaviour of their last-born. For all purposes he was a model son. He exhibited decent grades, perfect manners, was well spoken and extremely helpful. But as soon as he had started high school and found a new taste of freedom, he would stay out late, often not coming home at all. No amount of talking, reasoning, threats or punishments could put a stop his uncharacteristic delinquency. The only explanation Elias would yield was that he, “was out with friends”. Yet time and time again, his ‘friends’ whereabouts could be accounted for, whereas his could not. During this time he had remained as respectful as ever, he just wouldn’t adhere to curfew.

During one Sunday lunch that Derrick and Elias’ mother had invited her brother to, he had sat in silence staring into space, until his young nephew meandered through the door. Elias had greeted everyone in the room and after repeatedly calling to his Uncle, he finally plopped himself in a seat beside him, flung an arm around the man’s shoulder and said, “You know, you got a reputation for being insane, but if nothing else, I’m sure it makes for a good story I'd like to hear sometime. Hey do you want that steamed fish on your plate there? Crazy ain't enough of a reason to waste good food."

No one had ever dared approach Desi in such a manner, but Elias seemed to have a gift with words, he could say what no one else would, in a way that none could take offence to. He spoke truth from the heart, not from the ego. Desi had responded by suddenly focusing his gaze and slapping the fork from the young boy's hand just before it reached his plate. He looked Elias in the eyes, grabbed him in a bear hug, and burst into tear filled laughter. Since that day he seemed to suffer less intense bouts of depression and would often ask for Elias' company. They developed a mutual understanding and respect for one another. By the age of fourteen, Elias gradually went from staying over a couple of nights a week to unofficially moving in. None of the Kingsley's could comprehend their friendship, but it seemed to bring a bit of stability to Desmond's state of mind. Since the 'move', whenever Elias did stay at his parent's house, he now came home at a respectable hour. Or maybe Derrick's coinciding separation had played a part in that. No one had been paying close enough attention to notice.

The weekend prior, whilst at Derrick's, Elias had tried to encourage his brother to let bygones be bygones and come visit his Uncle; he had some important advice he needed to share.

Derrick politely declined all of his siblings coaxing until finally blurting, "And what the fuck, kind of advice do you expect me to take from that nut?"

Elias stared at him for a few seconds, before responding.

"You know what Derrick? You know what? Fuck you aiight?"

“What the…? Fuck me? Did I hear you correctly? Is that what you just said? You’re getting pissed at me for not wanting to play nice with the man who probably just wants to ask if my devil daughter has gone back to hell yet? I don’t buy that bipolar shit, not for a damn second. Every time he has been around my daughter, he’s comes out with some dumb shit, all the while sporting a cheesy grin, as if to say he is complimenting her. Matter of fact, last time we were in the same room he told me my wife got fucked by a man whose ability far surpassed my own and that I could learn a thing or two from him. And you know what I did Eli? I’ll tell you what I did. Nothing! I held it down, I didn’t fuck him up the way I would have been well within my rights to do. How you gonna tell a brother to learn to be man enough for his wife by taking lessons from the fucker she cheated on him with? He ain’t got no advice for me that I need to be taking.”

Elias could see there was no point in pressing him any further. He had never before argued with Derrick. But then again neither had he known the full extent to his brother’s bitterness toward their Uncle. Desi had conveniently forgotten to clue him up on this key aspect of his and Derrick’s dispute. He sighed in defeat.

“I’m tired of this shit, always the good guy. You all don’t even know. This ain’t about you, Maya or even Desi. I’m saying if he’s got some advice that could help cousin Teeny, you need to squash that ego of yours and take it. It’s been four months D., Teeny should have come back by now….”

Wisdom

"I believe in myself, but I am yet to know myself. I am the god I pray for the mercy of as I wait to awaken from this nightmare. I walk amongst mortals and other sleeping gods. I was born different, I know that much, but I don't know how or why. I have regular parents; I even have my own children and bills to pay. But I don't fit in. When I cry I do it alone, I don't want to answer questions about what hurts, because I truly do not know. I'm lonely when in a crowd; I'm different in a way they cannot understand. I feel them, I am them, but then I am not them. I am me, but who am I? I'm lonely, but never alone, because I can feel what it is to know god, I feel the strength most when I am weak. I'm making no sense, and perfect sense at the same time. It is so agonisingly difficult, yet ridiculously simple. I am young, but I'm older than I can remember. I have lived many lives before, but I make the same mistakes in this one. As I once heard a mortal say; 'same soup, different bowl'. I cannot comprehend how it is I feel such extremes and I wonder if I am going crazy, but I am the sanest person I know. Being human is so enchantingly painful. This is what hell must be like."

Mortal memories, the frustrations of a god incarnate.

Location: Dream Warrior Initiate's Temple.

16

N9ne Blood

Everything now made perfect sense. Zauba'ah, the soul that travelled through the vessel known as Teeny recollected memories of all that she had been prior to insemination. Zauba'ah belonged to a group of entities known throughout universes as N9ne Blood. Within the collective of elites, Teeny's soul had been N9nth Degree, the highest designation amongst spiritual beings, one degree below the formless Etherean. Higher evolved beings resident in All, did not use the base ten numerical system common to Earth and other similar civilizations. Instead they used the inter-galactic base nine. A simplistic method attributed to the principle of nine being the true highest number, all else were composed of a combination of lesser figures. The number epitomised balance as the resulting figure of any multiplication of itself, when added to become a single digit once again equated to nine. It resembled the expansion and contraction of universes that imploded and exploded, ever changing yet always remaining the same.

N9ne were physically incarnating spiritual beings that operated as one, demonstrating readiness to surrender individuality. They were another expression of All. N9ne were individuals within the simulated separation from All that had evolved to an extent of complete awareness. All maintained all, and nurtured those who sought to experience and know self. Thus these elite individuals were caretakers of infinite galaxies, essentially elders within the innumerable kin of Oneness. Guidance from of those within the higher frequencies of All, became misinterpreted as god by the sibling incarnations on lower frequencies. Where many refuted the attribute as misinterpretation, N9ne overstood it to be an endearing term for the state to which the less evolved desired to return.

In keeping with balance, N9ne were responsible for mentoring aspiring beings of lesser frequencies. These beings became known as Initiates. Degrees indicated the level of mental and spiritual evolution, each one bearing nine levels. Before her incarnation on Earth, Nana had been a N9nth Level Se7enth Degree Initiate under Zauba'ah's school of thought. Numbers within designations indicated that they were students, commonly addressed as Seekers or Initiates. N9ne was the only degree, in which the number replaced the letter to perfection, the removal of the letter 'I' bore testimony to the absence of individualism and completion of their physical cycle. Coincidentally – or not, the letter 'I' was also ninth in Earth's English alphabet. Thus the number and letter were often used as a DNA trigger for N9ne Bloods that incarnated within similar frequencies.

"I failed miserably," said Nana, her head hung low in shame. "I didn't realise the assignment would be so difficult. I mean, how hard could it be? Accompany you to Earth, and make sure I stayed focused enough to help you remember what you came to do. Instead I forget, while you remember and waste time trying to remind me. I held you back, I sabotaged the mission. I'm so sorry."

Imhotep rolled his eyes and reclaimed his mound. He continued with his favourite mental exercise of manifesting and manipulating a holographic image of a pipe, mimicking the burning of tobacco and swirling smoke that he eventually allowed to dissipate at his leisure.

"Do not be too hard on yourself," said Teeny "I selected you to escort me for a reason. You have great potential. I do not make such decisions lightly only to forsake my apprentice at the first obstacle they encounter. What matters is that you willingly assisted in my improvisation. Despite the damage you had inflicted to your body, your DNA retained instinctive memory and complied with my need to impregnate my genetics into yours. The fourth attempt to create a compatible genetic sequence was successful, and Maya became the perfect mothership vehicle for my return. As soon as my transport had been secured, I had to leave to enter a training facility that would keep me focused and endow me with the skills necessary for me to mobilise into the second phase. Whilst there I managed to activate triggers in many other Sleepers who had yet to awaken, but were guided on instinct to follow a path into the same training facility that they too might remember. Many of the Warrior Class that found their way into various armed forces are beginning to recall, but there have been many losses. Barely five percent respond to their genetic triggers set to cause explosions in their DNA and awaken them at the proposed time. A great number of those that didn't enlist in training camps have become proud and relish in the fear they induce in others as thugs and gangsters as they succumbed to the numerous opiates put in place by those who fear most."

Zauba-ah had hidden the unique genetic sequence characteristic of N9ne Bloods with the region of the human genome that Earth's scientists had termed junk DNA. On awakening, the body would literally resemble a vehicle that N9ne Minds could pilot, through deliberate manoeuvre of DNA and RNA transposons. That ninety-seven percent of the human genome had been rejected as 'junk' or 'non-coding', bore semblance to how little the species were aware of the vastness of All and its exhaustive populations of varying frequencies within its mass.

Full N9ne Mind memory and manoeuvrability of their incarnation could only be actualised through the completion of the process of physical maturation into an adult. During puberty, a N9ne incarnate's body underwent rigorous changes and conditioning that increased their resilience. It allowed them to manipulate their vehicle to perform acts that would, to the average human, appear to be feats of wonder.

In physical form N9ne Bloods, were still susceptible to physical and emotional urges. Many declined the option of incarnation through birth simply to avoid of the hormonal imbalances that naturally occurred during the pubescent period alone. Zauba-ah's reputation partly stemmed from the number of missions the soul had successfully completed despite having to experience the standard thirty-six month 'interlude of insanity'. Regardless of the rumours that led to Zauba-ah's school of thought being dubbed 'Sheol' meaning *hell*, many would-be N9ne Bloods strived to be worthy of the soul's tutelage. Of course it was common knowledge that there was no such place that bore the attributes of hell as described by religious fanatics. The only eternal fires a soul could be consumed by, were those fuelled by the need to burn out desires that had yet to be extinguished. Hell was the self-created mental void in which one suffered withdrawal symptoms of habits they had enjoyed whilst in the lower physical realms.

"Besides," the soul of Teeny continued, "though you remained asleep, you responded professionally, albeit in a basic instinctual capacity. My passage back was secured through the hospitality of your womb. You even presented my current incarnation with the blanket bearing a panther, thus showing your recollection of one of my key memory triggers. Your transfiguring into a panther to greet me is also duly noted. I thank you.

"That you fell prey to religion is barely worth mention. It happens to many, though usually not my Initiates. This leads me to wonder on your preparatory methods before deployment. It would seem you neglected to commit my guidelines to memory," said Teeny in the gentle, yet firm masculine voice of her male form.

"Should my memory become vague I was to research the numerous historical documents, detailing records of incarnations of previous N9nth Degree Elites and their Initiates," recited Nana. "But I did that, and still I forgot. I read the Bible and committed it to memory."

"Hmm, the Bible. The acronym of which creative minds affectionately address as being Basic Instructions Before Leaving Earth," Teeny mused. "The reference you selected was by no means conclusive, neither was it the best reference for information. The book is a highly contaminated document due to poor translation and over dramatisation, as well as being grossly manipulated as a tool of control. The only applicable sections to the assisting of your memory were the first five books and the one now known as Revelations. Despite its copious inconsistencies and contradictions, sufficient key words and phrases remain to at least trigger a sequence of questions in the reader to guide them toward their path. The first nine chapters in the book of Genesis are enough for those who it was meant to instruct. Even then the scripture resulted through the plagiarising of older texts that held slightly clearer accounts, the Enuma Elish and Atra Hasis, to name a few. Other supplications within the bible are predominantly addendum of junior Initiates of old, not unlike you. The remainder, a result of malicious tampering of data humans were too ignorant to fully comprehend. Alternative historical texts have experienced the same to either a greater or lesser degree. This is an unfortunate outcome," she that appeared as 'he' explained. "Earth is indeed a supreme being that seeks to evolve, but fear of the unknown keeps her in turmoil, a typical response to hormonal adaptation in any physical entity. The part of her that fears most holds her back, but it is time nonetheless. The only thing constant is change and she must evolve. Those of us here to oversee her rite of passage are also susceptible to her fears upon incarnating through her."

"How do you do it?" asked Nana. "How do you not succumb to the Illusion? And how is it you can speak to me in the image of your first incarnation, yet you are to return as a female child? Does it not confound you?"

"You forget - the soul is genderless. When we shed the body vehicle, hormones and external physical gender expression no longer determine us, there is nothing to imply sexuality or duality. Instead of choosing the gender of our subsequent incarnation in response to the experiences of the previous one, we choose that which might best mobilise us to complete the assignment, or that which we find most comfortable. The rest is simple. We allow ourselves to indulge just enough to enjoy our stay, without losing focus and becoming ridden with guilt. To put it simply, we maintain a balance in-tune with Gaia's fluctuating vibrations within our human body vehicles in order to receive the best performance out of them. We sight see, we interact, and partake. We experience and live in a manner that leaves no room for regret. This is how it is possible for us to not become bound into a cycle of karma that needs to be balanced across many lifetimes as a method of decontamination. All worldly desires must be relinquished before return to the frequency of Mind on which we vibrate. I sense your fear, but you needn't worry, your de-con will not take long."

"I thank you for your faith in me, but it may take many lifetimes. I was only incarnate for fifty-seven years, and look what became of me," said Nana woefully.

"I believe nothing. I know enough. You are present here, yet you remain bound to the concept of distance and time. You forget that it is irrelevant, another illusion. You still mourn for my previous incarnation and address me as David, yet that half of my assignment is complete and no more. You have forgotten both my name and yours. You are my responsibility and this was your first assignment in the physical. Know that I have not judged you. You will walk with me once more. We will speak again, but for now I will tend to other matters. I must return soon."

Nana nodded and exited through the waterfall.

17

Jamaican Ginger Cake & Soya Cream

Maya pulled into her driveway, appreciative that her last appointment had cancelled without advance warning. It allowed her to leave work early seeing as it left no time for another client fill the vacant slot. Either way, it had earned her a couple of paid hours off. She gathered her coat and bag from the passenger seat, and for no reason in particular, glanced in the wing mirror as she tucked her belongings under her arm. She saw a familiar reflection to the rear left of the vehicle and smiled.

"Hey sweetie, how are you? You just finishing from netball practice?" she asked Alysha as she climbed out and locked her car.

"Hello Ms. Maya, practice isn't on Thursdays this term. It's on Tuesdays now."

"Oh, I guess I'm a little out of touch what with Teeny missing the start of the year six." Maya felt awkward for not knowing something she would have committed to memory had Teeny been at school.

“Can I help you with that Ma’am,” asked Alysha, stepping toward her second mother, arms open offering to take Maya’s load. Alysha had always been a good influence on Teeny.

Maya opened the door to her home and let them both in. “You know you’re not a stranger here, go help yourself to a drink or snack from the fridge.”

“Thank you Ma’am, but actually, I came to ask you a favour.”

“Oh really? What’s on your mind?”

“Well, I was wondering if I could leave a message on The Wall for Teeny.” Alysha confessed sheepishly.

“Oh sweetie of course you can! I know she’d love that, and you know what? I’d love it too,” beamed Maya. The young girl’s request was a welcome breath of fresh air.

Alysha smiled and returned Maya’s bag, hung up their coats and took off her shoes before skipping up the stairs to her best friend’s room. Maya idly kicked of her shoes alongside Alysha’s then bent down to straighten them up as neatly as their role model neighbour. She walked into the living room and powered up her computer and pulled out her Dictaphone and notebook in preparation for typing up some case notes. Leah had offered to take them, but Maya had insisted she would do it. Every once in a while she liked to bring her work home and type them up personally. It wasn’t necessary, being that it was a part of Leah’s job description that she carried out to perfection, but Maya’s sentimentality had her tend to the job personally once in a while.

Maya padded to the kitchen to switch on the kettle, she turned around and jumped to find Alysha standing a few feet away from her. She hadn’t heard her enter. Unlike her own daughter’s loud footsteps, her soul-daughter walked with a quiet grace.

“Leesha! I didn’t hear you come in. Would you like a cup of tea?”

"I'm sorry, if I scared you. Ms Maya, um, Ma'am... I uh, I was wondering – well…" Alysha nervously shifted her gazed from the ceiling, to the wall and eventually settled for the floor, where she ground the ball of her bobby-socked foot into the tiles. "It's a Thursday night and well, if Teeny was awake, this would usually be the week that…" She brought her hands from behind her back so she could observe them as she resumed her fidgety tug of each finger. "Last week she would have stayed the night at mines, and this would be the week I'd spend the night… I know it's wrong of me to ask, but I was wondering if I could you know, stay over like I usually would. I just… I miss her Ms Maya. She didn't wake up for her birthday… and now all of a sudden, it's November and Mother is asking me what I want to do for mine… I just… There's no point you know? It's not fair."

"I know Alysha, I know. You are welcome to stay." It was the first time since Teeny's the unethical hiatus that Maya had openly witnessed the pain endured by her friend's daughter. She opened her arms and welcomed her sorrow in an embrace. The girl gasped a sigh of relief and thanks and cried out her hurt into her second mother's shoulder. Alysha was nearly as tall as she, when Maya found herself crying with her, she almost forgot who held who. She pulled herself back into parent mode. "Okay, I'll tell you what, how about you go get cleaned up, and I'll call your mother and let her know you'll be staying over. What say we have chickpea curry for dinner?" Maya smiled, thankful for a break from her new monotony. Alysha nodded, pulling a white cotton handkerchief from the tiny bag she religiously wore across her shoulder, she dabbed her tears with an eloquence that never failed to mystify her. She watched as her soul-daughter pivoted and headed back toward Teeny's bedroom, still weeping silently as she stepped.

After dinner, mother and soul-daughter together sat and watched Eastenders. Alysha cheered up considerably and even offered her soon-to-be-eleven-year-old wisdom to the characters as she sighed and told them off for "being so stupid". By the end of the programme she was smiling as she hugged Maya goodnight then politely excused herself.

Maya managed to type three quarters of her case notes, before the 'personal touch' novelty wore off. She sat back in her chair and blew aside one of her twists that had once again fallen into her face. She made a mental note to trim her hair the next time she took them out. She saved her work and decided to go check on Alysha.

As she approached her daughter's room she thought she could hear a conversation that took place on the other side. She pressed her hear to the door and heard Alysha's voice.

"Your mother hasn't given up on you either, she's still sad, but she doesn't show it so much. She did today though."

Maya thought she heard her sigh, but she was unsure.

"School isn't the same without you, in fact, in your words, 'it sucks.' I hate it there now. People are so negative. Big Jordan is really testing my patience, I wish he left and went onto high school like Toby. I almost miss him - he would have put Jordan in his place the moment he started back on the first day of the summer term wearing sunglasses. He would have popped him for sure." Alysha allowed a giggle to escape her, followed by another sigh. "Teeny, this isn't funny any more okay? You don't just abandon your friends like that, it's just not lady-like."

Maya stepped back. It hurt her to imagine how hard Teeny's ordeal must be for the young girl to cope with. She was an adult, a therapist, and she herself couldn't cope. She crept back downstairs to her kitchen wondering what she could do to help. She smiled and opened a couple the kitchen cupboard doors. Bless Elias, he had done shopping for her again, a ritual he had begun a week after her daughter's admittance to hospital. She grabbed a carton of soya cream and loaf of Jamaican ginger cake. She opened the packet and cut a few slices into three bowls and one by one heated them in the microwave.

"Hmm, something's missing.... a candle." She rummaged through one of the drawers and found a birthday candle and mismatched holder. She poured cream over the warmed slices of cake, threw in some teaspoons and in one of them she stuck the candle and lit it. She carried them up to Teeny's bedroom on a tray.

It was Alysha's turn to jump in surprise as Maya entered the room lit only by the bedside lamp.

"I know, your birthday isn't till next week, but I thought I'd bring up some of yours and Teeny's favourite."

Alysha looked up through tear filled eyes from the foam cube she had unfolded into a guest bed. She choked into her handkerchief, stifling an overflow of mixed emotion, clearly speechless. Maya sat knelt down on the floor beside her, placing one of the bowls on Teeny's bed and passed the one that held the birthday candle to the teary child. She sat down, legs tucked to the side, with her own bowl in front of her.

"Come on, wipe your tears and make a wish sweetie." Said Maya. "Let's do this how Teeny would like it done."

Alysha daintily dabbed her eyes once again and paused before taking a deep breath and blowing out the candle. She giggled.

"Thank you Ms. Maya, you really shouldn't have gone to the trouble."

"Nonsense! If I could have defrosted Teeny's cake at such short notice I would have, but I guess warm ginger cake and soya cream will have to do. Mmm, I quickly learning why you girls like it so much. If you have the room, you might have to eat Teeny's 'leftovers' if she is too full to finish hers."

Alysha giggled again, “This may well be the one and only time Teeny is too full to finish hers. I’m sure she will make up for it next time.”

Maya laughed. “Hey, why did you fix up the mattress? You could have slept on the bed.”

“Uh, well her soul might want to come home for a rest in her own bed,” Alysha reasoned trying to hide her embarrassment for entertaining such a notion.

“Ah, now that would explain why I wake up with a backache every time I sleep in here, her soul kicks around in the bed just as much as her body does. Seems like Elias was clued in about this too, he also refuses to sleep on the bed whenever he stays over. I offer him the spare room, but he always insists his preference is to sleep in here on the floor.”

Alysha smiled again, appreciative of Maya’s compassion. The two ate and chatted until the young lady fell asleep.

18

The Gift & The Curse

Derrick poked his head around the server room door as he always did at the end of every work shift. Everything fine, he went back to his office. There was nothing more that needed doing, yet he found himself half sitting, half leaning back on his desk to brace himself. He kissed his teeth and shook his head, dismissing the wave of dizziness he suddenly felt. Someone knocked on his open door, demanding his attention.

"Ay Ricky, some of us are going for a drink, you down?" It was Paul. "Damn, you look like shit! You alright?"

"Yeah. Yeah I'm fine," replied Derrick drawing his hand down his face, forcing himself to shake off his light-headed irritation. "Nah, I got some place I need to be. Thanks"

"Aiight, nex' time yeah?" said Paul and hurried off to catch up with his co-workers.

Derrick reached back into his top drawer and pulled out a bottle of paracetamol. He threw two into his mouth, grabbed his coat and case and walked out. He filled himself a cup of water from the dispenser in the hallway and swallowed down the pills.

The drive to the hospital was uneventful, but Derrick found himself cussing at a couple of careless drivers for being "fucking Neanderthals" that, "don't know what a bloody wheel is for". Each time he had to pull over to compose himself, aware that he was reacting to the frustration at the traffic other drivers around him projected. There was a time that driving had been a hobby, a form of relaxation and escape. He had once enjoyed spontaneous decisions to take off for a weekend to a place, destination unknown. On a whim, he Maya and Teeny would find themselves on the way to Cornwall, Kent, Bristol and other British cities, resorts and countryside. On one occasion they had even found their way to Snowdonia, Wales, but times had since changed. Now driving was a battle of wills. He'd find himself speeding despite having no place of urgency to be. It was as if he could feel an invisible force gnawing away at him, pressing him to go faster, faster. He'd even find himself cussing the driver ahead for driving too slow or causing him to unnecessarily remain in third gear. He reacted on, and vocalised the urgency of drivers around him.

As of late he'd catch himself gritting his teeth, something he never did. It was a habit he despised witnessing in others. The moment he caught himself, he would become aware of tightness in his neck and shoulders, the result of knots of frustration that seemed to have no explanatory point of origin. He would be hunched over the steering wheel, gripping it so tightly he'd have to focus deliberately on each finger to persuade them to release hold of it. He didn't manoeuvre with hands maintaining the recommended 'ten-to-two' position, instead his left hand would stay locked around the gear stick. Even when he came to realise what was happening, he found it extremely challenging to resume his own relaxed style of driving. His head would pound furiously, causing him on occasion, to unashamedly whimper for mercy. His vision would blur leaving him with little more than instinct, fine-tuned over years of experience to guide him to a safe place to stop and collect himself.

"Hey Teeny-Tiny," the father softly greeted his daughter that lay ignorant of her parent's desperate need to return to them. "I brought you a couple of magazines, seeing as we finished that book so quickly. I'm still checking around to see where I can find the next in the series. They got some cool articles in here. Seems like your peeps are real happy that skateboarding is gonna be recognised as an Olympic sport. Hey maybe you can compete against Nyjah Houston. Wouldn't that be cool? You gotta wake up though baby. Here, lemme read you the low-down."

Derrick pull his chair closer and stroked his baby girl's hair as he read both magazines cover to cover, pausing only to give running commentary between articles. Finally he closed the second publication and sighed and lay his head down beside her. The room was silent aside from the rhythmic beeping of the machine that monitored her vital statistics. He passed a few minutes playing idly with her fingers, before eventually raising his head. He felt sick. He acknowledged the warning of a rush of warm salty saliva filling his mouth, by quickly stepping into the adjoining bathroom, and held his head over the toilet. Thankfully this sensation didn't occur too frequently, but sometimes when he 'felt' too many people at once, he would find himself having to vomit. It was almost as if his body refused to continue without first discarding the excess it had involuntarily absorbed. At times he would throw up so violently his legs would buckle and he'd fall to his knees in submission as he did now.

"Fuck!" he spat angrily.

He's eyes watered and his stomach wrenched as if invisible hands that gripped him from within were wringing his insides. There was nothing left to bring up, but still he heaved till he gagged. He fell back into a seated position, resting his head against the door of the shower cubicle and closed his eyes, gasping for breath. He remained sat in the shadows for the next few minutes. In his haste he hadn't bothered to switch on the light, but the glow from Teeny's room was more than adequate. It wasn't like there was anything he particularly wanted to see anyway.

Derrick opened his eyes and looked around him. It wasn't a bathroom so much as it was a shower-room. The length of it would barely fit a full sized bath. Opposite the shower stall was the toilet, in between the two, was a tiny half-sized sink. He reached up to it and hoisted himself back to his feet, then washed his face and hands. He went back into the room, poured himself a cup of water and returned to the shower room to rinse out his mouth. After flushing the toilet, he returned to Teeny's side.

"Baby, Daddy's real sorry, but he's gotta go," his voice wavered, a mixture of guilt and frustration. "It hurts my head in here, it's just too loud. Man, all these people are deafening me." he winced in pain. "You know my heart is right here with you baby. The moment you wake up, you call my name. I promise I'll hear you and I'll come running." Derrick kissed Teeny's forehead, and then her hand, then picked up his things and left.

To his relief the traffic had died down somewhat. Derrick managed to refrain from hurling abuse as he drove to his home in Brondesbury, but his head was throbbing. As usual, the pain relief had had no effect. Popping pills had become more a reflex action in the hopes that there was a slim chance they might work, but they never did. By the time he made it to his driveway, the pain was so intense it he struggled to align his keys with the lock in order to get into his house. He threw his case on the floor and leant on the open door wondering what he had forgotten. He decided it didn't matter and picked himself up to close the door, then turned back to look at his car and remembered he hadn't locked it. He fumbled for his car keys and finally pressed a button on the remote lock key ring. His custom palladium silver sports edition C180 Kompressor responded with a couple of chirpy beeps and a flash of the hazard lights. He closed the door and staggered to his living room couch and flopped into it and closed his eyes.

Derrick opened his eyes on hearing the phone ring and reached out to pick it off the glass topped coffee table.

“Mmm,” he answered with grunt.

"Where have you been? I called you four times already. See how you let me go cook up your favourite and you don't even bother turn up. No phone call, nothing." shrilled a female voice on the end of the line.

"Mama? I said I was coming over. I only just got in, I'll be there soon." he replied wearily.

"Soon for what? It's past 11.30, there's no point again," snapped his mother.

"11.30? Nah, I just reach back, it's only past 7. I'll be there.” Derrick said as he patted down his body looking for his mobile phone to check the time. “Oh. Uh, I'm sorry. I only put my head down for a second."

“It happened again didn’t it?” His mother’s voice softened. “You blacked out again. Derrick, have you been to the doctor yet like I told you? What if it happens when you’re driving?”

“ ’im nuh need docta, mek ‘im tek de medicine how it meant fi tek nuh! ‘oman pass me de phone mek me talk likkle sense a ‘im.” Derrick’s father was in the background hollering his input. “Derrick, you haffi tek tree pill, dem piyan piyan likkle ting unnu tek nuh work pon we. Unnu baady too ‘trang, it a need bigga dose still.” Derrick’s father shouted in the background offering his advice through his thick Jamaican accent. Forty years living in London had had little success in softening his stubborn hardcore twang. “ ’im get ‘im baady strent fram me you know, Kingsley men dem is ‘trang an imma a Kingsley fi true.”

"Nuh badda listen a yuh fadda yuh know, fa unnu cyatch ova dose." His mother had switched from her perfect British accent to Jamaican patois to match her husband.

"Mama…" Derrick tried to get a word in.

"A wha di raas!" exclaimed his father in response to his wife contradicting him. " 'im cyant ova dose, 'im a Kingsley mi a tell you! Bwoy, betta still, tek four fi good measure."

"Pooppa…" he tried again, knowing his voice bore no weight when his parents got like this.

"Lard of his mursy! Yuh a try fi kill de bwoy? Listen to me, go an tek yuhsef to de docta!" his mother argued.

"Mama! Please, I'm fine. Really, stop worrying." Derrick cut in quickly.

"Fine? Bwoy fine nuh mek yuh fall sleep an miss yuh mudda Jerk chicken and rice. Unnu don't hear when we call all dis time? Dat nuh right yuh nuh!" his mother cried.

"A nuht nuh big ting. De chicken nuh was'e," piped his father.

"See yuh fadda greedy suh?"

Derrick's mobile rang. He looked at the screen.

"Mum, Dad. I have to go. Maya's on the other line."

"Wha? Why is dat fool gal calling yuh at dis time Derrick?" his mother cried.

"Mum, it's late. If she's calling me now, it must be about Teeny. I have to go." Derrick was getting impatient. He loved his parents, but sometimes even they hurt his head. He had long given up on telling them off for abusing Maya every time her name was mentioned. There was a time that Maya had been loved as the daughter they never had, but times had changed and Derrick's mother defended her son's broken heart with scorn.

Though his mother never admitted it, Derrick knew it was more out of the personal loss she felt at losing a cherished family member.

"Pass mi love to mi baby Tiny. Da Lard will heal her," she continued.

"Hmm, farty-two years marriage, an I never once look pan henny baady else!" his father added, no doubt preparing to tell a story that Derrick had heard more than a hundred times before. "Henny wey dat likkle girl a Kingsley yout', her baady 'trang like we."

"Das right! And mek me ketch unnu wid a nex' 'oman! Derricks mother started.

"Yuh 'ear dat? She nag nuff, but she a good 'oman and mi love her still. See unnu mudda dere, dat more dan enough 'eadache fi me," his father said fondly.

"Mek mi come show yuh 'eadache… bloody cheek!" his mother retorted.

"Mum, Dad. I gaan!" said Derrick and he put down the phone.

His parents seemed to thrive on winding each other up, but the love they shared was unmistakeable. They were like brother and sister, each as mischievous as the other. In their late sixties, they still held hands, and even swung them as they walked side by side. As a child reading aloud was never exclusively reserved for bedtime stories. His mother would read not only to him, but his father too, texts ranging from excerpts from the bible, to books penned by Louise Bennett. Since childhood, Derrick silently declared that he would experience the same affection with his own wife when he grew up.

His phone registered Maya's call as having being missed. He called her back.

“You just called me?” spoke Derrick into the phone as the call connected.

“D.! I know it! I know the answer! I asked for a dream, like she said and I though I might as well try, you know that’s how I used to do it before, it didn’t work at first, but now it has. It worked and I know what we have to do!” Maya spluttered excitedly.

“What? Slow Down M’y’, you lost me. Deep breath, start again.”

His ex-wife inhaled, then exhaled through pursed lips. “You know you said I knew the answer? Well, I went to bed early tonight, but before I slept I asked my subconscious to give me a dream that would tell me what I needed to know the help Teeny. It’s so simple! We have to do it, we have to try for Teeny’s sake,” said a still excitable, but more coherent Maya.

Spiritual

"Everything we need to become who we are meant to be is with encoded within us. Sometimes we struggle to become more, to become who it is we know exists deep down in that place where we allow ourselves to unashamedly dream. But what if that dream is the true reality, and life outside of the dream is a nightmare born of a lie? How do we know which is which in order to decide the one we must wake up to?

The answer is simple; the key is to try not to think so hard."

Inscribed on the door of the Ennead Chamber

Location: Ouranos; Mental Realm density level nine

19

TH.O.R.T.S

Teeny looked at her surroundings her vibration as N9ne Blood restored, the cavern no longer existed, as she now perceived beyond her Nana's rendition of 'heaven'. Instead she saw an expanse of white, a room void of mind-generated imagery. She could now see that she had been deep in TH.O.R.T.S, one of the numerous Thought Oriented Reality Transmit Simulation rooms, used predominantly for education, decontamination or debriefing purposes. The technology was based on the concept of the Mental Realm, creating tangible holographic environments that responded to thought commands. It took a highly disciplined mind to maintain the stability of THORTS environments, thus the presence of at least one N9ne Blood was necessary. For lengthy simulations, the presiding N9ne would manage THORTS via an external terminal used to document and generate a loop for consistent backgrounds. The garden, river and waterfall of Nana's mental creation, incorporated random variation to add to the realism of the effect.

As Teeny's memory had returned, the ghostly wisps solidified to become the tangible presence of others participating in the reintegration of various souls to the point of becoming statue-like. The discrepancy of dimensional frequency enabled many incidences of debriefing to take place in the same space and time without intruding on one another. The wisps could not distinguish Teeny in the same way she could see them. She had tactfully remained at the density level appropriate for the dimension to which she had been recalled. She looked to the direction of where the waterfall had been and saw her grandmother sitting motionless on a boulder of her own projection. The woman remained oblivious to all else that took place beyond her level of perception and looked peaceful in the mental confines of her own THORTS.

Even though Teeny knew she could not leave the decontamination chamber whilst in mid incarnation, it felt good to be back home. Home was the Ouranos space station, a trans-dimensional metropolis that spanned all seven major realms. She sensed her body that lay in the stasis chamber specifically adapted for N9ne Mind. It differed from other chambers deployed for similar usage in that it was nine-sided. An enneagon shaped pyramid room, each wall of which held one of nine pod-like capsules that could be utilised individually, or linked together to perform as one. The foot of the capsules pointed toward the wall, whilst the head pointed toward the centre. Each occupied section was lit by a black light that radiated a gentle purple glow. The populated capsule glowed a pale green if the N9ne remained a sleeper, and a soft blue if fully actualised.

When a candidate underwent a mission, they would enter a similar type of chamber in order to execute a process of mind, 'body' separation. Their physical responses would be slowed and consciousness altered to mimic delta and theta brainwave activities. Delta equated as the heart of theta, the unconscious mind where the all-knowing seat of the soul remained. This enabled the alpha and beta portion of their psyche to be near infinitely extended for insemination into a host body of the particular species they were sent to assist. There they performed at a conscious or beta level. The alpha, subconscious state functioned as a bridge between beta and theta frequencies, through which the candidate could maintain communication with their 'higher self' or original divine body. When incarnate, they would live and breath as the indigenous of the region to which they were deployed. Certain practices promoted the strengthening of the bridge, resulting in clarity of authentic memory and superior ability. Dutiful attention and focus ultimately led to a bi-directional path between the definitive soul essence and it's incarnate being. Beta, alpha, theta and delta frequencies were the anatomy of the soul, the primary vehicle that similar to the physical, could be shed. Any body the soul was inseminated into served as secondary or tertiary vehicles.

To be used as one, an Ennead - a group of nine, N9nth Degree beings of the same level had to occupy a capsule apiece, and each had to be self-aware in the time and place of their away mission. Only under these circumstances could each pod be connected so that the occupants could function as one mind. Each participating N9ne had to be fully awakened and mature, thus fully actualised for 'Unity' to be initiated. This served to prevent contamination of such as that experienced by Nana. Zauba-ah's incarnation as Teeny, did not qualify for Unity. She was prepubescent and amongst sleepers. It was possible for a fully actualised N9ne to sense others of their level and awareness in the field, though it was unusual that they would be located in close proximity to one another.

From an external view Ouranos appeared to be semi present, fully discernible only to N9ne Bloods. Lesser minds perceived it as a lifeless asteroid that it had been cloaked as, by way of THORTS. As such it remained undetected for generations, dismissed as being nothing more than a random constituent of the asteroid belt. Only recently was it discovered and later termed as a dwarf planet by humans who named it Ceres. It had been present since the incident that created the renowned belt.

An accidental collision involving Nibiru, the alleged twelfth planet of the solar system into another planet, Tiamat caused it to shatter. The largest portion of the planet that remained was thrown into a new orbit between Venus and Mars and became known as Earth whilst a smaller portion became its satellite, the moon. The rest of the of the planet's debris scattered, though retained it's original orbit and became the asteroid belt. Nibiru, the 'planet of the crossing' had alarmed residents of Tiamat who had mistaken its yet to be documented path, for an attack on their planet when the heavenly body's gravitational field heavily affected their environment. In retaliation they sent four battle class ships to eliminate the threat to their way of life. Their attack sealed their fate as the ships became trapped in orbit around Nibiru causing an erratic alteration to its original trajectory. One by one, the ships were haplessly thrown into Tiamat by their uncharted orbit. One split the planet in two, another crashed straight through the larger of the half, exploding on impact creating a central sun, another skimmed the planet to create the spectacle humans came to marvel as the Grand Canyon.

The accident necessitated immediate damage control in the form of regeneration and re-population of the newborn sphere. Nibiru travelled along a three thousand six hundred year flight path. During one such orbit, the activity of its passengers, a collective of scientists and researchers of superior mind and evolution, were documented by a few of Tiamat's survivors. The predominantly water planet was home to an indigenous Reptilian species, the more docile of which, recorded the entourage as a cooperative known simply as God, creator of heaven and Earth. The passengers of the mighty ship also referred to as Anunnaki, had been on a search for aurum; a naturally occurring element found on Tiamat, commonly referred to as gold. The Anunnaki had hoped to mine and collect the element to assist in the rebuilding of their planet's diminishing ozonosphere. However, after the calamitous event that destroyed their planet, the more aggressive of the Reptilians angered when they heard of the reason for Nibiru's crossing, more so of the plan to create a new species, a part Reptilian, part God hybrid that would serve two purposes.

The initial function was to repopulate the Earth, but when the Anunnaki's own refused to mine for how their company were physically incapable of undertaking such manual labour, the hybrid became a feasible option to assist in doing so for them. The Reptilian aggressors remained unimpressed by God's acceptance of responsibility and consequent attempt to reach an amicable solution for the catastrophe. So too did they remain unmoved by God's process of clearing the wreckage that obscured the new planet from the sun, leaving it dark and void. The proposed removal of debris, the terra forming, and also the creation of this new of life, spanned seven thousand years, which equated to seven rotations of the planet. It was bad enough that their species had been diminished, now they were expected to tolerate a new being that was supposedly a living symbol of peace between their species and God? A new being that served the interests of these intruders? Such consolation was unacceptable! Had it not been for the fact that a majority of Tiamat's inhabitants resided in the depths of her waters, they may well have faced annihilation. Besides, a similar being already resided on the planet, one that they had dominance over. Few remained since the crash, but that was inconsequential to the Reptilian way of life, they were seen as little more than a by-product of delinquent genes. But this newly proposed hybrid was seen as an insult, an abomination and a threat to their way of life and a rebel group devised a plan. They would interfere with the process of the new beings creation by breaching the purpose built laboratory environment known as Eden and contaminate the maturation process of the human male and female within.

What the Reptilians refused to comprehend, was that Earth did not bear the same characteristics of the planet they once knew. For any life to survive, a new macrocosm had to be created enabling the sphere to flourish once again. To balance the equation, she also required a new microcosm; this was the ultimate purpose of the new species, to maintain harmony. The contamination resulted in numerous defects varying from physical to mental and emotional instability, the latter of which made them prone to psychosis. The interruption of the maturation process led to initially less apparent traits including rapid aging, visual, auditory and auditory impairment, vulnerability toward sickness and infection. It caused problematic reproduction that brought forth more visibly apparent traits and defects. Unable to salvage the experiment in the limited time allotted for the task, God granted the new species self-determination and awarded them dominion of the planet. The humans were left with a promise of guidance toward completion for those who requested of their assistance. The Reptilians were dismayed at this result and sought to prove humans unworthy of the privilege.

Over time, an unexpected side effect of the contamination became apparent; the new species developed a genetic bias. The offspring that exhibited dominant God genes developed various allergies to the planet due to not having developed fully compatible immune systems and exhibited advanced capabilities. On the other hand, the offspring that favoured their Reptilian genes were mostly compatible and bore semblance in nature and were eventually accepted as being indigenous children of Earth's original species. They were also predisposed to the possibility of developing advanced capabilities, though at a slower rate. The subtle variations of the new species contributed to the segregation of that which was one, thus duality was formed. Over time God became associated with good or agreeable and all else bad or disagreeable and a planet scale tug of war ensued. A battle for righteous domination over the planet persisted; a fight that neither ever won. Instead 'God' and 'Bad' splinted into countless factions and religions, each preaching their version of how humanity came into existence in an effort to claim superiority. Through the ages, the story was retold and facts including the time line, distorted. Documentation of the historic event eventually became known as Holy Scripture.

The whole incident drew the attention of the Galactic Council; an impartial regulating and governing body consisting of the N9ne Council ambassadors of over one hundred separate star systems. At their decision, Ouranos had been created to maintain balance as well as ensure that such a calamity as the one caused by Nibiru's crossing never occurred again. The disunity on Earth was cause for concern for several reasons; the warring splinter groups had come close to wiping themselves out as their weapons of destruction became more sophisticated. Incidences like the deployment of the devastating atomic bombs, 'Little Boy' and 'Fat Man' on the cities of Hiroshima and Nagasaki respectively, necessitated an increased presence of higher evolved minds to maintain active vigil and counteract such destruction. Humans were naturally entering the next step of their evolution, but many were hindered by preoccupation with their quest for rulership. Indigo and Crystal children were the first manifestations of the species spiritual evolution, but the Reptilians had no desire to see humans evolve further. It was their belief that failure of the species would return Earth to their rule. As such, though they accepted the humans that showed preference for their genes, it was more out of the fact that it made it easier to manipulate them toward their own selfish ends. However, the Reptilians declined to acknowledge that unlike Tiamat, Earth was still undeveloped and required her new ecosystem to mature. If humans did not evolve, her growth would be stunted and impact the ever changing universe to which she belonged. Cessation of development would cause the planet and all life on it to become stagnant and eventually die. Change was the only unified constant; regression was not an option. In order to ensure planet wide evolution, various higher minds collectively assisted the natural progression by inconspicuously incarnating on the planet and balancing and neutralising destructive frequencies emitted by malicious intent and ignorant thought.

20

The Reptilian Agenda

The Reptilian were a proud race and the fateful accident continued to be a source of contention. Countless lives had been lost, including many great well-respected ancestors, known to humans as dinosaurs. A domino effect of the crash meant that the larger remnants of the planet became obscured from the sun, causing a spontaneous ice age. Their typically tropical environment, froze within minutes. If not for the heat radiated by the ship that had exploded in the centre of the planet, even their retreat to the deep may well have been futile. The impact caused the nuclei of the atomic particles that fuelled the war bird to split, resulting in nuclear fission. From there the motion had been set for a chain reaction, creating a lesser sun that burned in the midst of the devastation.

> "*And the earth was without form, and void; and darkness was upon the face of the deep. And the Spirit of God moved upon the face of the waters.*"

The first priority of God, had been to minimize the level of radioactivity and eliminate the potential for nuclear waste, through a process of recycling. They then turned their focus toward creating a subtropical environment of the new planet's now hollow centre. The major entrances to the subterranean world were located in the Northern and Southern Polar Regions.

In order to stop the planet from overheating through the combined rays of the inner and outer suns, the planet was tipped to rotate on a 23.5-degree axis. This realignment served to maintain two climate diversities. The inner bore semblance to Tiamat, the outer a variation of both warmer and cooler extremities. The colder expanses, though less hospitable, were necessary to balance those of higher temperatures and supported the supplemented ecosystem. The process spanned thousands of years and was finalised by the creation of the modernised human: a further evolved version to that which already existed, but had diminished in number. Earth was left to develop and grow to become a planet in her own right.

Tiamat's original orbit positioned the planet between Mars and Jupiter, its atmosphere effectively harnessed the rays of the systems heat-generating orb. Distance from the sun was not the determining factor for the temperature of a planet as humans mistakenly assumed. It was a planet's atmosphere that processed the intensity with which solar waves reflected and generated heat. This meant that Pluto's remoteness from the sun did not by default render it the coldest or least inhabitable sphere in the system. In the same token, Earth's closer proximity did not determine it to be a warmer climate than the planet that birthed it.

From that time to this, only one thing remained constant: The Reptilian's desire to fully reclaim Earth as their own. To that effect they made a persistent effort to deem humans unworthy of the dominion over the planets surface. Under the watchful eye of the Galactic Federation, there was little they could do to aggressively repossess what had once been their home. Their plan was subtle, yet incredibly powerful. It was a long delicate process, but the cause was worthy. The method chosen to achieve their goal was to coax the modern man toward a path of self-destruction. They corrupted historical texts, some directly, others by withholding full accounts from mainstream access. They made their plight fair seeming, not by way of outward lies, but by putting a slant on the truth in their favour. As humans splintered, new beliefs formed, making them difficult to indoctrinate. Observation of ritual shed light on the effectiveness of religion and it became the perfect tool to satiate the masses and instil a healthy dose of fear. It quenched curiosity, as belief became a substitute for truth, whilst facts were dismissed, accounted for by miracles and promises of salvation. The majority came to unite under monotheistic doctrine and the parameters for acceptable behaviour was drawn. Sin, as deviance from propaganda became known, earned penalty, while submission earned reward. An appeal was made to humanity's fear of the unknown. What became of them when their body expired? The answer was simple. Hell was the assured destination for those who did not follow the general consensus, Heaven the destination of the placid. Hell, if ever there was such a place, became known as being a place located below Terra; Latin for Earth, of burning heat. A tale spun on the presence of the infant solar orb that blazed eternally within.

Guidance was sent in the form of God incarnating as mortals on Earth, in an effort to offset the of the Reptilian's attempts to mould the future to their preferred outcome. Sin was simply an elaborate form of emotional and spiritual blackmail, and 'hell' the consequence of non-abidance. One religion under the rule of a single god with questionable sanity worked wonders, whilst three religions each with a single god by different names paid dividends. It promoted endless conflict amongst humans. They fought in the name of their Creator, who supported events involving atrocities toward human kind. The Jewish holocaust, the Christian's justification for slavery, the Muslim's perpetual state of jihad were all paradigm. Reptilians manipulated history by embellishing it with false hope and consequence and staging platforms for conditioned response.

As far as the Reptilian were concerned, the confidence in the successful outcome of their agenda to reclaim the planet was duly warranted. To date the end of the world – the age of man was on schedule. Their version of 'truth' was the status quo that the majority happily, albeit blindly, ascribed to. Promises of power and authority kept the most loyal of their followers satiated. Their existence remained controversial and unproven myths. Their subservient obediently executed the final stages of their plan by impregnating a deadly seed via knowledge of fuels 'safe' for human consumption. Expensive energy by which to propel and sustain the reliance of technological creature comforts, that came at a price beyond what greedy mortals could afford; their planet. The final undertaking of the Reptilian's agenda was to alter the ecosystem of the planet, warming the globe to become the tropical climate of their preferred environment. Their debunkers worked in their favour to negate any evidence presented to alert Earth's human populous to their imminent doom that could be averted if only they would acknowledge and take affirmative action to prevent such an outcome. Senators and scientists alike would 'pooh pooh' at the preposterous notion of global warming due the depletion of the planets ozone layer.

Yes, it was only a matter of time before they reclaimed dominion over the blue planet. Their only concern was the matter of N9nes and their Initiates mission to remove the veil of ignorance from the eyes of humanity. But when in their realm, in human form, even they were prone to the hypnotic spell that the great lizards had cast. Thus far, they had managed to suppress or distort belief in their existence.

21

Reunion

Teeny looked with unspoken request at Imhotep, who bowed his head in acknowledgement.

"I commend your compassion Zauba-ah, your reputation dictates otherwise. You are still affected by the active link to your incarnation?"

"I take full responsibility for my decision," she replied. Her soul vehicle acknowledged and appreciated Imhotep's deliberate address of its pre-human title.

"So be it. You do recall that on re-implantation, only memories applicable to your physical guardians reunion will remain? All else will become vague like a distant dream. Over the next few years your genetic memory will activate upon maturation of your human body vehicle. Only at such time will you remember more." he warned.

"This I know," said Zauba-ah confidently. "So my friend, you are finally going to be human!" she beamed. "I look forward to see how your disagreeable nature will translate in your soul exchange."

"I was merely complying with your wish that I be the N9ne Blood present to oversee your debriefing. Your apprentice however was too far-gone to fully reintegrate. It was our plan that she would be able to deliver the message to Earth as her next assignment, but it would seem I have no choice but to convey it myself. I find it hard to conceive that she was of Se7enth Degree, due for ascension to Ei8th. She now reveres me as a deity of sorts, oblivious to the fact that she herself is that which she worshipped as God whilst on Earth."

"That you allowed her the opportunity to deliver my debriefing shows compassion on your side, I am in mid incarnation, what is your excuse?"

"It was my hope that permitting her the privilege might assist in her decontamination process, but alas, she remains bound to the physical, to Earth."

Much to Imhotep's disappointment, Nana's recollection of her pre-human existence was sketchy at best, despite his sincere effort to assist in her reintegration process. The past Earth year had been spent trying to teach her how to access the information in the Mental Realm so that she might regain her memory. However Nana, for all her questions had been unable to decipher the responses, and insisted that all she could sense when she tried was an inert void that made her feel uneasy. On the one occasion she had managed to avail herself to be able to detect the incalculable knowledge, she found herself overwhelmed to the point of screaming hysterically until she finally collapsed into a foetal position and sobbed. She claimed to have been blinded by the intensity of an illumination that all at once was consumed by infinite darkness. Imhotep decided against requesting that she try again, concerned that it could cause her to reject the little she had remembered and possibly even render her catatonic. Even if he hadn't reached this conclusion, he doubted Nana would have willing entertained the idea, in fact he knew her response would have been obstinate, point blank refusal. Being the last remaining N9nth Degree presence in the region of the Mental Realm that presided Gaia's solar system, he had no choice but to incarnate as a human in order to deliver healing in the form of cures for many of the ailments her inhabitants suffered. The extent of Nana's dementia had rendered her unfit to carry out the mission as it had originally been expected she would return to Earth to implement.

Imhotep closed his eyes and tilted his head to focus his attention on the progress report he received from Rachael. "It would seem you are due to return. You should prepare yourself."

Zauba-ah complied and altered her ethereal presence to mimic that of the child of her incarnation. "My debriefing is incomplete. I am not fully reintegrated. Where are the remainder of us? I do not sense our Ennead presence here, are you all of us that remain at this juncture?"

"Affirmative," replied Imhotep. "Aside from myself we are all on Earth. We are four active, the remainder including yourself are four sleepers. Another 2econd level N9ne Blood is due take my place here and oversee my soul exchange, Rudwaan of the twelfth galaxy. His Council have recently completed a similar mission with success on one of the planets within. He will act as bridge commander on my departure and maintain our link."

N9ne Council presided in every galaxy. Councils were composed of Ei8th Level, N9nth Degree beings. Other councils consisted of each of the remaining levels in preparation for their relative ascensions to the subsequent echelons, under the guidance of the single predominant assembly. Only the presiding council was termed N9ne Council, all others were Council of N9ne. Imhotep and Zauba'ah were 2econd level N9ne Bloods of the sixteenth galaxy collective.

"Acceptable," Zauba-ah concurred. "Imhotep, where is my companion?" she asked suddenly.

“Your companion is in your midst on Earth. Toby Kwele, I believe.”

“What? Toby Kwele? Are you sure? That boy irritates my incarnation so!”

“Toby Kwele is indeed your soul mate companion. At present his memory is partial, thus most of his actions are driven by his subconscious. He does not yet recall who you are, yet he instinctively teases to justify reason to interact with you. At this time, even he does not know why, though he recalls enough to be attracted to you. For the sake of you not unifying before time physically appropriate to your incarnation, your genetic memory of each other remains dormant. Puberty will facilitate both your memories and you will eventually continue your missions side by side. You know this, which is why you were able to discern his essence amongst all others when you merged with the Mental Realm. It is time. Prepare yourself for reintegration.”

“Affirmative. I will address my ward once more before my departure.”

“As you wish. I will request her attendance,” said Imhotep. “Zauba’ah, I have no desire to partake of the illusion of loneliness that your ward describes. Should I fail to awaken immediately, find me. Do not allow me to suffer.”

“You will not be alone. I will find you.”

Imhotep nodded and once again altered his frequency to resume his watch over other concurrent decontamination procedures he was in the midst of overseeing. Though he appeared to dematerialise, in actuality he merely altered the density of his person. Thus allowing him to synchronise with other vibrations of existence, enabling the ghostly apparitions to once again perceive him as more than the statue he had become to them. He walked through the cavern wall and into the adjacent room to check the progress of a particularly tedious reintegration.

The Warrior Class were reputedly more difficult to process as they usually returned to the realm from a perspective typical of their physical death: Guns blazing, punches flying, swords slicing. Fortunately they were also a disciplined Class, respectfully identified as 'Souldiers', biblically referred to as cherubim or seraphim and sooner or later they would remember who they were, albeit rather sheepishly. If they perceived themselves as having failed due to having been distracted, misguided or simply forgetful, they almost always requested to be sent back for another chance to successfully complete the mission. Souldiers were usually deployed to protect premature or non-Warrior Class incarnations, recall rogue members of their faction, or accompany the recently deceased for post mortal processing. Their recall usually took the form of unsolved assassinations, where they would terminate the body vehicle of disruptive Souldiers who wreaked havoc in their confusion. Their reputation spread across different worlds in different forms. They were feared as the grim reaper, worshipped as Anubis - the Egyptian god of the dead and even mistaken as devils.

The reintegration of this particular Souldier had taken longer than usual and Imhotep's patience had worn thin. He refused to further participate in the charade by altering his appearance to appease the warrior's mental projection of the last battle in which he fought. As he entered a sword was plunged into his chest, he looked down at it, then up at the Souldier, rolled his eyes and sighed. "I grow weary of the continued animation of your residual memory. How much longer must I humour your barbarism?" Imhotep mentally cast away the sword causing it to disintegrate back into the origin of its projection.

There were several classes that resided on the station, each consisting of beings who found their purpose through the pursuit of that which pleased them most. Peace was a product of satisfaction. When an individual was happy following the path best suited to their innate nature, hatred and envy other products of dissatisfied beings were negligible. In a society where all were content, fear and anger had no nervous energy from which to materialise. None were considered lesser than the other as the members of each class were the elite of their profession and were respected as such. Classes were numerous: Amative, Warrior, Nurturer, Procreator, Scientist, Engineer and Domestic amongst others. The Amatives were an eloquent class innately versed in the art of seduction and deliverance of sexual satisfaction, much like the Geisha of Earth, Nurturers included medics and child carers. The associated Procreator/Breeder Class were not nurturing by default, but they were incredibly fertile. Within days of giving birth after an enviously graceful labour, their bodies seemed to heal without sign of ever having endured pregnancy at all.

It was not unheard of for an individual to bear temperament for more than one Class designation. Zauba-ah had been such a soul. She was both Scientist and Warrior, an interesting combination that assisted in her ascent through the degrees. She exhibited mind of excellence, yet at will could effectively terminate a life for reasons that were not immediately discernible to an unsuspecting onlooker. Her presence caused many to be at a loss for whether to fear or admire her. The essence of her designations made her a loyal, honourable genius at best and at worst, cold, ruthless and deadly. It was rumoured that during the first day of a new selection of Initiates to her Dream Warrior School of Thought, she had walked up to one student and stared at him intently, searching the depths of his soul. Without any explanation beyond the words “Not in this lifetime,” she thrust her hand in his chest and pulled out his beating heart. She then asked the horror stricken student to open his hand and placed his heart in it for him to observe, until he eventually collapsed and died. It was forbidden for any Initiate to discuss anything that took place in any N9nth Degree Academy, but the said student was never to be seen again. Outsiders speculated in hushed voices, though none dared to question the Initiates for fear of reprisal.

Zauba-ah altered her mental vibration, slowing her oscillation from N9ne Mind to 5ifth, allowing her being to correspond with the frequency on which her integration had taken place. Her preparation was necessary in order to engage with her Initiate at her density level.

Nana obediently returned through the waterfall. "It is time," she affirmed. "It would seem I have been granted new tenure, I too will be returning to Earth soon. Thank you for submitting the request that I be granted another chance. Will I see you there?

"You will walk with me once more and as before I will look after you. Prepare well."

"I will do better this time," Nana promised. "If I may, I would like to incarnate as a man this time. With what I know now and the role model I have in you, surely this time I will succeed. Not to mention it would be a nice change not to have to squat awkwardly to hover over public toilet seats! Ahh to be able to stand up, whip it out and urinate without the contortions we women go through for the sake of answering to nature's bellow," she laughed in reminiscence.

Zauba-ah smiled and beckoned Nana forward and held she that was once her grandmother's face in her hands and tiptoed to kiss her forehead. "Leave so that I might become One now."

"A question, if I may?" asked Nana.

"You may."

"I'm confused, As David you performed you mission with N9ne focus and discipline, yet you exhibited many... uh... habits." Nana deliberated on how best to respectfully fulfil her curiosity.

Her mentor overstood and smiled. "My squeezing the toothpaste in the middle and other habits of annoyance were my attempts to gently remind you to not take your incarnation so seriously. My quest was futile, but over time your response became a source of amusement. It tickled me to watch as you so perfectly performed your feminine lecture of righteousness, when the simplest cure would have been to buy a separate tube of paste that I could squeeze how I liked. In regards to the toilet, how easy would it have been to insist that we both exited the bathroom, leaving both the seat and the lid down in compromise? Such incidents became my human indulgence."

Nana wished she hadn't asked and quickly bowed her respects and exited once again. Zauba-ah stifled a chuckle and shook her head as she recalibrated in preparation for reinsertion.

Overstanding

"My every move is being watched, they know who I am. My presence is drawing the attention of 'those who fear most'. A couple of my patients have befallen unfortunate deaths. 'Accidental' of course, but the message is clear; even my human charges are at risk by association."

"How long before you abort?"

"I intend to be present to grant safe passage for Imhotep's incarnation, beyond that, I am unsure. I await further instruction, though termination is the most likely outcome."

"Have you been informed of the coordinates of his entry?"

"Yes. Souldier – you have kept me safe during the mission to recall Zauba-ah and I thank you, but I am no longer under your jurisdiction, you cannot defend me this time. I am to receive the delivery of this N9ne's soul in the United States."

"I cannot follow you. I am assigned to my N9ne here, my life is pledged to her security."

"My Ei8ht, you need not be concerned, I will be fine. I may not be Warrior Class like yourself, but we Nurturers are Souldiers in our own right - we do what ever it takes to survive for the sake of protecting those in our care. Be comforted."

Conversation between Rachael and Teeny's Souldier

Location: Eastbound Central Line Train.

22

Step To The Plate

Derrick stood in front of his car and then looked over at his bike. He had purchased it as a gift to cheer himself up soon after he had discovered Maya's affair. It wasn't long before he realised that not even the Kawasaki Ninja ZX 12R he had lusted after for so long, was enough to numb the pain. Since the increased intensity of his blinding headaches began a year ago, he decided it wiser not to give in to the temptation to ride it. Every time he stepped out of his house to take to the road, he'd look longingly at the bike and sigh before climbing reluctantly into his car.

He was tired. He and Maya had spent most of the night talking about her the revelations of her dream. A majority of the conversation consisted of him trying to find an alternative meaning to her vision, and her assuring her resolute faith in him. Any other time he wouldn't have doubted her word for a second, but the answer she had come up with, was an expectation he felt unable to live up to. At the best of times he didn't like to be put under this kind of pressure. The thought of it was nauseating, but it was for Teeny. If indeed what Maya said was correct, he had to try. With duty taking precedence over his reluctance, he deactivated the alarm for his car and stepped inside.

Maya was excited. After waking from her dream and finding herself unable to get through to Derrick, she proceeded to call the ward Teeny rested in, to arrange a visit. The night nurse in charge had patiently informed her that there would be no admittance permitted at such an hour, and advised Maya of the visiting times that she had already committed to memory. When Derrick called her back she recounted her dream to him, never once becoming disheartened by his lack of enthusiasm to perform his role at their daughter's side. She knew it was a lot to ask and that he would need convincing, but her dream had endowed her with confidence that everyone else around her seemed to have. Could it really be so simple? Would what she saw really be enough to wake Teeny from her slumber? Her soul said yes. She pulled into the hospital car park and ran all the way to where her daughter lay.

Derrick walked into Teeny's room and was met by a very hyper Maya who ran up to him to drag him directly to their daughter's hospital bed.

"Maya, I can't do this, I don't know how," protested Derrick, pulling back.

"You can Derrick! You so can!" enthused Maya. "You do know how, do it how I explained it. Just do that thing you do, but do it in reverse. Don't take it in, push it out. It's simple!"

"Simple? If it's so simple why don't you do it? I can't even control what ever it is I do. That's like telling me that even though I can't drive it'll be cool for me to reverse my way down a motorway. It don't make sense. What if I make things worse?"

Derrick was both stalling and trying to conceal the extent of his panic. Maya really believed he could heal his daughter? Why did she have to go dream such a crazy idea. Maybe her fear for Teeny wasn't allowing her to think straight. Maybe it was having an affect on her dreams and what she had seen was just some stress release mechanism. Somehow her theory sounded almost commonsensical, but this was beyond his logic. Logic to him was TCP/IP, subnet masks, routers, switches and servers. Even the way personal assistants would call one of his team mistaking them for computer support technicians in the hopes of saving the files they had absent-mindedly deleted made more sense than this. Now Maya was insistently claiming that the thing that caused him to experience dizziness, headaches and even blackouts, was what would wake Teeny up. This was more pressure than he could handle. The thought alone made his head hurt.

"Derrick," said Maya taking his hands in hers and looking into his eyes. "You have a gift. Everyone has the potential to heal, or do what you do, but not everyone is ready, or as naturally attuned. Your range of sensitivity is higher than most people's. You always believed in me, in my gift to see things even when I thought it was fluke. We've both had our doubts and kept it amongst ourselves, because we couldn't explain it. I still can't explain it, but I've seen what you can do and you've seen what I can do. Even if you don't believe it, trust that I have already seen you do it. Please don't doubt me now."

Derrick looked down at Teeny. He wanted so desperately to believe Maya. She was never wrong about these things, but to even put one foot in front of the other to position himself at Teeny's side seemed like an impossible task. He couldn't move.

"Come on, you can do it," said Maya seeing the doubt in his eyes.

She gently slipped an arm around his waist keeping hold of his hand with the other, and coaxed him nearer the bed.

"You didn't see me hurt her?" Derrick asked.

"Of course not D., all you are doing is sending her healing, showing her the way back home. It'll work, I promise."

Derrick raised his hands a few inches above the trunk of Teeny's body and exhaled. He closed his eyes and tried to focus. A few moments later he opened his eyes and looked to Maya for help.

"I don't know what I'm doing. I don't know what to focus on. What does healing look like? How do I send something I can't even see?" He said frustrated at himself, his head was pounding for being put on the spot.

Maya squeezed his hand "Derrick, you know love. You know your love for Teeny. You think of that love, imagine holding it in your hands and giving it to her like a gift. You can do this, we can do this, I can help, but not in the same way you can." She shifted to stand alongside him and hovered her hands parallel to his placing the one closest to Derrick's to rest on the back of his. She looked up at him. "Healing looks like..." She paused in search of the right expression, and then smiled as Elias' words suddenly made sense. "It looks like Teeny in mid air when she flies off the end of a vertical ramp and kisses the sky."

Derrick nodded slowly, moistening his lips as if to savour the taste of the unseen speck of clarity that landed upon them, "Okay, I think I get it."

Logic within the illogical. That could work, he reasoned, as he thoughtfully shifted his head from sided to side and liberated his breathing. He inhaled through his nose and out through his mouth and found release, his head suddenly didn't seem to hurt so much. He could feel heat from Maya's hand that lay above his. He almost felt as if he could feel a slight pressure beneath his hands and he opened an eye to check if his hands had fallen to rest on Teeny's body, but they hadn't. He closed his eyes again and tried to imagine encompassing the love he had for Teeny in an invisible gift-wrapped box that only she could see. He mentally replayed moments of awe he had experienced whilst watching is daughter on the ramps and he became lost in time.

The love he had for Teeny was bigger than him, he could almost feel how far it extend from his body. He sensed Maya's presence and felt her love pass through his hand. He accepted it and added it to the devotion he channelled to Teeny. He felt the love that was bigger than him, grow bigger still and imagined it surrounding his baby girl. He wrapped it around her like the mink blanket she was so fond of. He didn't notice the minutes as they passed, becoming five, then ten, then fifteen…

"Welcome home," Teeny breathed.

"OH MY GOD!" screamed Maya and threw her arms around her daughter. "Oh my god! Oh my god Teeny!" Maya showered her daughter's face with aimless kisses as she cradled her rocking back and forth. Derrick hesitated before opened his eyes afraid that what he would see might not match what he heard. He dropped his hands and began to tremble uncontrollably.

"I'm okay Daddy," Teeny said and held out her hand toward him.

Derrick grabbed and squeezed it then threw his arms around both Teeny and Maya. "Thank you," he whispered.

Neither of them noticed Rachael peer through the door and smile. She glanced at her pocket watch, which read 09.45. "December seventeenth 2007. Right on schedule." she muttered happily as she turned away and threw her backpack over her shoulder. "Mission complete, the rest is up to you now Destiny 'Zauba-ah' Kingsley." The Nurturer headed silently toward the hospital exit.

Dumbfounded doctors were no more knowledgeable of what caused Teeny to awaken, than they were of the grounds under which she lost consciousness in the first place. However they insisted she remain a patient until such time as they felt confident she truly was as unaffected as she appeared to be by her ordeal. Stranger still, all her motor functions seemed to work perfectly, maintaining excellent dexterity and coordination. Highly irregular for one that had been comatose for such an extended period, the length of which would usually be deemed a vegetative state. It was their concurrence that for the meantime, Miss Kingsley should undergo several blood tests, and various scans and a daily dose of physiotherapy, just to be sure she was over her ordeal.

Though the visit home to Ouranos lasted only a few hours, Earth whose orbit was closer to the sun meant that Teeny's absence translated to equate as four and a half months. She had since missed her birthday, and Christmas was a mere eight days away. By the time traffic stopping flowing in and out of her room, she was exhausted and moody. It was wonderful be in the arms of her parents, but all she wanted to do was meditate and consider how best to handle the mission she had been assigned. She had to remember. She did her best to meditate using the method her Nana kept telling her use to facilitate her memory. She closed her eyes and focused on her breathing until she surrendered to fatigue and fell asleep.

23

Is A Friend Indeed

"Teeny, wake up!"

"Alysha, please let her rest, we can always come back later," chided Nia.

Teeny stretched and opened her eyes and smiled to see her mother, Nia and her best friend, Alysha surrounding her.

"She's awake!" squealed Alysha as she clambered onto her best friend's bed without pausing for invitation.

Teeny squealed back and held her tightly. The two hugged and squealed as if they had been apart for years.

"Hey Sweetie, its wonderful to see you awake. I didn't doubt for a second," said Nia, beaming widely.

Hugs were exchanged between Teeny and her visitors as well as recounts of recent events. Eventually Nia and Maya conceded to the young friends need to gossip and left to refuel on some coffee in the hospital restaurant.

"Hey isn't it a school day today?" inquired Teeny, suddenly realising it that not only was it a Wednesday, but it had only just gone ten o'clock.

"Uh, yeahhh…" drawled Alysha. "I kinda got sent home from school for 'disruptive behaviour,' she said rolling her eyes up and mimicking quote marks with her fingers.

"No way! Who framed you? You are the ultimate Miss Prim and Proper!" said Teeny unconvinced.

"Well, I've chosen the route of bad girl," Alysha flicked her head in the air so that the novelty hair bands that tipped her braids shook.

The duo collapsed in fits of laughter, knowing full well Alysha's impeccable reputation as a role model student, was matched only by her overtly perfectionist attitude. She abhorred disarray and rowdiness. Her hair and clothes were always immaculately put together as if she was always dressed for Sunday school.

"Really though," Teeny giggled, "what happened?"

"We were in assembly and Mrs Portland announced to the school that you were still in hospital and we should say a prayer for you. Anyways I heard Jordan two rows down, laughing and disrespecting the prayer. I'm thinking he's got nerve, so when we go out for playtime I went to him and asked what was so funny about you being in a coma, and he says he thinks you just busted your head on your skateboard and that you wouldn't be likely to wake up any time soon. Next thing I knew I was being dragged away, and he was on the floor crying. All I remember was Miss Priestly telling me to calm down, and she was pulling me towards the school office and I was screaming about how I'd beat down anyone who didn't believe you were coming back and that when you did, we'd beat them up again together. Mother was called to come get me and they told her I was obviously 'emotionally distressed,' by what you were going through for me to be the cause of such uncharacteristic behaviour. They told her I should stay at home for the rest of the week."

"Uh… I'm sorry, you're trying to tell me you got into a fight? And with Big Jordan of all people?" Teeny rolled her eyes in disbelief. "Nope, I don't believe you."

"I got his blood on my skirt at home to prove it," said Alysha, nonchalantly leaning back onto her elbow feigning scrutiny of her self-manicured nails.

"You made him bleed?" Teeny's voice raised an octave.

"Sure did. I may be a lady, but when it comes to defending my sister, I will happily break a nail." Her friend held a solemn look on her face for a couple of seconds, before doubling up in laughter.

Teeny kicked her legs in the air, as she too fought to control laughter she was unable to contain.

"But guess what?" said Alysha turning on her singsong, 'I got juicy gossip' voice. "A while after school would have finished, you know for them goody two shoes students," she fluttered her eyes sarcastically, "I hear a knock at the door and Mother calls me down to speak to someone who's come to see me. Well, brace yourself; it's only Toby Kwele!" She paused to relish in Teeny's response

"No - way. Now you *are* lying!" Teeny grabbed and shook her friend in demand she told the truth.

"This lady does not lie, thanking you much!" Alysha said snootily. "So, Toby Kwele comes to my house and asks to know how you are doing." She giggled as Teeny threw herself back on her pillow as if to faint, then leapt back up again, eyes wider than ever. "I asked him how he knew where I lived and he said that idiot brother of mine told him. Anyways, he gives me this card that he has so blatantly made and tells me to give it to you, that it's from some kids at school, and he walks off. Uh – Hello! He's in high school now, so I don't know what kids he's talking about. Well you know me, I looked inside it and it said something about hoping you get better soon and how everyone misses you, except he's just signed it with an 'x' and there are no other signatures. So I call out to him to let him know he needs to put his name on it. You know I'm just trying to help, but he comes back, grabs it from my hand, tears it up and tells me to forget it. Then he tells me not to dare tell anyone - like that's really gonna happen, and he storms off in a huff."

"You are such a bad liar Leesha," said Teeny dismissively, to which her friend dramatically gasped and jumped off the bed.

"On my honour as a lady!" said Alysha with a curtsey. "I tell no lies!"

The door opened and the girls jumped. Their mothers had returned.

"Alysha, I can hear you halfway down the hall," Nia said in a loud whisper. "I'm not impressed with this new disruptive behaviour trend you seem to be following. We've been asked to leave and let Teeny rest."

"Noooo!" cried Teeny.

"Don't worry, I'll see you tomorrow," said Alysha as she climbed back onto the bed to give Teeny a cheek-to-cheek bear hug.

"I don't think so, you're staying with your Grandma tomorrow and Friday, I have work to go to. Today was a special occasion. That's it. Shhh! Uh uh!" Nia added seeing her daughter open her mouth ready to plead unfairness.

Her daughter slinked off the bed, with a sulk coordinated to Teeny's and bid her sister-friend farewell.

"I'll be back again in the evening okay sweetie?" said Maya, trying her best to hide her disappointment at having also been asked to leave to allow her daughter rest. "Here, I bought you some magazines and a couple of muffins."

"Okay Mummy. Thank you," replied Teeny, equally disappointed.

Teeny lay back on her bed and replayed her and Alysha's conversation in her head. "Toby Kwele," she whispered to herself, sounding his name syllabically.

24
The Mouth of Babes

“Mummy did you record all the episodes of Eastenders I missed for me? I’ve watched some, but I can’t find any more,” asked Teeny, bolting through the front door and into the living room before her mother could respond. They had just returned from the last of her physiotherapy sessions. She had only been in attendance for two and a half weeks before the therapist admitted that it was unnecessary for her to continue. He had never seen anything like it and could see no reason for the young patient to maintain the appointment schedule. Teeny had, as usual whined incessantly for the duration. It was obvious to her that she suffered no lasting effects to her mobility. In fact, she had already ridden her skateboard a couple of times. Her first time back on the ramps had been challenging, but even the new bruises acquired as she reacquainted herself, were like a breath of fresh air. Now that she had been fully discharged from hospital care, she was home, really home. Maya began to wonder if the last few months had been a dream as she saw Teeny dart from the living room to the kitchen at break neck speed.

“Is there any plantain left?”

“I got about a months worth backed up, but I stopped when Nia mentioned something about Alysha recording it for you. And no, there is no plantain left, I could make some later if you want?" Maya called back as she hung up her coat and put Teeny's rucksack she carried to rest in a corner at the bottom of stairs.

"Cool, we can have it with Granny's jerk chicken Daddy promised he'd bring later," called Teeny. "Ooh!" She found apple in the salad compartment of the fridge she had been rummaging through and bit into it.

"Teeny! You didn't even rinse it!" cried Maya, seeing her daughter stuff the apple into her mouth on her second bite. "You don't even like fruit."

Teeny paused to look at the apple in her hand and shrugged. "I'm hungry," she reasoned.

Maya watched her daughter, shook her head and smiled.

"What?"

"Nothing. Nothing at all. Only that you are just so beautiful."

"Hmm, mushy much?" said Teeny, sticking out her tongue that had still held flecks of semi-chewed apple.

Maya laughed. "I love you!" she sighed, and planted a kiss on her forehead.

Teeny stopped chewing and squinted her eyes in concentration trying to remember something she was sure was important. She shrugged again and continued chewing.

"Mama," Teeny said thoughtfully, "I'm gonna go lie down for a while. If I fall asleep, will you wake me when Daddy comes?"

"Of course honey, you go rest."

Derrick pulled up his car outside his old home. He stepped out and reached back in to scoop up the flowers and the food saver container that lay on his passenger seat, locked up and went to ring the doorbell. He heard Maya's footsteps approach as she came to let him in.

"Here, this one's for you." He thrust a bunch of yellow of roses at her. "To say thank you," he explained in response to the look of confusion he caught on Maya's face as he stepped across the threshold. "I never did say thank you. What happened at the hospital that day is still messing up my head, but I appreciate what you did. For Teeny, for believing in me."

He followed Maya's lead into the kitchen. She sniffed the roses and shook her head. "It was you. I should be thanking you for trusting me. You brought our baby back. I don't know what I would have done if we…" she trailed off not wanting to vocalise the fear she had lived over the past five months.

"I know - I feel you. She sleeping?"

"Yeah, I told her I'd wake her up when you arrived." Maya said, turning to head out of the kitchen.

"Not yet," Derrick urged and sat down at the table resting the second bunch of flowers he held beside him. "We need - I need to talk about the things that have been happening. Nobody else would understand. Hell, I don't even understand, and I really need to. Something wild happen the day Teeny woke up and you are the only one I can talk to about it. Shit. Am I making it up? M'y' sometimes I think I'm going crazy, then something like this happens. I ain't gonna lie, this is fucking me up. Since that day… I mean Christmas, it was like none of us bothered to wrap up the presents."

Derrick, Maya and Teeny had celebrated Christmas on New Years Day. After all the excitement that surrounded the awakening of their only child, there had been no time to plan for anything sooner. Their attention had been focused on other numerous happenings. To the ex-couple's disenchantment, their daughter had eventually been released as an outpatient late on

Boxing Day, exactly nine days after she had first opened her eyes. True to her word, Teeny had walked out on her own two feet adamantly refusing all offers of assistance.

As they passed around the gifts that sat beneath the Christmas tree, Teeny excitedly thanked them for the clothes, computer games, and every other present before having unwrapped them. She herself seemed oblivious to the surprised glances her parents exchanged as she accurately named the contents of every parcel. At every gift-wrapped item she was handed, she'd scream with glee her appreciation, or happily exclaim how badly she had wanted the such and such it concealed.

Maya sat pulled up a chair beside Derrick and held his hand, propping her elbows on her thighs. "What happened sure was wild. I saw it, I knew in my heart it would work, but I haven't taken the time to question it, because… I don't know. I just don't have a clue. I've started having flashes like a split second images jumping in my head. Like when I'd tell you if Walter was gonna be in a good mood, except I can't hold onto what I see long enough to make sense of it. It started the day after you did that thing for Teeny. As for Christmas, I lived the highlights of the day before I woke up that morning." Maya paused to squeeze her eyes closed and open them again. "And there's something else. Since last week I… My eyes. I'm looking at you now and I see this big thing around you. It's like a bubble. Just like a bubble down to the way patches of colour shimmer off the surface. I see it around Teeny too. I try to touch it and its as if can vaguely feel something, but there's nothing there. If you think your going crazy, I'm right there with you."

"You're seeing the natural energy fields that surround all living things. They are called auras," said Teeny, who now stood at the kitchen door. She rubbed her eyes and smiled. "Hi Daddy, I knew I heard your voice. Did you bring the chicken? I'm starving." She climbed into his lap and hugged him.

"Yup, and these," said Derrick handing her a white lily bouquet. "Congratulations on being officially home free," he smiled.

Teeny looked down at the flowers. She cautiously touched one and bit her lip.

"You don't like them? I thought they were your favourites," said Derrick

"No, they are beautiful. I love them, really. Thank you," said Teeny and kissed her father's cheek. "It wasn't a dream. It's a sign, almost like a trigger. Lilies. They're one of my triggers!" she whispered to herself.

Maya had barely gotten over her daughter's 'aura' explanation for the strange hazy outlines she had begun seeing around things. She wondered if Derrick had been able to hear what Teeny had mumbled. She looked over at him and as if he felt her, he raised his eyes to meet hers. He gave a slight twitch of his head, his discreet way of saying he was none the wiser. Teeny slipped off her father's lap and placed the lilies back on the table and walk toward the kitchen door. She looked back at her parents, saying nothing, but silently requesting that they accompany her. They stood up to follow their daughter's lead into the living room. Teeny sat in the middle of the sofa, and spread her arms so that her hands touched the empty seats beside her.

"Teeny, what's wrong baby girl?" Derrick asked.

She closed her eyes and deliberated the best way to deliver the message to her parents. "Mum, Dad. Please sit down. I need to tell you something." She paused as her parents obediently located themselves on either side of her. "I need you to listen, and I mean really listen. And more important than anything, I need you to believe me." She looked at each of her parents. The looked at each other, then back at their daughter and nodded. "When I was asleep in the hospital. I saw Nana…"

Teeny continued to explain in detail the answer to questions that neither of them had dared to ask of the things they could do. About how it was that her mother could glimpse future events through dreams, images and signs. How her father was a universal empath and potential telepath. How if they owned their abilities instead of dismissing or disregarding them as coincidence, they would grow into them, allowing her father's to pain ease and her mother's second sight to become vivid. She spoke at length of the power of fear and it's ability to mask love and made it falsely appear to cease existing.

"Mummy, there is something else you need to know too." Teeny gazed at her mother intently. "Nana said she never told anyone this, but Granddad - your father, he never abandoned any of you. He loved you all. It's not that she lied to you - it's just that Nana didn't know back then what she knows now. Granddad is still with you, just not in the way you might need him to be."

Maya gripped the seat tightly with one hand and with the other she covered her eyes then drew her hand down to cover her mouth. She whimpered, uncontrollably rocking her body back and forth, trying to contain the rush of years of emotion accumulated from having been a fatherless child. She was taken aback. Derrick was locked in a trance, his gaze seemingly fixed on Teeny, but he didn't see her. He was fighting to find logic in all that she had quietly spoken of. Believing everything his daughter had said wasn't the problem. Accepting it was. Everything suddenly seemed so clear as he retraced incidences of his blackouts and pain episodes and was able to synchronize the occurrences to specific events and situations. His baby had just casually explained the solution to the enigma of why no amount of medicine had been able to take his pain away, and why he placed so much value on his moments of elected solitude. How he had known of Maya's affair and why he would suddenly feel pain in various areas of his body for no apparent reason, only for someone to claim to ache in the exact same place a few moments or even days later. And Maya; how she could close her eyes and see things that the average person's eyes failed to perceive. Their lives had been influenced by the additional senses with which they experienced the world around them. Though they had never spoken on it, it had brought them closer together. They simply accepted and understood each other, taking for granted how it enhanced their rapport to know that few else could truly relate to them on the same level.

Like Derrick, Maya didn't doubt her daughter's words, but it didn't make them any easier to swallow. She had a huge lump in her throat as if alongside truth, Teeny had actually administered her an oversized dose of reality. The words she had used, the way she had spoken; so eloquent, so adult and so unashamedly raw. Whilst at the same time with a deliberate softness that made Maya's heart pound fiercely, forcing her to accept that she wasn't dreaming.

"Teeny," Derrick finally broke the silence. "I believe you, but baby this is… this is huge. It's a lot to take in."

Maya nodded her concurrence. "It is…" She tried to find the words to adequately express herself, then gave up and simply exclaimed, "Wow!"

"Thank you," said Teeny. "For believing in me I mean. But I need you both to trust me again. I need to ask you to do something I know you wont like." She looked at her father and held his hand. "I need you to empathically bond with Mummy," she turned to face her mother and held her hand also. "Mummy, I need you to think of the moment that made you and Daddy fall apart."

Both her parents withdrew their hands simultaneously. “Whoa!” recoiled Maya in horror. Likewise Derrick leapt to his feet, throwing his hands out in front of his chest in defensive protest.

“Teeny baby, we have a problem right there.”

“Sweetie,” cut in Maya, “we both believe you, honestly, and we know that us getting divorced was very painful for you, but this is something you’re just a little too…”

“What? Too young to understand?” demanded Teeny. “Too stupid to see how afraid you’ve become of each other, but how much it hurts you both to be apart? Yeah, I remember I’m only eleven after all, what do I know? I’m too deaf to hear how you cry yourself to sleep at night and too blind to see how Daddy works double shifts to avoid coming home to a house without us in it. Hey, I’m even too much of a brat to mean it when I say that if you don’t do this one little thing and face your fears together; you will ruin all our lives, because it means you need your fear more than you need each other or me!”

Teeny stormed out and stamped up the stairs ignoring both her parents pleas that became demands for her to return. The walls trembled in response to the severity with which she slammed her bedroom door in defiance. Maya was now on her feet, mouth agape, looking at the rebellious young girl’s trail in shock.

Derrick’s eyes and mouth were jolted wide open in equal disbelief. He turned to look at Maya. “You know she gets that bullshit from you!” he said finally.

“Uh uh, that’s your daughter right there, sulks just like her daddy.” Maya rebutted.

Derrick grabbed the back of his neck and raised his head, in thought. He turned and paced the laminate flooring. “This is fucked up," he said out loud to himself. "She didn't lie though." He looked at Maya.

"She didn't lie," she affirmed with a barely audible whisper, and pushed her fingers through her hair, allowing her hand to drop and slap her thigh. "I don't want to hurt you any more D., you deserve better than that," she said shaking her head.

"I deserved you," he replied solemnly, and raised his hand and held his mouth as if trying to censor what he really wanted to say. "Fuck it, you know what? I need to know why I stopped deserving you. Lets do this." He opened his arms and nodded for Maya to step into them.

"No. Uh uh. I don't want.... I can't... not again," said Maya, her face ashen with fear.

"It's cool lets do it," Derrick insisted. "You owe me that much. I know I didn't want to listen before, but seeing as our life's mysteries are being solved, we might as well let it all out. Now or never." He didn't know if he had it in him welcome his ex-wife any more than he did now.

Maya hesitated, before stepping over warily, almost expecting him to pounce. She took position in his arms. This time it didn't feel like home, the place she had once felt most safe. Her heart raced, she held her breath in the hope of slowing it down.

"Breathe. Relax," instructed Derrick.

Maya complied, though with rigid hesitance.

"Relax!" he repeated impatiently. "Focus on the night."

He closed his eyes, shifted his head from side to side, took a deep breath and exhaled slowly. He flinched as through Maya, he felt a gut-wrenching sorrow as she mentally replayed the events leading up to her fornicating with a total stranger. Tears rolled down Maya's cheeks as Derrick's body trembled behind hers. The sound of his breathing became louder and his heart thumped to match the intensity of her own. She stiffened as if doing so might turn back the clock and change the events of the incriminating night and allow him to see other than the mental recount of the pivoting moment of her life that cause her to fall from grace. She winced against the thought that he might even feel the way her body had responded to the stranger's touch. How for a split second she wanted to completely surrender to his seduction and how she had even thrust herself back, beckoning him to go deeper.

"I'm so sorry," Maya sobbed. Derrick remained silent as he dropped his hold on her and staggered backwards. He shook his head and stormed out the house leaving the front door wide open behind him.

The Awakening

"Who am I to BE? How dare I express the right to be me? My smile must be tainted with a frown, lest my happiness make you uncomfortable. My intellect makes you feel inadequate, so of course I must have a superiority complex or some other psychosis to ease your discomfort. My sincerity must be an act, for surely no one is this real? My objection makes me a rebel who must be educated in the etiquette of conformity. I must keep my head bowed low, be mediocre and not draw attention to myself. Dumb down so I can slip through the cracks and land amongst the dregs of society that you are happy to ignore so long as they don't threaten your blissful ignorance. If I am not too young, I am too old. If I abstain from drink, drugs, fornication and other legally permissible stimulation, I need to live a little and stop being so uptight. If I indulge, I have dependency issues and problems with self-control. If I am too black, I am an activist, if I am too white I am an oppressor. Where amongst your unspoken rules can I possibly fit in? Where amongst you do I belong?

I'll tell you, I am all of your stereotypes, every last one of them. They are my cover, my disguise - they keep you guessing. You never boxed me, I boxed you, kept you caught up in my femininity then by my lack of it. Do you think I was born a young black female by accident or chance? I chose it. I chose to be the one you deem weak, so you would never see me coming. I am known as Zauba-ah – 'The desert sandstorm', pray that you never feel my wrath."

25

The Ties That Bind

Nana inhaled deeply, she was pleased to have been granted the opportunity to return to Earth, though she had come to fall in love with her rendition of paradise. She didn't care that it was merely a product of her own THORTS. To her it was heaven, even if only a temporary one. She gazed at everything, taking note of the minutest detail in hopes she would remember it well enough to be able to return to it in the dreams of her new incarnation. This place was beautiful, not just the paradise of her creation, but all of it. Try as she might she was unable generate any vivid memories of her life as Se7en. She felt small things, though too vague to fully ascertain. She only knew it to be a heaven even more incredible than the one in which she stood now. It was a utopia, a place she longed to experience again, but how could she? It was little more than a memory that taunted her inability to recall it. She no longer belonged. Earth was her home how, a place where nonsense made sense, it was familiar, and it cradled her like the worn springs of an old armchair. The utopia that was Ouranos, was now a reward she felt unworthy of accepting. She felt inadequate, unprepared, no longer qualified to fit in. She wanted to earn the reciprocation of her embrace of it on the glorious day of her readiness. To do that, she had to let go of her regrets, her guilt, her need to relive poor choices in search for more favourable outcomes. She only hoped it wouldn't take too many lifetimes.

She was aware of Imhotep's irritation at her state of mind, and had spent much time defensive against his accusatory remarks and snide comments. Then on one occasion, with nothing left by which to retaliate, she listened to his words and slowly came to understand the source of his frustration. He was not so much insulting her, he was complimenting who she had been. Slowly she had come to recall her mission debriefing as outlined by Zauba-ah. Only then did she finally accept Imhotep's rationalization. She had fallen prey to the condition that she had been repeatedly warned of, but always scoffed at. Even now she was still unable to associate herself with what was she had been informed was her class designation and her real name, *Lanying*.

"I am victorious?" asked Nana of Imhotep as he approached.

"That remains to be seen," replied the great ape, taking position beside the woman. "We have no way of knowing at this time. While I detect unfavourably elevated levels of stress in Zauba-ah's incarnation, it is difficult to fully determine her status. Without being fully awakened she cannot communicate with us directly."

"Can you not perceive her with more clarity by observing via connection with the Mental Realm?"

"Indeed she is N9ne, but so soon after recall, it may trigger her to actualise prematurely. It is a heavy burden for one so young to have to bear. No, it is preferential that for now, she is permitted to BE. Thus far, she has done well, though not enough to secure her awakening."

"My genes will prevail," affirmed Nana confidently.

Imhotep looked at his fellow N9ne's Initiate and wondered if her confidence stemmed from factual knowledge or religious belief. He hoped it was the former. Her condition was a form

Alzheimer's disease of the soul body wherein cognitive deterioration manifested in the form of her being of Se7en Mind one moment, and then of frail human mind the next. Her regression was easier to pinpoint when she slipped into a trance-like state to replay fond memories of her Earthly incarnation. Other times it was less obvious. At times he wondered if she could actually see him when they spoke, or whether he became a person she once knew during her time spent on Earth. Despite his frustration he felt an inexplicable pride for her determination to complete her mission. She had done exceedingly well.

At the outset, Imhotep had recoiled at the thought of having to constantly monitor an Initiate. Like Zauba-ah he too was of bi-designation, Scientist and Engineer Class. Far removed from the ranks of the Nurturer Lanying had once been. Still, he had softened and even grown fond of her. He couldn't help but respect her after the time they had spent together since the expiration of her human vehicle. Monitoring her had become less of a chore and more of a pleasurable encounter he had gained much wisdom from, like an informal history lesson taught by a senior Earth citizen to a reluctant know-it-all teen. After witnessing the delivery of Lanying's performance in spite of her inept memory, he had become even more impressed.

"Actually, it is not your genes I am concerned for," Imhotep finally replied. "To that end, you are victorious. I congratulate you."

Nana looked at the gorilla questioningly. "I don't understand, you say victory remains to be seen, yet I am victorious. How can that be?"

"Reassignment to your mission was successful in that Zauba-ah was able to recall her authentic self and separate from the illusion of her incarnation. Her re-insemination was successful and she has set upon the task of reuniting her guardians. Thus far, all is well. Maya Kingsley's potential has now been secured by way of your genes. However Derrick Kingsley is another matter. His fate, and that of his family now rests in his hands." Imhotep turned to face Nana, who to his horror had knelt down head bowed as if in prayer. He gritted his teeth and shook his head, his mouth twisted in struggle to deny his urge to curse at her foolishness. He let out a sigh. "Please tell me you are not praying to god."

Nana nodded, without uttering a word.

Imhotep sighed again, this time more audibly, unable to contain his exasperation. "Oh really? And what might be the name of this god of yours?"

Nana paused and looked up at Imhotep as if he had asked a stupid question. She furrowed her brows as she answered plainly, "Derrick Kingsley, who else?"

26

Time To Get Taught

Derrick caught a glance of the silver sports car from the corner of his eye and skidded his Mercedes into a free space a few meters away in the private underground car park. He's heart pounded fiercely, his blood on fire from the rush of adrenaline that surged through his veins. He paused only long enough to rummage through the glove compartment for his tyre repair kit, before jumping out of the car, not even stopping to turn off the engine, let alone shut the door. He stormed over to the sports car and bent down to unscrew the valve cap on the front wheel tyre of the driver's side and shoved the valve tool into place and deflated the air. He repeated the process with the remaining wheels and turned back toward his car. On reseating himself behind the wheel, he turned off the engine and closed the door. Now he just had to wait.

The phone rang, making a rattling sound as it vibrated across the dashboard he had slammed it on earlier, prior to embarking on his mission of revenge. The caller ID on the screen of his phone read 'Home'. Another surge of adrenaline boosted the previous one, the effects of which had slowly begun to subside. His first impulse was to open his door and throw the phone as hard as he could and wait for the satisfying smashing sound it made on the concrete. He pressed 'answer'.

"Maya, I ain't tryna talk about shit with you right now, I ain't hearing it aiight?"

"Daddy, it's Teeny. Please come back home!" she exclaimed excitedly.

A split second of shame drenched him for the way he had snapped into the phone, allowing his baby girl to hear him swear and witness the anger he had intended for her mother to feel the brunt of. He sniffed and blew a gust of air through circled lips in an effort to contain his anger long enough to apply a little damage control to the situation.

"Teeny, I'm busy right now, I got something I need to do here. Lemme get at you later okay?"

"No Daddy, I need you to come home right now. Please!" Her voice changed from excitement to unadulterated desperation. She spoke fast as if she were in a race against time. "I know you're why you're mad… I know all about Mummy's mistake. I know you are hurting Daddy, but Mummy's hurting too and she's really sorry, I know she is. Daddy, please come home, we can make everything right again. Please Daddy, Mummy wants to make it better. She needs… I need you to help her get better. She's really sad Daddy, please come home right now!" Teeny's voice sounded weak, overwhelmed by the onset of uncontrollable sobs of despair"

His heart could have snapped right there. Her words struck him like razor sharp daggers that must have punctured his lungs, because it suddenly became hard to breathe. A lump swelled in his throat that he tried to swallow down, but couldn't as his mouth had become unexpectedly dry. He didn't know what blew him away most, Teeny's words or how much like they sounded like Maya's. He remained silent, the only sound that informed the other that they both still on the line were Teeny's tearfully wet sniffs and his breathing that he fought hard to regulate.

“Daddy?”

He still couldn’t answer.

“Daddy, you once told me that the difference between a god and a nigger was that a god responds, while a nigger reacts. God can make this better, my god can make our family right again, but if you don’t come home the nigger will destroy us all. He’ll destroy us all because he’s been alone, living in fear and ignorance for so long, he doesn’t know any better. I don’t want to lose my Daddy, I’m on my knees praying to you now god, don’t take my Daddy from me, please show him a sign. God, please come home now so we can be a family again.” Teeny had stopped crying. Her voice was now calm and sombre between sniffs.

The sound of a car alarm deactivated pierced the second moment of silence. Derrick turned to see the chocolate skinned man with neatly braided hair, stop in his tracks as he quizzically inspected each of his tyres.

“I hafta go Teeny; something I gotta do,” he ended the call and stepped out of his car.

“Sumthin up wit’ your ride Paulie?” Derrick hollered sauntering over to where the man stood cussing under his breath as he circled his car for the second time. “’Sup Derrick, I thought you left work early today. Glad I was wrong, you mind if I beg you a ride? Some wanker’s let the air out my tyres,” Paul spat the last sentence with disdain, still focused on his car.

“It’s that right? Bwoy… maybe you pissed some wanker off by fucking his wife huh?” Derrick replied casually shrugging his shoulders, slightly flicking his arms out from his sides as if to welcome Paul’s reasoning for the dilemma he now found himself in.

Paul looked up at Derrick. “Shit!” He threw his head back slightly as if to say, ‘that’s all I need’. He dropped his head forward, stroked his goatee and bit his lip as the took a bold step in his manager's direction challenging him to do something about what happened that night two years ago. "So you just clocked the play huh? Yeah I fucked her." Now he mimicked the arm flick motion, daring his senior colleague to 'bring it'. "What, you think you could just walk into Systech, take my promotion from under me and not expect some kind of payback? You'd barely joined the company a year before. I, on the other hand, had been busting my balls for years to earn the right to climb the ladder."

Derrick screwed up his face and swayed his head from side to side, in another place and time his motion could have been mistaken for that of a man seriously feeling the rhythm of an old school jam he struggled to remember the words for. "FUCK!" he exclaimed, jerking his head in a violent nod of affirmation. He tilted his head to the right supporting it in with his hand, thumb under chin, in contemplation. He squinted his eyes and raised his left arm, and flicked the air in front of his chest as he enquired for clarity's sake: "This is about my being promoted over you?" He saw Paul's challenging step and raised it by advancing even closer so they stood barely three feet apart from one another.

"Damn straight. You took what was mine, so I took what was yours. I see you figured it was me who gave her the flat tyre?" Paul said eyeing Derrick's handiwork, his disappointment now tinged with a slight admiration. "Before you rolled in, I literally owned the company, all I had to do was focus the right kind of attention on the right players and persuade them to see things my way. I got it like that you know. I can feel people, make them do things. But you… You were different; I couldn't do it with you. Took me a while to figure out why, then I realised it was because you're like me. You can feel people too, strong mother fucker at that. Still, it sweets me to see you out of control, popping pills, like a fucking idiot. Them headaches are a bitch though, ain't they?" he smiled at the memory.

Two years was a long time ago. Since then, Paul had found himself unable to justify why his colleague shouldn't have been promoted over him. He had even come respect the skill and professionalism he dedicated to the position of seniority and in due course realised that Derrick wasn't the enemy who prevented his ascension through the ranks. He was simply the better man. At times he found himself regretting what he had done to the man he had begun to respect as 'blood'. What he had done had been a malicious outburst that bordered on childish. He was gutted that he now stood before him confronted with his transgression, but he wasn't about to bow down and beg forgiveness. What was the point? What was done was done; there would be no adding insult to injury by apologising. Better to go out like a man than a coward. Like so many men before him, his definition of what it was to be a man had more to do with image than the genuine acquisition of respect through conscious deed.

Derrick swallowed at hearing Paul's words. So many pennies of realisation were dropping all at once in his mind. He was in the presence of a mental empath, and by the sounds of it, a highly skilled one.

Attuned with his empathic nature, Paul never had to suffer the pain that came with resistance of one's true nature, but on observation, came to realise how many others did.

"Mmm hmph, Mayaaaa," Paul drooled, licking his lips and nodding in satisfaction.

That was all it took for Derrick to lose the little composure he had. He grabbed Paul by the neck and threw him onto the bonnet of his car. "This is a game to you? You fuck my wife, break up my home and think it's some kinda joke? Watch me show you who you're fucking with now," he growled, as he drew his fist back for good leverage. Just as he was about to exert the full extent of his rage all over Paul's face, he noticed something that caused him to hesitate. The car. Paul's car was a silver Porsche 911.

"Please show him a sign."

Paul squirmed, and gave a nervous laugh. "Go the fuck ahead, free your inner-nigga, bitch!" Perhaps Derrick wasn't so different from him after all.

"You once told me that the difference between a god and a nigger was that a god responds, while a nigger reacts."

Derrick looked down at Paul, further infuriated by the way he seemed to relish in his moral demise.

"My god can make our family right again, but if you don't come home the nigger will destroy us all."

Derrick felt a war raging within him as his head struggled to apply logic to this equation. His ego screamed for justice while his heart and mind stipulated for peace. For the past two years he had suffered the humiliation of everyone's sympathy. Heard the hushed whispers of gossip that would suddenly cease when he hung out amongst friends. Cussed those that dared write off the woman he loved as being nothing more than an undercover harlot. And most of all, he had experienced the embodiment of his worst fears - failure and loneliness. In his grasp now he had the opportunity to ventilate all his pain and anger on the one who instigated it. But Teeny... how could he face her if he did? Especially after the way she had pleaded warning to him over the phone. His daughter's words now haunted him. Not just the urgency it conveyed, but the wisdom that seemed to be embedded in her intonation. It held a familiar knowingness he trusted implicitly, Maya's. The woman he loved. He lowered his fist and released his grip over Paul's neck. He took a step back and sighed heavily. He knew himself well enough to admit that his anger would not concede at the first blow, rather it would magnify and mutate into something ugly. Besides, a conviction for grievous bodily harm would equate to further sacrifice of his life that Paul didn't deserve. He turned back toward his car.

"What? That's all you got? I got your bitch right here." Paul hollered, grabbing at the region of his genitals. "Bitch couldn't say no. Nigga I took your shit! You ain't been able to tap that pussy since I fucked it good 'n' proper you faggot arse mother fucker!"

Derrick stopped in his tracks and shook his head. "Teeny, sometimes god just gotta teach them heathens who not to fuck with," he muttered, and turned around to furnish a loud resounding slap that reverberated on the walls of the car park. Paul fell to the floor, unable to withstand the blinding combination of shock and obliviousness to the speed of lightning strike to his face. Derrick stood over him and looked for a second before squatting to meet his subordinate's body that lay sprawled on the concrete.

"I got promoted because your fuck lazy self didn't have what it took to step to the plate and be god. And as for my wife, you got nothing. Taking from a goddess what don't belong to you doesn't give half as much pleasure or satisfaction as when is given because you *are* her god. You may have walked away feeling sweet, but she walked away pissed because you couldn't even make her cum. Biatch!" Derrick got up and continued back towards his car. "You're right about one thing though," he called over his shoulder, "this god is a strong mother fucker fi real."

27

Time To BE

Teeny sat on the bottom step with a tear-streaked face, still holding the phone in her hand. To the left of her she could see her mother sat in the living room on the sofa, hugging her knees, through the arched door-less entrance. She too had stopped crying. Now she just stared into space, frozen in time like a statue.

Maya sniffed, stiffly unfolding her arms from around her legs and eased one leg down, slowly followed by the other. She looked at the ball of tissue she had crumpled in her fist before reaching out for the arm of the sofa for its support as she pushed her self up and off it. She looked again at the ball of tissue and idly pinched her fingers around it, hesitant to face Teeny whilst she felt so emotionally drained and physically dishevelled. She took a deep breath. It was time she at least make an attempt to bring back some kind of normality to the evening. It was already an hour past Teeny's bedtime. She walked towards the living room doorway, tossing her tear soaked tissue into the bin that lay to the right of it.

"Time for bed Teeny," Maya croaked. She cleared her throat and tried again. "Come on, up you get, it's past your bed time." Her voice adjusted enough to sound a little clearer. She forced a deliberate cough to straighten it up a little more. Teeny got up and turned to obediently climb the stairs toward her room. Her mother followed.

"Tuck me in?"

"Of course sweetie," replied Maya, her voice back to normal, albeit a sad version of it.

Teeny had prepared herself for bed shortly after her dramatic departure to her room. After she heard her mother crying as she closed the front door, she had spent a few minutes deliberating on what to should do. Finally she had crept into her mother's room, picked up the phone and mustered up the courage to call her father.

She jumped into bed and waited for her mother to come to her side. Maya pulled her daughter's blanket over her shoulders and leaned in to kiss her goodnight. Teeny sat up on her elbow. "Mummy, everything's gonna be alright isn't it? If you say everything's gonna be okay, I know it will be."

Maya bowed her head, avoiding her daughter's wide inquiring eyes. "I don't know Teeny, I - I can't answer that."

"Yes you can, you can feel it with your 'mummy radar'. It says everything's gonna be fine, right?" she urged.

Maya gave a faint smile and shook her head. "The 'mummy radar', doesn't quite work like that. It's just a feeling that some mothers get to tell them if something isn't right with their children to a certain extent, is all. It doesn't do the same for daddies."

"Yes it does, you can feel him if you close your eyes and think about him!"

Maya was not in the mood for this. "Destiny, that's enough, time for…"

"Mummy, humour me! Please just close your eyes and think of Daddy!" Teeny refused to settle for hearing no.

"Humour you? Child please, you need to get yourself to sleep and stop this nonsense, school starts back on Monday. That means we only have four days to back into our routine. Sleep – now!"

"Please Mummy," Teeny whispered, she knew she was pushing her luck by testing her mother's patience, but how much worse could things get?

Maya could see this was going nowhere. She gave an exasperated huff and closed her eyes for two seconds, then opened them. "There, satisfied?" she asked on the brink of losing what little cool she had left in her.

"Mummy, you didn't even try!"

Maya glared, daring the obstinate youngster to keep pushing.

Message received loud and clear, she backed off, throwing her head back into the pillow and her arms into a fold across her chest on top of her covers. Maya got up and walked towards the door. Teeny stuck her tongue out at her mother's back in frustration.

"Oh, the 'mummy radar' works just fine for that sort of thing!" she called in just before closing the door behind her.

Maya turned and walked to the end of the hall for the bathroom. She stood in front of the sink and stared briefly at her reflection, then pressed her lips together and slowly shook her head at herself, before switching on the tap and throwing cold water over her face. She fumbled on the adjacent wall for the towel to dry her face, then gave up and settled for using the white tank top she wore. *Fuck it,* she thought, and snatched off her clothes, dropping them on the floor, and stepped into the shower. She shivered under the cold water as it warmed up and became a source for the mist that climbed the glass walls of the cubicle. She cried all over again. Her tears ceased almost as soon as she turned the taps off ten minutes later. She sighed and leant her wet body on the wall of the stall and watched droplets of water roll down the door in front of her. She closed her eyes and thought of Derrick and sighed again. Suddenly she jumped up from where she leant, grabbed her robe and hastily stepped out of the shower.

Still dripping she ran down the stairs and stood in front of the front door before she caught herself.

"This is crazy, what am I doing?" she murmured, and then looked up as headlights filled the window of the door. "Come on Maya, don't be silly, the 'mummy radar' only works with Teeny. You couldn't have just seen Derrick driving down the street," she muttered trying to convince herself that her eleven year old was just talking mess. She cupped her hands over her mouth and nose and nervously shifted from one foot to the other, then back to the first foot again. Her heart jumped at hearing a car door slam shut and footsteps approaching the door. "Shit! It's him! It's Derrick. Nah. No way! It can't be." She wrung her hands and took a deep breath and snatched the door open before she had time to talk herself out of it. Derrick stood in front of her, his arm outstretched about to ring the doorbell. "Shit! Destiny was right!" she gasped.

"Maya?" Derrick's eyebrows arched in surprise. He looked at her wet face, that a drop of water rolled down, then at the tiny puddles that had formed on the floor around her feet and stepped inside.

"Its okay," he assured. He turned slightly to close the door, taking his gaze from the floor, sweeping it up her robe. Maya had tied it closed as she leaped down the stairs, still, she lowered her eyes in embarrassment, as she wondered how ridiculous she must have looked. She pinned closed the top of her robe with her right hand and nervously rubbed her left palm on her thigh. Derrick advanced toward her, reaching out to gently pull aside her hand. He peeled back the robe and softly cupped her breast in his hand and caressed it lovingly.

"What are you...?" Maya started, but was interrupted as he hushed her and stepped so close she could feel his nature rising. He kissed her tenderly and with his other hand, pushed between her thighs tracing his fingers upward to massage her swelling lips before pushing them gently inside her. She moaned and felt more tears begin to swell, as he edged her toward the stairs guiding her to lay back. Maya looked into his eyes, for approval to continue in her quest to undo the fastenings of his trouser in an effort to free his member from the garments that kept him from her. They made love. Love that said I'm sorry, I forgive you, I was wrong, take me back. And again she wept. This time tears of joy and ecstasy.

That night Maya dreamt again, but the nightmare revealed itself to her as the prophecy it had intended to be. She answered to the voice of Teeny's cry, but it wasn't her daughter at all. It was destiny that called to her, requesting that she walk along its path. She took heed and saw the emergence of a rainbow that spoke, requesting that she lend herself to guide its many hues that would soon smile across the planet. Maya humbly accepted and then watched as children rained from the sky. A new day was dawning.

Teeny woke up eyes closed, focused on remembering the details of her dream. She stretched out her arms and rotated her hands until her body felt release, then smiled until the smile became a giggle, and then giggled until it became a laugh that became a squeal of delight. She opened her eyes and listened for confirmation of what she sensed within. Down the hallway she heard the door open and her father's voice say something she couldn't quite hear, followed by the familiar sound of her mother's slippers smacking the undersides of her feet. Teeny squealed again and jumped out of bed and rushed out into the hall to meet her new family. She paused for a moment as she passed her vanity table that had become home to her lily bouquet. She ran her finger along the edge of one of her flowers and watched as the petal complied with the issuance of new choreography of its molecules and transformed from its white colour to a vibrant indigo. She smiled and hurried into the hallway.

"Daddy, you came home!" she screamed diving into his chest causing him to lose his balance and grab for the wall.

“Yeah, Daddy’s home, Teeny-Tiny.” he smiled.

Before he had the chance to put his arms around her, she had already darted toward her mother and thrown her arms around her waist. She glanced up at her mother’s face and gave a cheeky grin before cupping her hand on her mother’s stomach and whispering: “Hey Grandma, I got your message. Congratulations on your new mission. It would seem we were successful and your conception has just been guaranteed. I’ll take care of you just like I promised. Bet you didn’t think I’d remember huh? That’ll teach your cheeky Se7enth Degree self to threaten to take away my Eastenders. That’s my vice for this lifetime!”

Her parents stared at each other as she clung to her mother’s waist. Maya raised her arms in a shrug at Derrick in answer to his silent request to be clued in on whatever was going on. Teeny kissed her mother’s belly then released her and skipped off toward the bathroom. She stopped just as she reached the door, spun round.

“Mum, Dad, I think Ya’alaam would be a real cool name for my baby brother. It means ‘He who knows’, and believe me; he will.” With that she stepped in closed the door behind her, then as an after-thought snatched the door open again, poked her head round and hollered, “By the way; we’re running low on mayonnaise, we’re gonna need a lot of it over the next few months!”

Derrick and Maya stood frozen on the spot in bewilderment.

Everything seemed so brand new. Teeny skipped all the way to school, this time without her traditional beg and whine session she performed daily for her mother to permit her to skateboard to school after having the privilege revoked. She was serving the first week of her month ban that had come as a punishment for not adhering to her mother’s hard fast rule of not skateboarding across roads. She knew the rule was for the sake of her own safety, but Teeny preferred the theory that her mother didn't trust the skill with which she could handle the board. Today that didn't matter though, because she was on a high from whence nothing could possibly bring her down. Today, she didn't need her board to fly.

"Oi, Kickybum! Kick-kick-kickayyyyy!" Toby wailed through hands he funnelled around his mouth to help his voice carry.

Although Toby now attended high school, he had not had to alter his journey at all. The place of his secondary education was located behind the primary school he had recently left. The institution had not been his parent's first choice, but he had been inexplicably delighted to hear of his acceptance there. He never would have admitted his joy being attributed to the fact it meant he would remain close to Teeny. It enabled him to continue seeing her everyday and relish at her annoyance of his incessant taunts.

A couple of Toby's friends laughed at his jeering. Teeny spun round and marched up toward them. He styled out a flinch and wondered whether he had finally hit a raw nerve on a bad day and was about to receive a dose of long overdue retribution. Teeny stopped and stood in front of Toby and his crew and threw her hands on her hips.

"You know, today is one of those days that not even *you* could ruin for me Toby Kwele."

Teeny stepped right up to the boy's face, grabbed him forward by his shirt and planted a kiss on his cheek, then leaned in further and whispered, "It's okay Toby, I think you're cute too." She turned on her heel, head held high and walked off without another word.

EPILOGUE

"Greetings." Welcomed Imhotep as Rudwaan emerged his personification from the ethers. "How is your journey prevailing?"

"All is as it should be, I am well taken care of," the N9ne Blood replied. "My physical is due to arrive within the next rotation of the station. You are happy to remain until I arrive?"

"More than. In fact I wondered if you might like to take my place in the soul exchange."

"With respect I decline, I have little desire to incarnate again in the form of a low frequency being so soon after my last mission. I am informed that the humanoid inhabitants of Earth face much turbulence at this time."

"Your sources are accurate. They are a particularly disparaging species. It is with regret that I find myself weighted with the responsibility of delivering the message," Imhotep lamented.

Rudwaan's presence was a thought projection that was only perceivable in the dimensions of the station that vibrated on the frequency of the Mental Realm. His body was still in transit, travelling through hyperspace at tachyon speed under the guardianship of two Ei8th Degree Souldiers. He had been placed in stasis to facilitate his mental projection to arrive ahead of his physically tangible form.

Rudwaan bowed graciously and raised his hands to touch the sides of Imhotep's temples inviting him to do the same of himself. The pair closed their eyes and merged consciousness, mentally debriefing one another on the events of each of their assigned domains of responsibility within All.

Zauba'ah's consciousness had successfully been reinserted within the human vessel. Though having being programmed for her memory to reach full status during puberty, this N9ne had insured against the possibility of failing to awaken by assigning a vast array of new triggers to her DNA. The decision was a prudent measure that might at least remind Teeny of her temporary recall back to the Mental Realm. Upon regaining consciousness in the hospital, she had instinctively begun to request to know what had happened. In her solitude she had meditated on the little things that niggled in her mind, though she could not quite make out what they were. Toby Kwele, Alysha's dramatic persona, her mother's kiss on her forehead, lilies, her skateboard, the panther on her mink blanket, Eastenders and numerous other minute details had contributed to her regaining her memory sooner than anticipated. How might this affect the mission bearing in mind her current physical and mental immaturity? Surely that she was N9nth Degree should balance out the odds of her premature awakening? Yes, thus far she had maintained diplomacy when relaying the message to her parents and had spoken only of what concerned them at this time. Teeny had every intention of completing her mission with the professionalism of N9ne Blood incarnate, but she had no intention of passing up the pleasures of her age related practices of human rites of passage. When in Rome…

The N9ne Degree entities separated and finalised with unified concordance that all was well.

Imhotep prepared himself to meet with the soul whose body he was to be integrated. Word of affirmatin had been conveyed as to the readiness of his human Earth vessel.

THE BEGINNING

Mind over matter is simple… as long as the matter don’t mind.

Consciousness resides in All.

www.N9neCouncil.com

Lightning Source UK Ltd.
Milton Keynes UK
17 September 2009

143833UK00001B/17/P

9 780955 748301